THE CHARIOTS OF CALYX

Also by Rosemary Rowe

The Germanicus Mosaic
A Pattern of Blood
Murder in the Forum

THE CHARIOTS OF CALYX

Rosemary Rowe

headline

First published in 2002 by
HEADLINE BOOK PUBLISHING

A Headline hardback

10 9 8 7 6 5 4 3 2 1

British Library Cataloguing in Publication Data

Rowe, Rosemary
The chariots of Calyx
1. Libertus (Fictitious character) – Fiction 2. Romans – Great Britain
– Fiction 3. Great Britain – History – Roman period, 55 BC–449 AD
– Fiction 4. Detective and mystery stories
I. Title
823.9'14[F]

ISBN 0 7472 7099 6

Typeset by Avon Dataset Ltd, Bidford-on-Avon, Warks
Printed and bound in Great Britain by
Mackays of Chatham plc, Chatham, Kent

HEADLINE BOOK PUBLISHING
A division of the Hodder Headline Group
338 Euston Road
London NW1 3BH

www.headline.co.uk
www.hodderheadline.com

To Ann Gower

Author's Foreword

The Chariots of Calyx is set in 187 AD, a time when most of
Britain had been for almost two hundred years the northern-
most province of the hugely successful Roman Empire:
occupied by Roman legions, subject to Roman laws and
taxes, criss-crossed by Roman roads and presided over by a
provincial governor answerable directly to Rome, where the
increasingly unbalanced Emperor Commodus still wore the
Imperial Purple.

Provincial government was centred in the then new capital
city of Londinium (London), which the Romans, with their
superior engineering skills, had founded soon after the
conquest on unpromising ground at the lowest practicable
bridging-point of the Thames, where no real settlement had
stood before. The new capital was intended to impress.
Visitors write in awed terms of the magnificent basilica – one
of the finest in the Empire – while the safe, navigable waters
and the well-planned network of supporting roads made it a
successful trading centre from the outset. There was also a
considerable military presence. The exact size of the garrison
at the time of the story is disputed, but it seems clear that
several thousand troops were quartered in the city, although
that number may include the personal staff of the governor
whose personal bodyguard, as well as his numerous clerks,
secretaries, messengers and attendants, were all officially
army personnel. Perhaps this is not surprising; after the
almost-successful Boudicca rebellion of a hundred years

earlier, when much of the new city was destroyed by fire, there was always a substantial legionary presence in towns controlling the tribal areas of the rebel Iceni and Trinovantes. For instance nearby Verulamium (St Albans), which also features in this story, housed a sizeable military garrison of its own.

Londinium, like any city of the time, relied upon the twin necessities of corn (in the Roman sense of edible grainstuffs) and water. Corn fed both people and horses, and water was vital for life and industry, as well as the transport of goods, and this story reflects the importance of these essentials. (Oil, mostly olive oil, was then the 'third necessity' of civilisation – used for cooking, cleaning and light.) Corn supplies were a constant area of discontent – especially in a city like London which (unusually) had no extensive grain-fields adjacent. Instead, grain had to be brought into the city, usually by water, and following a series of disastrous gluts and famines was now stored in granaries until required – under the control of the town authorities, who were distinct from (although subject to) the provincial government. Stored grain often rotted and spoiled and there are plaintive accounts from all over the Empire of the excessive price demanded for inferior grain, but the Roman commercial precept of *caveat emptor* was held to prevail and any man taking possession of goods in exchange for money had no recourse once the transaction was completed. 'Let the buyer beware' indeed. For two centuries successive imperial decrees had attempted to control the price and distribution of grain, and then of bread, but the system was still subject to considerable abuse, and the *frumentarius* (corn officer) was traditionally one of the 'most hated, most fêted' officials in any city – usually rich, often corrupt and not infrequently the subject of riots in which the hated officer was dragged around the streets in effigy. Such is the figure of Caius Monnius in this story.

Horses, too, required a lot of grain and the city revolved around the use of horses for transport, power (horse-driven mills were not uncommon) and entertainment. Chariot racing was one of the most popular spectacles in the Empire – as witness the colossal Circus Maximus in Rome – and although no chariot circus has ever been conclusively identified in Britain it is certain (from accounts and other related finds) that such contests were equally popular here and even attracted famous charioteers from other parts of the Empire. The 'circus', with its purpose-built track and turning posts, was a racecourse, not to be confused with the amphitheatre for gladiatorial 'games', of which many British examples have been identified. Serious chariot racing was professional, although local towns might also have amateur meets. Racing drivers (as the Latin translates) often began as slaves, but were traditionally allowed to keep at least a proportion of the handsome purses they won, and – if successful – were soon able to buy their freedom, although they were usually still subject to a 'contract' with their team. Huge transfer fees were paid, and successful drivers often rose to be exceptionally wealthy, idolised by their fans and, unusually for the lowly born, accepted into the best society. The four (later six or eight) teams, or 'colours', were not politically neutral. The Green team was at this time associated with anti-imperial feeling and unrest, while Reds were the pro-government team, and so on – although it was not unknown for drivers to change teams at the end of a contract, or even to buy themselves out. The parallel with modern football – even to the rivalry between, say, Celtic and Rangers – is almost irresistible.

As mentioned above, the exact location of the circus in London is unknown. One dubious theory places it north of the river near the Cheapside baths, and this hypothesis has been accepted for the purposes of this story. Equally uncertain is the identity of the Roman governor at this period. Helvius Pertinax was appointed as governor in the early eighties, and he was clearly in Britain in early 187, but it is not certain at what date he relinquished his command. Following the uncovering of a plot against Commodus, the just, severe and incorruptible Pertinax enjoyed a meteoric rise, to be first Governor of Africa and then Prefect of Rome, two of the most powerful posts in the Empire. He was actually acclaimed Emperor by the loyal soldiery after the murder of Commodus – although he was insufficiently corrupt to hold the post for long and was assassinated soon after.

What is remarkable is that this man – who was the son of an ex-slave and began as a teacher of grammar until found a military posting by a rich sponsor – has no identified successor to the post of Governor of Britain, and no clear dates are available for his departure. One possible theory is that no successor was ever named, and he continued to govern by proxy until his appointment to the Prefecture of Rome, when his own nominee was awarded the post and the records (otherwise complete) begin again. For the purposes of this story, this not entirely unprecedented arrangement is presumed to have evolved in late 187, and Pertinax is here portrayed as planning a farewell tour of the province.

Apart from Pertinax and Commodus himself all characters in this story are fictitious. The Romano-British background to the book has been derived from a wide variety of (sometimes contradictory) written and pictorial sources, as well as interviews with specialists on the period. However, although I have done my best to create an accurate picture, this remains a work of fiction and there is no claim to total academic authenticity.

Relata refero. Ne Iupiter quidem omnibus placet. (I only tell you what I heard. Jove himself can't please everybody.)

ROMAN BRITAIN

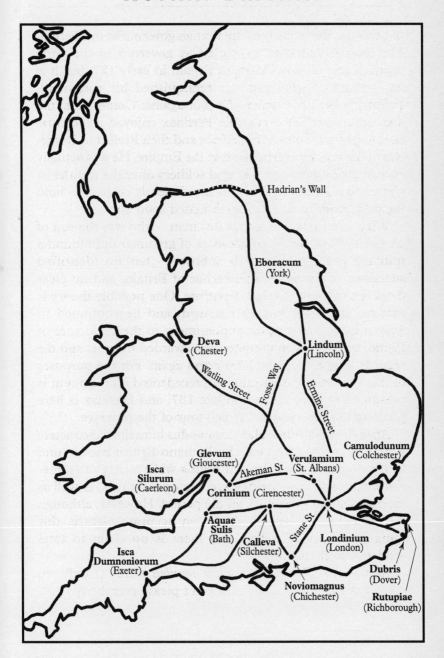

Hadrian's Wall

Eboracum
(York)

Deva
(Chester)

Lindum
(Lincoln)

Watling Street

Fosse Way

Ermine Street

Camulodunum
(Colchester)

Glevum
(Gloucester)

Verulamium
(St. Albans)

Isca
Silurum
(Caerleon)

Akeman St

Corinium (Cirencester)

Aquae
Sulis
(Bath)

Calleva
(Silchester)

Stane St

Londinium
(London)

Isca
Dumnoniorum
(Exeter)

Noviomagnus
(Chichester)

Dubris
(Dover)

Rutupiae
(Richborough)

Prologue

In the opulent town mansion of Caius Monnius Loveinius, one of the wealthiest officials in Londinium, everyone was asleep. Or almost everyone.

It had been a Roman holiday – the birthday of one of the deified imperial dead (or perhaps not dead, since emperors were now officially immortal) – and Caius Monnius, like everyone else of importance, had marked the occasion with a feast.

But the remains of last night's banquet had now been cleared away: scores of slaves, for whom a Roman holiday was no holiday at all, had worked for hours by oil-light moving the last platters from the tables and sweeping scraps of roast peacock from the mosaic floors, but now even they had finished. The fine pottery eating bowls had been scrubbed clean with sand and ashes, the oil-lamps replenished for the night, and the elaborate food libation to the gods – fragments of gilded swan and of delicate honeycake – had been duly shared, as custom permitted, and the weary servants had gone gratefully to their sleeping spaces.

The invited revellers were long since gone home, replete and benevolent in their carried litters: while the master of the house, stupid with lust and wine, staggered to his lady's quarters and by the light of two lamps held by a pair of unwilling slaves, roughly and repeatedly violated his beautiful young wife. Then he too had lumbered to his bed in the adjoining room, posted one slave to sleep outside his door

1

and the other outside his wife's, and had fallen at once into a drunken slumber without even removing his toga.

Elsewhere, the whole household was asleep. Even the doorkeeper had succumbed to the powerful draught he had unwittingly taken in his glass, and had nodded into oblivion, still sitting on his stool, his head resting against the painted plaster wall of his waiting niche. In the darkened corridors nothing moved except the flickering light of a few feeble oil-lamps suspended from the rafters. The tiny wicks, in their open bowls, cast a faint glow upwards but did little to illuminate the area beneath them, and most of the exquisite tiled floor and elegant passageway of interconnecting rooms was a pool of darkness and sinister shifting shadows.

Strange, since in any well-run city household there is always at least one servant awake and watchful, to keep guard.

But tonight there was no one watching. No one to see a single shadow, darker than the rest, detach itself from the gloom of the *librarium* and move silently and stealthily towards the room where Caius Monnius lay. It hesitated a moment outside the lady's door, guarded by the sleeping female slave. The servant was old, and breathing heavily. The shadow bent over her, but the woman did not so much as stir.

The shadow moved on to the master's room. The wretched page sighed and turned slightly in his dreams. The shadow paused. There was no one to see the hands that flashed out suddenly, the fingers that lifted the head by the hair, or the savage tightening of the close-linked silver chain around the throat of the unconscious slave. The sleeping draught had done its job so well that the boy did not even give a grunt as he died.

The shadow let the boy fall gently back, and stepped silently over the lifeless figure into the room beyond. There was a long, long pause. Caius Monnius was a substantial man, and he did not die without a struggle. But a pillow muffled his gurgling and at last the woven chain – its three strands supple and strong yet together no wider than a man's finger – accomplished its deadly work again.

Then the shadow edged soundlessly to the connecting door which led to the bedroom of the lady. The door inched open. A knife gleamed dully in the gloom. The shadow moved towards the bed.

But the lady Fulvia was not asleep. She lay back on her pillows, eyelids shut, and as the knife was raised she seemed to tense. Then, as the blade came down, she moved her arm so that the savage edge merely slashed across her flesh. She opened her eyes and stared about, but before she could even force herself upright – gasping with pain and clutching at the wound – she knew she was alone. She heard the knife clatter to the floor. And then the lady screamed, and kept on screaming, so loudly that the sleeping servants in the attics woke.

A moment later the stairs rang with the sound of their footsteps, and the passages glowed in the flare of their hastily lighted tapers. A dozen slaves rushed into the lady's room, to find her sitting up on her bed, clutching her blankets to her with bloodied hands. She was pale and shivering, and gesturing wordlessly towards the inner door and to the bloodstained knife which still lay glittering on the floor nearby.

'The master!' someone shouted, but Caius Monnius would never come to his wife again. He lay slumped upon his bed, the pillow by his side, with his crushed festal wreath still grotesquely on his head and the chain so tightly wound around his neck that here and there the hammered metal had bitten into flesh, and blood was oozing between the narrow links. The shutters at the window-space had been forced open. A servant cried out in horror.

3

Fulvia struggled to rise. 'I must attend my husband!' But she collapsed into the arms of her slave-woman.

Frightened slaves rushed outside at once into the dark. The garden was walled, but the lights of their torches soon revealed a crude ladder set up against the wall in the furthest corner. There was no one in the garden: no one in the street. The shadow, whoever it was, had merged into obscurity and vanished.

Of course, I didn't know all this at the time. Like every other honest citizen in Londinium, I was fast asleep in bed.

Chapter One

Unlike most of those respectable citizens, however, it was not my own bed that I was occupying. In fact when the household slave arrived to call me, it took me a few moments to work out where I was.

'Citizen? Libertus? Pavement-maker?' I came to my senses to find somebody calling my name. Unnecessarily loudly and close to my ear, I thought. I had been dreaming that I was an emperor, resting on cushions of down.

I opened one eye and shut it again instantly. That's a powerful oil-lamp, I thought crossly, as the brightness seared my sight. What idiot had brought it inches from my eyes?

'Longinius Flavius Libertus!' The voice was insistent. 'Are you awake?'

I forced the eyelid open again. No oil-lamp, I realised painfully, just sunlight streaming through the open shutters. But my fuddled brain refused to deal with the implications of that. I simply turned on my pillows and tried to drift back into oblivion, muttering crossly, 'Go away.'

'Citizen mosaic-maker! His Excellence the Governor enquires if you have slept.'

That woke me. I sat up in bed so suddenly that I narrowly escaped oversetting the bowl of scented water that the slave was carrying. For a moment I goggled at the painted walls, the carved table, the fine wooden shutters standing open at the window-space, the terracotta paving on the floor. And this bed! Not cushions of down, exactly, but the next best thing – a proper bed with a woollen mattress on a splendid stretched goatskin base. A far cry from my usual humble pile of rags and reeds. And the young slave at my bedside was not my own cheerfully scruffy Junio, but an elegant stranger in an exquisitely bordered tunic.

Of course! This was not the wretched attic over my mosaic workshop in Glevum. I was a house-guest of His Supreme Excellence Publius Helvius Pertinax, supreme commander of the legions and governor of all Britannia. I was in his palace in Londinium, and judging by the broad daylight pouring through the windows I was guilty of a serious breach of etiquette. Most Roman households rise at dawn, and all important citizens expect to begin the day by receiving their *clientes*, the retinue of humbler citizens and freemen who call each morning to offer their homage in return for patronage, favours and even – occasionally – breakfast. I should have been awake, dressed, and ready to attend upon on my host hours ago.

Governor Pertinax is a just and even-handed man, but he is also noted for his punctiliousness and sense of duty. I could only hope that this morning his generosity was more in evidence than his severity. I tumbled out of bed at once and began fumbling for my fine new toga to pull on over my humble tunic.

'His Excellence is asking for me?' I attempted to drape myself hastily in the great length of crisp white cloth. That was a mistake. As anyone who has ever worn a toga knows, putting on that most Roman of garments is not a matter that can be hurried. Loose folds were already detaching themselves and escaping into droopy loops around my knees. But I felt the need to hurry. The governor had shown me great favour by inviting me here at all – to be so late to greet him seemed like woeful disrespect. Better men than I have doubtless been flogged for less.

The slave watched me for a moment with a kind of pity and then put down his bowl on the carved ebony table and came to my aid.

'Permit me, citizen. After all, that is what I am here for.' It was true, of course, but the man had such an air of supercilious elegance that I had been ashamed to ask him. Now I had made myself look additionally inept by failing to manage the wretched thing myself.

He stepped forward with a lofty smile. The snaking toga at once arranged itself into obedient folds in his hands as he unwound me from its coils. 'There is no need for such haste,' he said, in the manner of a tolerant tutor-slave. 'His Excellence has ordered me to bring you water for ablutions. My master understands that after your long journey from Glevum you were naturally weary. And you no doubt wish to wash before you go to see him.'

I ignored the implied rebuke and breathed out a little. I had been weary, certainly. The journey to Londinium had taken days, and even in an official carriage on the military roads travel on that scale is hard on the bones, especially when you are nearing fifty, as I am, and unaccustomed to such journeying. 'His Excellence is gracious,' I said. 'And perceptive.'

The slave smiled thinly as he laid aside my garment. If he was appalled at the sight of my second-best tunic, frayed and mended (my best one was at the fuller's, itself being washed after the journey), he betrayed it only by the flicker of an eyelid.

'Perhaps His Excellence observed your deportment last evening,' he remarked, picking up the bowl again and coming to sponge my head and neck expertly with the cool water. 'It was noticed that you were almost asleep at dinner.'

My heart sank. Another breach of good manners! I had hoped that my weariness would pass unremarked, but the truth was I'd found it difficult to keep my eyes open at the table – especially after my lingering visit to the bath-house, and the relaxing massage with scented oils I had been given to take the jolts out of my joints. The rich food had not helped, either, nor the plentiful supply of Roman wine. I am not accustomed to such luxuries. Perhaps it is as well that the governor is famed for keeping a comparatively spartan table – some banquets would have proved too much for me altogether.

I had rather prided myself on how well I had kept awake, right through the floor show and the sacrifices – at least when Pertinax was watching. I had even remained sufficiently alert to avoid swallowing any of that dreadful fish sauce which the Romans insist on serving with everything. Yet evidently my drooping eyelids had not escaped detection. No doubt the table-slaves had noticed.

I wondered if my behaviour when I was shown into this guest-room had also been reported to my host. Probably it had. I had made no attempt to observe the proper formalities – I have no recollection even of lying down. One moment I was surrounded by slaves, being relieved of the festive wreath around my forehead, helped out of my smart new toga (itself a present from the governor) and assisted somewhat un-steadily towards the pillows: the next, it seemed, I was being awoken by this servant. And now the governor was asking for me.

I thought about this as I permitted the slave to splash cool water over my legs and arms and dry me with a towel. A trickle of apprehension ran down my spine, far colder than the wash. 'He called for me by all three names, I notice?'

That was more than an idle observation. It is the mark of a Roman citizen to have three Latin names. As a Celtic noble captured into slavery, I had acquired mine ten years ago, when my master died and bequeathed me his own coveted status together with my freedom. Nevertheless – like that wretched toga – it was a badge of citizenship which sits uncomfortably on me and which I avoid using as far as possible. Even the governor last night had clapped me on the shoulder and called me simply 'Libertus'. By using my full title now, it seemed he was offering me a rebuke.

The young attendant ignored the implied question. He folded me deftly into the toga and fastened it with a clasp at my shoulder. 'There, citizen,' he said, standing back to admire his handiwork. 'Now you are fit to attend upon His Excellence. You may eat, first, if you wish.' His tone suggested that, at this hour, food was a luxury which it would be wisest to forego.

I sat down on the bed again while he fastened my sandals. I was hungry, but I was obediently ready to decline the offer of breakfast, when the slave went on, 'My master ordered that food should be prepared for you, and naturally I arranged for bread and fruit – though your slave now tells me that you would have preferred oatcakes.' A preference for oatcakes, his manner implied, was the ultimate mark of a hopeless barbarian.

'Junio?' I said. In the anxiety of the morning I had overlooked the fact that my own young slave had accompanied me to Londinium and would be somewhere in the building. Probably resting after the journey. As a guest, I had naturally been provided with a servant from the household as a matter of courtesy, but that did not preclude me from having my own slave attend me too.

Suddenly I felt aggrieved. I had rescued Junio from a ruffian of a slave-trader when he was no more than a terrified, half-starved child. Surely he could have contrived to come and wake me up at a less socially embarrassing hour? 'Junio!' I said again. 'Where is he?'

The elegant slave looked disapproving. 'He is waiting

outside with a tray. In case you should have wanted that light repast I spoke of . . .'

I guessed that Junio had insisted on bringing me breakfast himself. I felt a little better. Somehow with Junio at my side I would feel more comfortable, even in these grandiose surroundings. But my feeling of irritation did not altogether disperse. Junio had been there all this time, hovering outside my door. He could have spared me the humiliation of being washed, dressed and condescended to by this elegant creature.

'Perhaps I will have an apple, after all,' I said. 'It would be singularly inappropriate to appear before my host with a stomach grumbling from hunger. You may send Junio in.'

The slave hesitated a moment, then with a look of reproachful disdain he crossed to the door and flung it open. Junio came in, carrying a tray. The sight of that slight familiar figure with its tousled curls and irrepressible grin gave me a sudden confidence.

I nodded imperiously to my erstwhile attendant. 'You may leave us, thank you. And take that dirty water with you. I will call you again when I require you to lead me to His Excellence. Oh, and . . .' I reached my hand into the leather drawstring purse at my belt and drew out a coin. It was more or less obligatory to tip the servants if one visited a strange house. All I could find was a five *as* coin – little enough, but I would have been glad of it in my own slave days. Not in this household, however. The look on the young man's face was almost comical. I really think for a moment he considered giving it back.

'My thanks, citizen,' he said gravely, and bowed himself out.

Junio put down his tray on the inlaid table, his grin broader than ever. 'Your gift did not impress him, master?' The tray, I saw, carried a platter of fine fruits – figs, dates, medlars, plums and apricots which must have come from all over the Empire. There was nothing so humble as an apple.

I ignored Junio's remark and picked up a small brown medlar. It was mellow and ripe, and I sank my teeth into the fragrant flesh.

Junio watched me in mock horror. He had been raised as a slave in a Roman household, and seemed to share our conquerors' misconception that because a ripe medlar looks half rotten it cannot be good to eat. 'Chosen like a Celt,' he grinned.

'Enough of your impudence.' I spoke with as much severity as I could muster. 'Why did you not come and rouse me earlier, you young scoundrel? You might have saved me the embarrassment of being late for the governor.'

This time his surprise was genuine. 'Wake you, master? But it was His Excellency himself who gave orders that you were not to be disturbed. You'd had a long journey already, he said, and it is a long way to Eboracum.'

That was true. I had been invited to Londinium by the governor on purpose to accompany him to Eboracum. Pertinax had learned from my patron in Glevum that I wished to go there to look for Gwellia – the wife who had been torn from me some twenty years earlier when we were both captured by pirates and sold into slavery – and had arranged to take me with him as a reward for solving a politically embarrassing killing. What Pertinax did not know was that my reasons for making the journey had become redundant. I now knew that Gwellia had been sold on. I had even glimpsed her for one tantalising moment, bound hand and foot on the back of a cart with a whole consignment of other female slaves, being driven south. By now she was probably somewhere in Londinium itself.

But it was too late. My promised reward was Eboracum, and to Eboracum I would have to go – although it would break my heart to have to leave the capital without searching for her. I had even considered pleading with my host, but of course realistically that was impossible. No sane man dares to appear ungrateful to the governor. All I could do was try to make a few discreet enquiries in the day or two before we left, though in a city this size there was very little hope.

I sighed.

Junio misinterpreted it. 'I am sorry, master, if you wished me to attend you. There were strict instructions sent to the servants' quarters. You were to be allowed to sleep.'

'But that slave woke me. Said that the governor was asking for me.'

'So he is, now,' Junio said. 'But only because of this murder.'

'Murder?'

It was Junio's turn to sigh. 'You mean that supercilious slave didn't even tell you? Pertinax was receiving his *clientes* this morning when the message arrived. An important official was killed last night in his own home. One of his slaves was murdered, and his wife – who only married him a few months ago, poor thing – had a narrow escape. There was an intruder, it seems, although the man's mother is full of accusations.'

I frowned. 'But surely this is a matter for the courts? Why does Pertinax want me?'

Junio grinned. 'You underestimate your reputation for solving mysteries, master. Marcus must have sung your praises to good effect. The whole household here has heard of you, even the slave who cleans the stables.'

I might have guessed as much. Marcus Aurelius Septimus is my patron in Glevum and a particular friend and confidant of Pertinax – in fact, he is the governor's personal represent-ative in our part of the province. I knew that he boasted to Pertinax of my little successes in clearing up one or two earlier unpleasantnesses: not surprisingly, perhaps, since as my official patron Marcus himself received much of the credit. Without that, I would never have found myself in Londinium now, enjoying my 'reward'. And now Pertinax himself wanted my services! That was alarming in itself, although no doubt it explained the use of my three-fold name.

I shook my head doubtfully. 'But those affairs with Marcus were political matters – or they appeared to be. This is hardly the same thing. A domestic murder . . .' I said it without much conviction. The murdered man had been an important official, Junio had said, but it only made me all the more reluctant to become involved. If I was occupied with that kind of investigation, there was the end of any hope of looking for my wife.

Junio smiled. 'Not all that domestic. There is also the little matter of some missing document or other. To say nothing of an awful lot of tax money. Or so the servants here are saying – one of them overheard the messenger. So if you have quite finished with that medlar, master, perhaps you had better let me wipe your chin and then you can call that slave and go and see the governor. No doubt he will tell you all about it.'

Chapter Two

The governor was waiting for me.

I was shown into his receiving room – a vast, pillared chamber dotted with statues, silken hangings and wonderful carved and inlaid furniture. At once His Excellence waved away his remaining *clientes*, rose from the magisterial couch and stood at the top of the shallow steps on the receiving dais to welcome me in person. Only his private bodyguard – half a dozen huge auxiliaries from the African provinces, the muscles in their naked arms rippling under their smooth brown skin – remained, silent and watchful around the edges of the room. However, I was favoured. For the Roman governor, this counted as a private audience.

The governor himself was an imposing sight. Publius Helvius Pertinax was of course a soldier – general-in-chief of all the cohorts and legions in Britannia – and he had chosen this morning to dress like one. He was only of middle height, and no longer young, but in that uniform he looked every inch a governor. Somehow the glittering breastplate and leather skirts made him seem far more imperial and intimidating than the splendid Roman robes he had worn to the banquet the night before. Add to that the watching guards, and his own naturally rather severe face and formal manner, and you will see why, despite Junio's assurances, my agitation about being late was in no way allayed.

'Ten thousand apologies, Mightiness,' I stammered, hurrying up the steps as fast as I could, and flinging myself abjectly

15

to my knees upon the topmost one. Uncomfortable, but unexpectedly effective. I had intended to make the humblest of obeisances, but in my hurry to prostrate myself I caught my kneecap on the edge of the stair. I bit back the exclamation that rose to my lips, but when I raised my eyes towards my ruler the tears in them were genuine.

He must have noticed them. The stern face softened to a smile. 'Citizen pavement-maker.' He extended a hand, upon which so many rings and seals were set that they looked like finger-armour. 'Do not distress yourself. I am glad to find you rested.'

I accepted this as an invitation to rise, and having duly pressed my forehead to the hand I did so, although with difficulty. The blow to my knee had deprived me momentarily of all power of intelligent speech, so I simply nodded in what I hoped was a dutifully grateful manner.

The governor wasted no time. 'I am sorry to have wakened you, my friend, but I am in need of your advice. No doubt you have heard about this unfortunate business in the city?' He sat down on the couch again as he spoke, picked up an elaborate ebony-handled fly-switch from the table (a memento from his service in the Syrian legions, perhaps) and gestured to a footstool at his side.

I sat down where he had indicated, and said carefully, 'I heard that there had been an unexpected death.'

He eyed me shrewdly. 'A death, certainly. Of one of the city's senior officials too. How unexpected it is I could not say. There have been so many plots and counter-plots lately – as you know, since you so brilliantly helped to uncover one.'

There was no decently modest answer to that, so I said nothing, and merely attempted to look at once grave and deeply interested. In fact, every alarm-goose in my head was already hissing urgent warnings. Ten minutes ago I had been

16

concerned lest I had earned Pertinax's disapproval – now it was his approval that worried me still more. And with reason. I had been lucky to escape from that last investigation with my life. If the governor was about to ask for my help – as I had a terrible premonition that he was – I could soon find myself playing political *ludus latinorum* again, with my head once more as the stake.

A stake that I would be very likely to lose. I could see that. The penalties for killing a senior public official are so horrible that people will do a great deal to avoid facing them. Like murder me, for instance; to anyone who has already disposed of a man of wealth and influence, the life of a mosaic-making ex-slave would mean very little. On the other hand, it means a lot to me. I have no wish to find myself prematurely designing pavements for Pluto. And yet I could hardly ignore the orders of the governor.

'What kind of man was he?' I asked brightly, as soon as Pertinax had finished outlining what he knew. 'This Caius Monnius Loveinius? Do you know if he had enemies?' If I asked enough questions immediately, I reasoned, I might deflect His Excellence from issuing any specific orders or from asking any favours, which – coming from the governor – would amount to very much the same thing.

The governor looked at me keenly. 'Enemies? Half of Londinium held grudges, I imagine. He was *frumentarius* for the city – and doing very well out of it.'

I nodded glumly. 'I see.'

I did see. No man ever became a *frumentarius* in the hope of making friends. When one individual is responsible for the constant provision, warehousing and sale of corn, even for a smallish town, resentments are inevitable. Here, in a large city, it must be a thousand times worse. The best a *frumentarius* can hope for is to avoid being dragged in effigy on the hook around the streets – by the inhabitants every

17

time there is a famine, and by the farmers and carters whenever there is a glut. No one loves a corn officer.

'Only half Londinium has a grudge?' I said, with a smile.

Pertinax did not acknowledge the jest. 'Everyone needs grain, and it is impossible for a *frumentarius* to please everybody.'

No doubt it *is* an unenviable job, given the British vagaries of wind and weather. Doubtless, too, there are corn officers who are ornaments to their office, trying to ensure good-quality grain at a reasonable price to all comers, and whose accumulation of golden treasure is limited to the edible variety in their granaries. I can only report that I have never met one. On the other hand everyone, from baker to town official, cavalryman to cook, will seek to bribe and flatter a *frumentarius*, at least to his face. As the governor so rightly said, everybody needs grain.

'Well,' I said, 'he isn't doing so well out of it any more.'

Pertinax regarded me severely, rebuking my unseemly levity with a glance. It reminded me of schoolmasters I had known. I remembered that Pertinax had, in fact, once been a teacher of grammar – before his father's patron found him a place in the cohorts and set him on his rise to power. He must have been a formidable *paedagogus*.

He sounded like a schoolteacher now, weary and patient. 'Libertus, you know that I have applied to be relieved of this appointment and be posted elsewhere?'

I nodded. I did know. The proposed journey to Eboracum was to have been part of his farewell procession around the major cities of the province. 'The Insula Britannica will miss you, Mightiness.' I meant it. To have a just and noble governor is every subject's dream. To have an intelligent and upright one – however severe he might be with wrong-doers – is an unusual privilege.

'Then, my friend, spare me your wit and use that patternmaker's brain to better purpose. Assist me to leave the province in good order. If the provincial council refuses to pass the customary vote of thanks on my departure, there will be an imperial enquiry into my governorship. That could be serious. The Emperor is becoming more' – he glanced towards the guards, but they stood motionless and impassive as the statues which surrounded them – 'more – shall we say – "individual" at every turn. For instance, did you know that as well as renaming Rome Commodiana in his own honour, he has now decreed that the months of the year are also to be changed? August is to be Commodus, September Hercules, October Invictus . . . and November has disappeared in favour of "Exsuperatorius" – all named after His Imperial Divinity, of course.'

I had not heard of this latest excess, although the Emperor's increasingly 'individual' behaviour was whispered throughout the Empire. I tried to make light of it. 'At least the changes will keep the imperial scribes busy.'

'He is becoming less and less forgiving of any kind of civil unrest,' Pertinax went on, as if I hadn't spoken. 'He sees it as dissent against himself – and the local governor is held responsible. This murder would not look well at an enquiry. This is not a joking matter, Libertus. My future as well as yours may depend on it.'

I could see why the governor was alarmed and I hastened to redeem myself by sounding businesslike. 'The question is, Mightiness, whether any of these grudges that you speak of were personal – directed at Caius Monnius in particular – or were merely irritation with the corn taxes in general.'

Pertinax nodded thoughtfully. He began fanning imaginary flies from his face with the horsehair whisk. 'They might be both, I imagine. Caius Monnius introduced some new measures which have won him little popularity: big drying houses by the river, for instance – the local landowners didn't like that – and his system of compulsory loans for the corn trade almost caused riots in the street.'

'Compulsory loans?' I did not live in Londinium and this was the first time I had heard of this.

'If a man wants money for seed corn, or to build a warehouse-granary, or merely to purchase large quantities of grain, he is now obliged to borrow it from the town treasury – at a high rate of interest, naturally.'

'Part of which finds its way into Caius Monnius' private coffers?'

The governor almost smiled. He toyed with the fly-whisk, and his tone was ironic as he said, 'I imagine so. I could not really say. That is a matter for the city, not the state. As provincial governor, it is hard for me to intervene, unless specific charges are brought against him – as, of course, they never have been.'

Of course they hadn't. A man would have to be exceedingly desperate, or influential, to bring an accusation like that against the city corn officer. For one thing, under Roman law, there can be no trial unless the accused can be physically brought before the courts – difficult with a wealthy, influential, well-guarded man like Caius Monnius. For another thing, the accuser still has to eat. As I said, everyone needs grain.

One thing surprised me, however. I had always regarded the Roman governor – second in command only to the Emperor in matters relating to the province – as having almost unlimited powers. Of course, like every other major city, Londinium was a republic in its own right, with its own urban administration, but it had never occurred to me that Pertinax might have to tread with care in order not to offend the sensibilities of the civic council.

Like Pertinax a moment earlier, I glanced towards the guards against the walls and lowered my voice. This matter might be sensitive. 'That would explain the money which is missing? Some disaffected borrower, perhaps, pressed beyond the limit? Taking forcible possession of what he believes is rightfully his?'

Pertinax put down his whisk and leaned a little closer. He too was aware that slaves have ears – perhaps because his own father was once a slave himself. He was unusual in that: most Romans regard their servants as 'vocal tools' – merely part of the furnishings and as incapable of independent thought as a chair.

The governor, however, was more circumspect. His voice was a murmur as he said, 'It might be so. And the document too. That disappearance worries me, though it is not clear exactly what it was. A list of transactions, perhaps, or a register for taxation. No one knows. It was merely noted that there was a sealed official scroll locked into his study chest last evening, and it is not there now. His slaves confirm it.'

'Confirm it? Then who noticed the disappearance in the first place? And how, if the chest was locked?'

This time the governor did smile. If it were not for his general air of dignity I would almost have said that he grinned. 'Caius Monnius' mother went into his study this morning and discovered the money was gone. The chest was open – and empty, though the slaves swear that it was locked as usual the night before.'

'Caius' mother lives with her son?' I said, more to show intelligent interest than anything. It is not unusual, if a woman is widowed, for her son to take on legal and financial responsibility for her and offer her a home.

'More than that.' Pertinax leaned back on his couch expansively. There was no attempt now to disguise his amusement. 'Caius Monnius has built an entire wing for her attached to his mansion, though she did inherit quite a sizeable estate in her own right somewhere out towards the sea. No doubt Monnius hoped to get his hands on that estate, but his mother insists on running it herself – through a steward, of course. A lady of decided views and personality. She is quite a figure in the town. She is the one who sent to me with this information.'

I said nothing. You didn't have to read the entrails to see where this was leading. An awkward political situation, falling between the province and the city. Sensitive papers missing. An hysterical woman demanding justice, and the governor not wishing to seem involved. And, of course, a foolish pavement-maker with a reputation for solving mysteries.

I was right. Pertinax regarded me benignly. 'As to how she discovered the document was missing, you will be able to ask her yourself. I have promised her that you will look into it – I would prefer not to involve the legal officers at this stage. I am sure you will handle things discreetly. Her name is Annia Augusta, and she is at the mansion, waiting for you, now. I have made the necessary arrangements.'

He gestured towards one of the massive bodyguards, who seemed to come mysteriously to life. The man clapped his enormous hands three times. The sound rattled the statues in their niches. At once, the supercilious slave appeared at the doorway.

'There is a litter waiting for this citizen,' the governor said. 'Accompany him wherever he wishes, and make sure he has everything he wants. And you may have them show in the last of my *clientes*.' He rose to his feet and extended the ringed hand to me again.

I knelt and kissed it and then got to my feet and stumbled off down the steps to follow the slave. I was dismissed.

As I passed one of the huge, impassive, brown-skinned guards, I would have sworn that I saw the corner of his mouth twitch momentarily as if in sympathy, but when I looked again the face was immobile as ever.

My heart sank. It seemed like an omen. What devilry, I wondered, were the Fates hatching for me now?

Chapter Three

Londinium is an awe-inspiring city, even when viewed from the uncomfortable vantage point of a swaying litter carried by two sweating slaves. From the moment we lurched past the ornamental fountains and the crowd of curious onlookers, and out of the gates of the governor's palace, I began to understand why this provincial capital is spoken of in awed terms by all who visit it.

I had glimpsed something of its wonders the evening before, though because of the imperial festival there had been little commerce on the streets. Even so, as we arrived in the failing light the mere expanse of tiled roofs had impressed me, and so had the vast numbers of houses, shops and colonnades. This morning, in slanting sunshine, the city was about its business again and the sheer quantity of people made me gape.

There are rumoured to be ten thousand men in Londinium, and as we turned away from the so-called Wall Brook and on to the main road across the city, I felt that all of them must be out here on the streets.

I am accustomed to crowds – Glevum is a substantial town and so is neighbouring Corinium – but I had never seen so many men together at one time in the same place, except for military processions or religious festivals. But this was an ordinary working day.

There were people everywhere: rich men in togas giving orders; lesser ones in tunics lifting bales; others, in little more than rags, attempting to sell their pitiful baskets of wild herbs and berries, or offering to hold a horse for a bronze *as* or two. Boys hustled by with handcarts laden with pigskins; women passed with firewood bundled on their backs. And creatures too. Dogs and donkeys loitered in doorways, caged birds whistled from a vendor's stall, and pigs, sheep and cattle called plaintively from the butchers' pens in the distant market, while mules and horses plodded in the gutters, laden with every cargo known to man, from olive oil to oysters, candlesticks to cloth.

'Where does it all come from?' I muttered, half to myself.

The supercilious slave was trotting beside my chair, obedient to the governor's orders, and heard the remark. 'All unloaded from the boats that come up the river,' he informed me breathlessly.

The pace that the litter-bearers were setting meant that he had to scurry along in a rather undignified manner to keep up, to my secret amusement. His name was Superbus, he told me proudly, 'meaning excellent', and that caused me to smile even more. 'Superbus' does mean 'excellent', but it also means 'supercilious'. Governor Pertinax had his own sense of humour, then, under that stern exterior.

The slave was not looking very excellent now. The pace was telling on him – he was already turning red and panting slightly, to the visible detriment of his self-esteem and the scarcely concealed amusement of the litter-bearers. (I half suspected they were doing it on purpose, so I was unreasonably pleased to notice that Junio, who was striding along on the other side of the carrying chair, appeared to be managing the brisk walk effortlessly.)

Junio caught my eye and grinned appreciatively. 'A little bigger than Glevum, master. Look at that basilica!'

I could scarcely help looking at it. We had just turned into the street which fronted the forum, and the building which

Junio was excitedly indicating would have been hard to miss. It dominated the entire neighbourhood with its lofty columns and gracious portico. The whole dignified edifice – town offices, function halls and courtrooms, flanked by temples and official market halls – was set back across a spacious public square, itself dotted with mighty statues and surrounded by a colonnade where independent vendors had set up makeshift stalls.

'Great Mercury!' I exclaimed, as all this came fully into view. 'Whoever built that intended to impress!'

'It's said to be the biggest basilica in the Empire, outside Rome,' Superbus informed us, as loftily as his heavy breathing would allow. Despite his scarlet cheeks he managed to sound as if the glories of the city were to his personal credit.

'Imagine!' I gave him a cheerful smile, hanging on to my chair with both hands as my bearers navigated a pile of turnips spread out for sale on the pavement. 'Hard to believe that less than two hundred years ago there was nothing here but a swamp.'

Unkind, perhaps, although it was nothing less than the truth. Everyone knew that the Romans had built their elaborate city on virgin land. None of our Celtic tribes had ever bothered with the place – the lowest practical crossing of the river, certainly, but the soil for miles around was too poor to support farming. Superbus, however, saw any comment on the city as a blow to his own self-esteem, and he deflated like a punctured pig's bladder. His face became more scarlet than ever and he said nothing further until we had arrived at our destination.

This proved to be a substantial mansion in the north-east of the city, the door already hung with a wreath of funerary green. It was a large house in possession of a privately walled rear garden with – as far as I could tell from a glimpse over the high wall – a long, low addition on one side. The 'wing' in which the fearsome Annia lived, I guessed. After Pertinax's description, I was looking forward to meeting her.

I had not long to wait. I had hardly set foot to paving before a small, stout woman with folded lips and greying hair had brushed aside the doorkeeper and was waiting in the corridor to greet me. From her wine-coloured stola and imperious air, and the pair of maidservants skulking nervously behind her, this was clearly a lady of some account.

I was surprised to find her there, since I am not a person of particular importance. It is not at all customary for a householder, particularly a female one, to come hurrying out personally in this fashion. Usually the visitor drums his heels in the atrium first, nibbling at dates, while a slave goes through the pretence of summoning the master – or mistress – who will arrive only after a dignified interval. One expects these conventions.

'Lady . . .' I stopped, lowering my eyes respectfully. 'The citizen Libertus, at your command.'

If I had supposed, even vaguely, that her unexpectedly prompt appearance was due to womanly anxiety and grief for her dead son, her first words were enough to disabuse me. 'Well, citizen, so there you are at last. Oh, get up, get up – we'll have none of that time-consuming nonsense here.' I had attempted to kneel before her with bowed head, a conventional gesture of respect towards a Roman matron in mourning. 'There's work to be done. That female has conspired to have my son done away with, and I want you to prove it. It may not be easy. They are clever, she and that lover of hers. That's why I sent to Pertinax. I said I wanted the best.' She inspected me, discontentedly, like a cook at the market appraising a fowl and finding it tough and scrawny. 'And he sent you. Are you the best?' I half expected her to reach out and test the flesh on my forearm.

'I will *do* my best,' I said, foolishly, still startled by the nature of my welcome. We had not moved from the entrance-way, and Annia Augusta – if that was indeed who it was – was still standing before me with folded arms, as forbidding as the Nubians at the palace. 'To find out who is guilty, that is.'

'It is not a question of finding out who's guilty,' she said sharply. 'Fulvia Honoria, my daughter-in-law, and that wretched Lividius Fortunatus of hers – they are the ones who are guilty. Any idiot could guess that. *Proving* it will be the problem. That is why I sent for you. What do you say to that?'

I had nothing to say to it. I was too taken aback to make any sensible reply. After a death, especially a violent death like this, one expects emotion – shock at least, or grief – and most of all from the mother. There was no sign in Annia Augusta of anything except scarcely concealed impatience.

She was looking at me pityingly now. 'It seems you're not as sharp-witted as I was led to believe. Well, since the governor has sent you, I suppose you had better come in. Come on – all of you!' She made a sharp gesture with her hand, then turned and led the way into the atrium. We followed her like a flock of docile sheep – her attendants, myself, Junio and Superbus, who by this time was smirking all over his face at my discomfiture.

I tried to ignore him, and concentrated on my surroundings.

The atrium was as tall, classic and gracious as Annia Augusta was not. It was roofed, as most atria are in this most northerly of the provinces, but someone had added an ornamental pool, in imitation of the Roman fashion, with a central statue, a few scattered plants and one or two lethargic fish lurking in it. I wondered what Herculean efforts by the servants were required to keep that little feature constantly cleaned and replenished.

The walls were of painted plaster, depicting hunting scenes, and the room had been elaborately furnished with more expense than taste. On one wall a huge and heavy gold-crusted table groaned under a pot-bellied onyx vase; on another a gigantic marble statue of Vesta squinted down at us from her plinth in a painted niche; and the whole floor boasted an elaborate mosaic, depicting lumpish nymphs and sea creatures in an intricate design of quite exceptional ugliness. What caught my attention, however, was a small plain table in a corner of the open *tablinium* beyond, on to which a young page was carefully placing a tray containing a selection of fresh fruits and a jug of watered wine.

Annia Augusta glowered at him. 'What are you doing here?'

The boy stopped, platter in hand. 'The mistress,' he ventured. 'She bade me . . . for our guest . . .'

To my surprise, Annia seemed to accept this, although ungraciously. 'Oh, very well,' she said impatiently. 'Put it on the table and leave it there.' The boy did as he was ordered, and escaped from the room with evident relief.

'My daughter-in-law,' Annia said. 'Giving herself airs.' She smirked – a little smile of satisfaction. 'Well, let her wait until the will is read. That will put a stop to her tricks. Filius will be the heir, and we shall see who is the mistress then.' She turned to me with a tight little smile and gestured to the plate. 'Though I suppose you may have some of this if you desire, now that it has been prepared. I don't like to see good food wasted. I would have offered you refreshment myself, if I thought you wanted it. But you have come from the governor's palace. No doubt you are already fed and watered satisfactorily?'

This was so outright discourteous that for the first time since I had entered the house and encountered this extra-ordinary woman I abandoned all attempts at the delicacy one normally displays in the face of sudden loss. I squared my shoulders and tried to look as masterful as I could.

'Madam citizen,' I said, with punctilious courtesy, 'I shall be grateful to accept your hospitality.' She was right, of course: I was neither hungry nor thirsty, but I felt that if I did not take a stand, and soon, I would lose my precarious authority altogether, governor's protégé or not.

Annia Augusta looked affronted at my words – I guessed she was not often defied by anyone – but she signed to one of her maidservants to fetch a stool, while the other led Junio and Superbus off to wait in the servants' room, as the custom was.

'And while I am enjoying your generous welcome,' I added, following up my earlier social swordplay with a calculated thrust, 'you mentioned a number of names. Perhaps you could explain to me who these people are?'

'People?' She sounded as if she had never mentioned a person in her life.

'This . . .' I searched for the name, 'Filius, did you call him? And Lividius Fortunatus, who is he? The only Lividius Fortunatus I have ever heard of is a racing driver in the circus.'

I said it with a suppressed smile. That Lividius Fortunatus was known to every man in the province. Drivers of racing chariots may be of humble origin – indeed many of them begin as slaves – but those who survive the training soon earn enough to acquire their freedom, and the successful ones are among the most highly paid men in the Empire, even if they are still tied by contracts to their teams. 'Living like a driver of the Blues' has become a synonym for conspicuous extravagance – and there are few drivers more successful than Fortunatus.

Even here in Britannia, that young hero of the circuit was rumoured to be paid more gold for a single race than a successful wool-trader might make in a lifetime. And it was not just the money. Young women (and sometimes nubile young men) were said to haunt his dressing rooms, to throw themselves at their idol's feet (or any other part of his anatomy). Rich men fêted him, poets praised him and vendors of his favourite wine and olives would not only give him samples of their wares, they would sometimes pay the charioteer handsomely to be seen consuming them in public.

So Annia would hardly be talking about *that* Fortunatus. There were, no doubt, many others. There has been a fashion recently for newly created citizens to choose their own Roman names, instead of necessarily taking their master's, the Emperor's and a nickname, as I had done. It prevents the world from being full of men called Julius, and having a Marcus Aurelius Something-or-other at the end of every street – though I wonder how the great and the famous react to finding their almost-namesakes everywhere. This was some racing enthusiast, probably, or would-be charioteer, naming himself after his favourite hero.

'I am a stranger in the city, madam citizen. Who is this other Lividius Fortunatus? I'm afraid I do not know the man you are talking about.'

I had begun to think that Annia Augusta had exhausted her ability to surprise me, but I was wrong.

'Of course you do,' she said sharply. 'That is the very man I mean. Lividius Fortunatus, the racing charioteer. Oh, don't stare at me in that disbelieving slack-jawed fashion. I am perfectly serious. I don't know how he did it, but I'd wager a thousand *denarii* that he murdered my son. And that, my dear citizen, is what I want you to prove.'

Chapter Four

I stared at her. It had already become clear to me that Annia Augusta was eccentric. It had not occurred to me till now that she might actually be mad. Lividius Fortunatus? Public idol, golden champion of the circuit, with managers of every team outbidding each other in offering him fat fees to transfer to their colour? A murdering thief? The woman might as well have suggested that she was a racing charioteer herself.

Annia seemed to read my thoughts. 'You don't believe me. Oh, don't bother to deny the fact. I can see what you're thinking. I'm an old woman and I learned long ago to read men's minds in their faces. That is why I don't trust Lividius Fortunatus. But you don't believe me. You think I am a foolish, tiresome old goose who suffers from delusions.'

It was, in fact, almost exactly what I had been thinking – although the word 'goose' had not been part of it. However, I could hardly tell her that. I began to murmur something deprecating like 'The courts would need more evidence, madam . . .' but Annia was not to be appeased.

She snorted. 'Well, so much for Pertinax's clever thinker! If you come here with your mind already made up you'll never arrive at the truth.'

What did the woman suppose? That I would make an instant arrest based on her distrust of a man's face?

'Madam,' I said carefully, 'it is precisely in order to arrive at the truth that I must weigh your accusations carefully, and judge the facts for myself. I can scarcely decide that the man is guilty simply because you tell me he is. It seems unlikely, don't you think, that a rich man like Lividius Fortunatus – however much he desired your daughter-in-law – would trouble to steal money and documents about the sale of corn?'

Annia flushed an angry red. 'No doubt he took the money to make everyone suppose that theft was the motive,' she said impatiently. 'It would not have been difficult. Fulvia must know where Monnius kept the keys – he never could keep anything from her. And she would tell Fortunatus. It seems to me an obvious deduction.'

It seemed much less than obvious to me, and my doubts must have shown in my face, because after a moment Annia went on in an affronted tone, 'I assure you, citizen, Fortunatus is quite capable of something like this. You don't know the man as I do.'

'I don't know him at all,' I agreed mildly, 'except by reputation. I have no preconceptions. Perhaps that is why the governor called on me.' I looked around helplessly, wishing that I could at least have started on the refreshments: not that I particularly wanted them, but the diversion would provide some sort of relief from the full blast of Annia Augusta's personality. In vain. There was still no sign of the maidservant with the promised stool.

'Lividius Fortunatus is a conniving wretch,' Annia said. 'Even you must know of his reputation with women. I warned my son that he should never have offered him hospitality, but of course he wouldn't listen. Where Fulvia was concerned he couldn't see beyond the end of his nose. He was absolutely besotted with that woman, though it was obvious to everyone else what was happening, even if her poor stupid husband couldn't see it. If he had listened to me . . .' She began elaborating on the advice she had given her son before his marriage. The recital had the momentum of a downhill cart, and once Annia had started down this track I could see it would be difficult to stop her. Yet there was much more I needed to know.

'Fulvia is Monnius' wife?' I said, as soon as Annia drew breath. I knew the answer already, of course, but I was hoping to slow that imaginary cart. I almost succeeded, for a moment.

Annia sniffed. 'His widow now,' she said grimly. 'Though much good it will do her! Filius inherits everything of importance – more work for me in the end, but that doesn't matter. We'll manage. Except that Fulvia will make a legal fuss, no doubt. I always said no good would come of that marriage.'

I made another attempt. 'Ah yes,' I said. 'The will. The money goes to . . . Filius, I think you said? He is a relative? A brother?' From Annia's words, she clearly hoped to have some control of the money.

'A relative, certainly, but not a brother, no.' She pursed her lips again, and glanced at me triumphantly. 'Filius is his son.'

'His son! But surely . . .' I broke off, aware that what I was about to say sounded indecorous. Surely I'd heard that Monnius had been married for only a few months? And then a solution occurred to me. 'Adopted, perhaps?' It is not uncommon for childless or unmarried wealthy men to adopt an heir to ensure that their estates do not entirely disappear into the imperial coffers. Since Monnius was so much older than his wife, some such provision would have been a sensible precaution – though of course if there had been children of the marriage there would have had to be a new will.

Annia was staring at me again, as though I were the eccentric one. 'Adopted? Nonsense. Filius is his natural son. By his first wife – his real wife – the one he ignominiously got rid of in order to marry that stupid Fulvia.'

'Monnius had been married before?' I interrupted.

It was as stupid a question as it was possible to ask, given what Annia had just been saying to me, but to my surprise she made no unflattering comment. Instead she folded her hands and lips and heaved a great disapproving sigh. 'Indeed he had. And to a proper sort of woman, too. Neat, clean, respectable and respectful. Not like that creature he divorced her for – full of her own ideas and importance, and interested in nothing but jewellery and clothes. Always prinking and preening in front of her mirrors, and wanting perfumes and fine silks from the markets. I could see from the start what sort of woman she was. It's not as if she even brought much dowry with her. But would he listen to his mother? No! He was determined to have Fulvia – just because she flashed her eyes and legs at him once at a banquet—'

'Good morning, citizen.' A soft, musical, delightfully modulated voice came from somewhere behind me. 'I regret that I was not informed of your arrival sooner. Please pardon my late appearance – welcome to my house.'

I turned. A woman was standing at one of the inner doorways, attended by two young pages. From her words, her sombre dress, and the poisonous glance which Annia gave her, this was clearly Fulvia, the woman whom Monnius had braved his mother's wrath to wed. A single glance was enough to tell me why he had thought the prize worth the penalty.

She was in the prime of marriageable womanhood – perhaps sixteen or seventeen – and strikingly beautiful, even in the drab colours and costume of ritual grief. Not virginal in the tall, pale, aquiline Roman fashion, but with the kind of shapely, dimpled, and bold-featured beauty which, offered at the slave market, would make any brothel-keeper in the province start loosening his purse-strings. She moved, too, with the kind of supple grace which somehow suggested a hired dancing girl rather than a respectable Roman matron.

I remembered Annia's earlier words about flashing her legs at a banquet, and for a moment I almost wondered. But of course there was no question of that. If Fulvia had really ever been an entertainer, Monnius would not have needed to trouble himself with marriage; he would simply have purchased her and that would have been that. This girl was clearly too well born for that. Yet there *was* something of the dancing girl about her and she had not brought 'much dowry' with her.

No wonder Annia disapproved.

I made the due obeisance and stole another look at the widow. She was dressed conventionally enough, in a simple dark-coloured stola, with a soft black drape covering her hair as befitted a woman in mourning, but she still radiated enough physical femininity to make me remember that I was a man – even if an ageing one. The stola was made of rustling stuff – demure, but just sufficiently high cut at the hem to reveal a perfection of ankle, and just low cut enough at the throat to hint at the soft milk-white swell of the breasts below. A woven girdle cord of soft black silk artlessly emphasised the waist. Curls of blonde hair escaped enticingly from under the dark hood, and as she raised her blue-green eyes to meet mine I saw that they had been carefully outlined with kohl, now smudged (not unbecomingly) with weeping.

Beside me Annia Augusta almost hissed with suppressed fury.

But Monnius' wife was at least a match for his mother. This was, at least until the will was read, her house and she emphasised the point again. She paid not the slightest attention to Annia as she said sweetly, 'Twice welcome, citizen,' and extended both hands towards me.

I gasped. Her left arm, until then hidden by the folds of her cape, was heavily bandaged. The stark whiteness of the linen bindings was almost shocking against the supple

37

darkness of her dress – except where, I noticed, there was on the outside of the upper arm a dark red stain that was more shocking still.

'Lady . . .' I began awkwardly. 'I am sorry to find you hurt.' I gestured towards the damaged limb, but she brushed my concern aside with a brave little smile.

'It is nothing, citizen. Deep enough – but I was fortunate. When I consider . . .' She shook her head. 'Even now I cannot believe it. If it were not for my faithful slaves . . .' Her teeth, I noticed, were small and uneven, like a child's. Somehow that flaw in her beauty made her seem more appealing than ever.

'Your slaves!' Annia Augusta said with a sniff, interposing herself between us. 'I only wish they were a little more efficient. We are still awaiting the arrival of a stool, so that this citizen can have his refreshment. I sent one of those useless slaves of yours to fetch one, some little time ago, but there is no sign of it.' She clasped her stout hands self-righteously across her chest and glared at her daughter-in-law. 'If I had been permitted to bring my own servants with me, we shouldn't have had this trouble, I promise you. They knew their duty. But I have no say in anything. No doubt that is the problem – someone has countermanded my orders!'

'Not I, Annia Augusta, I assure you,' Fulvia said drily, with a glance at me which suggested that the older woman was imagining things as usual. She turned to the young pages. 'Go, boys, and see what you can discover about a stool.'

But it seemed that Annia Augusta was right, after all, although not in the way she imagined. Hardly had the slave-boys left the room when they were back again, each carrying a stool, and followed by a thin sallow woman, all in black, with a plain, pinched face and an anxious expression. She bobbed me a greeting but her eyes were only for my older companion.

'Oh, Annia Augusta, good madam.' She was still almost bobbing in her anxiety to explain herself, although by her clothes and the handsome necklace round her neck, this lady was a citizen and not the apologetic servant she appeared. 'This is my doing. Which stool was it that you wanted? The one with the ivory inlay, or the gilded wood? I couldn't decide. In the end I had them bring you both . . .'

I looked from Fulvia to Annia, and from Annia to the newcomer, who was still wringing her hands in apology.

It was Fulvia who spoke. 'Ah,' she said. 'Citizen, I see that you have not met Lydia. My husband's former wife.'

To say that I goggled would be an understatement. When a Roman divorces his wife he sends her back to her family (if she is not to be punished for unfaithfulness) and generally expects her not to darken his doors again. Yet here was Lydia, only a few hours after Monnius' death, in his house, already wearing mourning, and agitating the servants about stools. 'His former wife?' I found myself saying. 'How . . .?'

Fulvia Honoria gave me a strange wry smile. 'You see, citizen, Lydia lives in the house – or at least in the annexe, which amounts to very much the same thing. Annia Augusta brought her here three months ago, after her brother, her legal guardian, died. Together with that wretched Filius of hers. Monnius fought against it, naturally, but he had a duty to the child, and Annia claimed she needed a companion.' She showed those small uneven teeth again.

'Of course . . .' Annia began, but Fulvia ignored her.

'An uncomfortable situation, do you not think, citizen? For all of us? I do not think even Lydia was keen, but of course she does everything my mother-in-law tells her, and where else did she have to go? Annia Augusta can be hard to resist when she puts her mind to something. Even Monnius gave way in the end, otherwise she would have made his life unbearable.'

Her voice was composed, and she was still smiling, although she was beginning to look strained, and she moved her hand to her arm as if her wound was troubling her. She was still dignified.

The wretched Lydia, however, had clapped her skinny hands to her skinny face and was rocking to and fro in misery, muttering, 'Fulvia, no! By sweet Mercury, you must not say these things!' Annia had gone red, and was puffing herself up like an outraged turkey, and even the servants – although not daring to move another muscle – were exchanging horrified looks from the corners of their eyes.

And I? I did the only thing a man could do, in the circumstances. I gestured to the slave with the inlaid stool, as imperiously as I could. He hastened to set it down by the table and I installed myself upon it, importantly, signalling to the boy to pour some wine.

It had the desired effect. At this demonstration of masculine authority, the women seemed to recollect themselves and stood back.

'Thank you for this hospitality,' I said, with what I hoped was a dignified smile. 'Now I am sure there are a hundred preparations to be made in this household, as there always are after a death. I do not wish to keep you from your unhappy tasks. If, perhaps, you could send my own slave to attend me, and continue to lend me one of your own? I am sure with the body to attend to, and the funeral meats to prepare . . .?'

I saw the women glance at one another. They were about to begin bickering again, I realised with alarm. Probably about whose responsibility it was to organise the rites. I went on, hurriedly, 'Otherwise, please ignore me. Call the funeral arrangers by all means. I will try to intrude as little as possible. Expect that I should like to see the body before the anointers begin, and I shall want to speak to everyone, one at a time.

Starting with you, perhaps, Fulvia, since as his widow you must begin the lament. Unless his son is old enough . . .?'

Fulvia's face, which was looking pale and strained, lighted with a small, triumphant smile. 'Filius is scarcely more than a child – he is only just old enough to wear an adult toga. He may close the eyes, if he wishes, but the duty of opening the lament will fall to me. As for the funeral arrangers, I have already sent for them. Some of them arrived before you did, citizen' – of course they had: I had noted the funerary wreath at the entrance – 'and by now they will be bathing the body.' She glanced victoriously at Annia, who was crimson with fury. 'But I will instruct them to suspend their ministrations a little. I am in any case going to my room. I shall be there if you need me, citizen, and you no doubt wish to speak to me – in private? After all, I was the only witness of what took place last night.'

Annia spluttered something, incoherent with rage.

Fulvia ignored her. 'I will retire, then.' She closed her eyes suddenly. She did indeed look faint and faltering, I thought. 'My servants will attend me. Enjoy your refreshment, citizen.'

Annia glowered after her. 'Making the arrangements, just like that – and his mother not even consulted!'

Beside her, Lydia began to sob, hiccoughing and snivelling wretchedly. 'Poor, poor Monnius. To think that he should come to this. And if that woman is arranging it, they will not even let Filius lead the mourners.'

Annia put an arm round her, and with a final glare in my direction led her from the room.

I sat back on the stool and permitted myself to be served with some refreshment. By this time I was quite glad of my beaker of watered wine.

Chapter Five

Junio arrived just as I was finishing the fruit (slices of apple, at last!), and he stationed himself beside my chair with a cheerful grin.

'I hear you wish to view the body, master? I have been given instructions to lead you there.'

I got to my feet, holding out my hands to be rinsed and dried by the house-slaves who had been standing by with ewer, bowl and towel for the purpose. I dashed a few drops of water on my head, too, as a sort of purification, and took the time to go and pour the dregs of wine on to the altar of the Vestal shrine. I am not usually a superstitious man, especially in regard to Roman rituals, preferring my own ancient gods of tree and stone, but this household worried me. If I was to be visiting Roman corpses, I felt, I could do with all the supernatural support that I could get.

I nodded to Junio. 'You know the way? Then lead me to him.'

The interlinking rooms and passages we passed through were as grand, and as lavishly decorated, as the atrium we had left, and everywhere there was the same disregard both for cost and for artistic restraint. Everything was bigger, heavier, more jewel-encrusted, and more ostentatious than its counterpart in any household I had ever seen. Even a simple gong-stick, hanging on a wall in a short corridor, appeared to be made of ivory, inlaid with gold.

43

Junio led the way into this corridor. It was a spacious passageway, almost a little lobby, from which three gilded folding doors led off into the rooms beyond and a stout wooden staircase gave access to the floor above.

'Servants' quarters,' Junio said, following my gaze and nodding upwards. 'And a few store-rooms up there for linen and candles. Nothing much else.'

'In spite of that grand stairway?'

He grinned. 'In spite of that grand stairway. That's where they took me to wait. I contrived to have a peek behind a few doors on my way back to you.' He gestured towards the nearest entrance. 'I think Caius Monnius is awaiting you in there.'

I nodded, though I might almost have found my way unassisted, from the pungent smells of funeral oil and herbs already eddying in the smoky air.

I pushed open the door. I found not only Caius Monnius awaiting me, but also half a dozen of the undertaker's men and women, engaged in preparing the body for its last procession. They had drawn back the folding window shutters while they worked (although they later would be discreetly closed again in deference to the dead) and muted daylight illuminated the room. It was an incongruous place for death, with a painted frieze of grinning satyrs round the walls, and a large bronze statue of a well-endowed Priapus standing in the corner by the door.

The undertakers, however, seemed oblivious. Evidence of their work was everywhere – the water with which the dead man had been ritually washed, the aromatic oils, the first of the sacred herbs and candles already pungently burning in pottery containers at each corner of the bed. A fine funeral bier was being readied, too, to carry the body to lie in state in the atrium when the preliminary rituals were finished. At our arrival, the funeral workers abandoned their tasks and stood obediently aside. Fulvia had evidently been as good as her word.

But it was already too late. I exchanged glances with Junio, who shook his head sympathetically. There was little point in my lingering here. Monnius had been stripped, cleansed and covered with a clean white cloth. His banqueting robes had been carefully folded and laid on one side, with the wilted festive garland on top of the pile. The fresh linen and new boots in which the corpse would be dressed for its final journey were already set out and waiting on the bier. I sighed. Any information that I might have gleaned from examining the body or clothing had long since disappeared under the ministrations of the undertakers.

I made a show of it, however. I inspected the fat neck, where the cruel marks of the silver chain were still clearly visible. Pertinax's account had clearly been correct.

Someone had twisted the chain tightly from the rear, and the face was horribly contorted. There were bruises around the shoulders, too, as if someone had knelt on him to hold him down, although I could see no other marks on the body.

I walked over to the window-space. It was large – effectively a door – and looked out into the garden: a paved peristyle colonnade, protected by high walls, with a little formal enclosure of plants and flowers in the centre and a painted shrine at the further end, with a ladder still leaning drunkenly against it. The left-hand wall was clearly formed by the back of the famous annexe, but there was no access to the garden from there or even any window overlooking it. This was a private space for Monnius and his wife, though if Annia *was* excluded there was nothing much to see.

I turned away and was about to leave the bedchamber when one of the undertaker's slaves sidled up to me. 'You want to see the chain that did it, citizen?'

I gaped at him. Of course I wanted to see it – I had merely

45

assumed that the murderer, whoever he was, had taken it with him.

'Still round his neck when we found him, citizen. And quite a trial we had to get it off, without damaging him further. But his wife insisted. Said it wouldn't be fitting to send him to the Afterworld in that. So here it is.' He picked up a small roll of cloth, lying among the oils and unguents on the large iron-bound chest in the corner.

'Show me.'

He did so, unrolling the cloth with a flourish. 'Only be careful, citizen. We have not cleaned it yet.'

It was a triple strand of silver, set with tiny gems at intervals, the metal hammer-worked so that the links were doubly strong, and the whole supple chain would lie neatly flat against the wearer's neck. There were fragments of its latest wearer still adhering to it.

The undertaker's slave smiled grimly. 'You see what the lady means, citizen? Hardly a fitting thing for a senior civic official to be wearing for his journey across the Styx.'

I did see what she meant. It was an element of the killing which had not been clear to me. At the mention of a 'necklace' I had half imagined a heavy Roman torc, or some stout ornamental chain designed to hold seals or keys. This was a feminine necklace, the sort of personal jewellery that only women, or effete and handsome slave-boys, ever wear. To discover such a thing on Caius Monnius was as startling as if he had been found wearing a stola, or with ochre on his cheeks and lamp-black darkening his eyelashes.

'Don't ask me whose it is,' the man said, anticipating my question. 'His wife has got one very like it, it seems, but this one isn't hers. She's got that safe and sound in a casket in her room – first thing she did when she saw him was go and look for it. And there's another funny thing. You see those feathers?' He pointed to a handful of them, lying in an open wooden bowl nearby. 'Found those when we came to wash the body. There's the pillow, there. It had been pushed down so firmly over him that the silk split at the stitching. We didn't know what to do with it all exactly, so we've put the things here to burn them with the funeral offerings later.'

'I will take the necklace with me. It may help in my enquiries,' I said, rolling it up again and slipping it into the folds of my toga. The undertaker did not protest. If anything, I think he was glad to be relieved of the responsibility. I nodded in what I hoped was a suitably thoughtful manner. 'And the knife?'

'That was apparently Caius Monnius' own, citizen.' He showed me where they had placed it, carefully, with the rest of the dead man's personal belongings. It was a fine knife: a sharp blade set in an elaborately carved horn handle – the kind that wealthy people often carry at their belts, especially at large banquets where there are rarely enough knives for all the guests. I carry a knife myself, though mine is a more humble article: if you rely on the *scissor* – the slave who cuts up the meat – you often have a long wait for his services.

I examined the knife. 'I see you have cleaned the blade,' I said.

'It did not seem respectful, citizen, to leave it as it was. It will be offered as one of the grave-goods to be cremated with him. He left instructions with us long ago, when he ordered his memorial stone. His knife, that household statue of himself, and a *mobius*, the official corn-measure, as a symbol of his office.' He peered anxiously at my face. 'I hope we have not done wrong, there, citizen? After all, the knife was actually not used to kill anyone, and it was not like the necklace. It just required wiping, sharpening and polishing with red earth.'

So there was nothing to be learned from the knife either,

47

except that it was Monnius' own, and had presumably been in his room the night before. That explained how the killer had picked it up – I had wondered earlier why Fulvia's attacker had not simply used the chain again. But my inspection of the body had answered that question at least. The necklace had bitten so deeply into Monnius' fleshy neck that it would have been well-nigh impossible to remove it again, in darkness and in a hurry.

I nodded. 'Very well, your people may carry on here. I have seen all that it is possible to see.' I turned to go.

The chief undertaker came after me, smiling ingratiatingly. 'I hope we have been of some assistance, citizen? They tell me you were sent here by the governor?'

The man wanted a tip, I realised. I fished into my purse again and parted with another five *as* coin. It was a large sum to me, but he did not look any more delighted with my bounty than Superbus had done. I began to hope that I would not have occasion to reward many more servants in Londinium. I have only a modest income, and giving gratuities in this city was clearly a very expensive business.

I summoned Junio, who had been waiting in the corridor, and was about to make a dignified exit when we were all interrupted by a disturbance in the street. Somebody was shouting.

I abandoned all pretence at restraint and went to the window-space to listen.

'What means these words, Caius Monnius is dead? I do not believe this telling. He was yesterday perfectly well. This is some plotting of his to avoid to see me.' The angry man – whoever he was – had hesitant Latin. His meaning, however, was abundantly clear to anyone for half a mile around. I longed to climb the ladder in the courtyard and peer over the wall into the street, but dignity forbade it.

Someone, clearly, was trying to calm the outburst. There

were muffled voices for a moment, and then the tirade began again.

'Well, you listen me, my friend. You tell your master, is he alive or dead, that Eppaticus Tertius is arrived to see him. And if Eppaticus does not see somebody very soon, then Eppaticus will take his matters to the court. Twenty thousand sesterces, he owes to me, and he promised me today.'

More apologetic muttering. The doorkeeper evidently.

'No, I will not make less loud my voice. All Londinium can know these things. And the other things will I tell, that Caius Monnius wishes I should hide – those things I will shout from the steps of the forum, if I do not have my money in my hand today. Now, stand back and let me see him, or by all the gods of the river, you will be the one which is dead.'

There was a scuffle, a shout, a bang and a groan. I glanced at Junio, and a moment later the two of us were hastening back towards the atrium the way we had come. Eppaticus, however, was too quick for us.

We met him coming towards us, in one of the inter-connecting rooms. He was a huge man in a plaid cape, with shoulders like an ox and a red bull face under a thatch of light brown hair. In one great hand he had hoisted the unfortunate doorkeeper by the neck of his tunic, and was half carrying, half pushing him along; while with the other (which seemed the size of a fire-flail) he brushed aside the two burly household slaves who tried to detain him, as though they were no more than a pair of troublesome sheep.

He was still bellowing. 'Dead, you say he is? Then you will show me him. Dead or alive, I will see Caius Monnius.'

'Ask this citizen,' the doorkeeper squawked, his toes scarcely touching the ground as he was thrust along. 'He is an emissary from the governor.'

Eppaticus stopped, looking me over from haircut to toga hem. 'So? Another Roman? What the governor wishes in this

49

house? What things that cheating Caius Monnius had told against me?' He was working himself up into a rage again, and for a moment it looked as if he might forget himself, and lay violent hands on me.

'I am a Celt, like yourself,' I said, speaking in my native tongue. 'And they are telling you the truth, Eppaticus. The man is dead. They are even now preparing him for his funeral.'

He put down the doorkeeper, and stared consideringly at me. As he turned his head I saw with surprise that he wore his hair in an old-fashioned Celtic pigtail at the back, although his forehead was not shaved as it would have been in my own tribe, and he lacked the long waxed moustache that would have suggested noble descent. His dress, too, was a mixture of traditions. He wore a Roman-style tunic, rather than trousers, under his Celtic plaid.

He was gazing at me with suspicion, but he replied in the same language. 'You are not from these parts, citizen? Your dialect is strange to me.'

'As yours to me,' I said. It was true. It was almost as difficult for me to comprehend his barbarous Celtic accent as to follow his fractured Latin. Nevertheless, the discovery that I was a fellow countryman had some effect. It had stopped the furious bull in his stampede and I hoped it forged a kind of fragile bond between us, though he was obviously still extremely wary of me. The tribes of Britain have often nurtured worse enmities between themselves than were ever felt for our conquerors.

I said to reassure him, 'I am from the farthest south-west corner of Britannia.' That, I hoped, was safe. Tribal tension is always greatest between immediate neighbours.

Eppaticus nodded his huge head slowly. 'And I am Trinovantine.'

I had heard of them. One of the most warlike and

quarrelsome tribes in the country: at one time, they had even joined forces with the Iceni to revolt against Roman rule. Of course, that was more than a century ago, and old scores had been officially forgotten – at least in public – but men still spoke in whispers of the terrible revenge which the Romans had inflicted on the warrior queen Boudicca and her daughters, and the razing of the cities (including Londinium) which had supported the rebels. I imagine that the Trinovantes have little love for a toga.

No surprise, then, to find Eppaticus clinging to Celtic ways – in fact it was more surprising to see the extent of his Romanisation. And he could hardly welcome an emissary from the governor. Indeed, he was staring suspiciously at me.

'Ah, yes! A Trinovantine. The barley ear,' I said, to cover my frantic thoughts.

I meant nothing particular by that – any trader in the island might have said the same. The original coinage of the Trinovantes was marked with an ear of barley, and therefore everyone in the province associated the name with the symbol, but the effect on Eppaticus was startling.

He let out a roar that rattled the wall-hangings. 'What has Caius Monnius been telling you? It was an arrangement – he was as much to blame as I was. It was a private matter, between ourselves, and now he tries to incriminate me! I'll kill him!'

I looked around the corridor. The slaves were watching the exchange with expressions which ranged from horrified amusement to blank incomprehension.

'Eppaticus,' I said, 'be careful what you say. Many of the servants here speak Celtic.'

He gave a snort of contempt. 'I care not which hears me,' he bellowed in Latin. 'He betrays me to the governor. I said before and I say again, I kill him. I throttle him. I wring his dirty Roman neck!'

'Eppaticus,' I said gently, 'you are too late. I told you. Caius Monnius is dead. Someone has throttled him already. That is why the governor has sent me here.'

He seemed to understand the message for the first time. He stared at me a moment. 'Murdered?'

Then, surprisingly swiftly for a man of his stature, he pushed the slaves savagely aside, and – still roaring like a bull – before anyone could stop him he fled headlong from the house.

Chapter Six

As soon as they had picked themselves up and pulled themselves together, two of the house-slaves ran out after him. I followed, a little more slowly, as my age required.

But as I arrived at the front entrance they returned, panting.

'It is no good, citizen, he had a horse outside, being held by a beggar. He was on to it and away in no time. We almost caught him, but he was too quick for us.'

I frowned. 'Who is he? Apart from being called Eppaticus?'

They looked at each other, shrugging. 'I do not know, citizen. He is not a man we've ever seen before.'

'Not as a dinner guest? Not among your master's *clientes*?'

They shook their heads in unison.

I found myself in a quandary now. I was here to investigate the death of Caius Monnius, and Eppaticus had apparently not known about that, so I had no reason to detain him. Yet his behaviour throughout had been so extraordinary – barging into the house uninvited, and barging just as abruptly out of it again – that I was reluctant just to let him go.

I turned to Junio, who had followed – like a good slave – at my heels. 'Fetch me Superbus,' I said, with sudden determination. 'He can go and ask a few questions for me. I want to know more about that Trinovantine.'

'Superbus, master?' Junio sounded stricken. 'Are you sure that he will ask the right question—'

I interrupted him. 'Send me Superbus,' I said firmly. 'You

53

cannot be everywhere at once, and there are more immediate matters here which I want you to help with.'

'As you wish, master,' Junio said, and did as he was bidden, although with an expression which suggested that he still had the gravest doubts about the wisdom of my decision.

'And be quick about it!' I shouted after him, largely for the benefit of the assembled servants, who had been watching this unslavelike exchange with fascination.

'Well,' I said, rounding on the others briskly. 'Have you no work to do? Back to your stations at once, and report this intrusion to your mistress. You!' I elected one of them at random. 'Escort me to the lady Fulvia. If she is well enough I think I should hear her account of what happened last night.'

'Yes, citizen,' he murmured dutifully, as the others shuffled off to their posts. 'If you would follow me . . .'

He led me back towards the master's quarters. Only just in time. As I turned away, I could already hear Annia's voice raised in outrage. 'You worm! You offspring of a circus trainer's pimp! How dare you not inform me of this sooner!' While Lydia wailed plaintively, 'Another intruder! Great Mercury defend us. We shall all be murdered in our beds.'

My attendant shot me an embarrassed smile and led the way back to the painted passage where I had been before. The smoke was thicker now, and more pungent, but we passed the master's room and the slave tapped timidly at the second door.

'Enter!' said Fulvia's voice, and we went in.

It was a luxurious room, beautifully decorated with roundels of painted flowers on the wall. Fine bed, fine cushions, fine rugs upon the floor: a great bound chest near the door for clothes and ornaments: another at the foot of the bed: an elegant footstool: a little brazier and a dozen lamps: an exquisite small shrine upon a stand, and a small shelf built into the wall where there was such an assortment of phials and pots, boxes, mirrors, combs and bowls that you might have thought the lady was going into the cosmetics business herself, and had made a collection for the purpose.

As in every other part of the house, no expense had been spared, but here there was evidence of a discerning eye. The garments that an elderly maidservant was folding fussily into the storage chest, too, were not only of finest wool and linen, but in the subtlest colours to be had in the Empire – mossy greens, soft blues and amethyst – each one a tribute to the dyer's art. And to the depth of the buyer's purse, I thought.

Fulvia was lying back against her pillows. She had removed her veil and silken belt and placed them on a stool beside the bed, but otherwise she was dressed as before, and her dark robes were in starkest contrast to the beautiful pastel shades around her. One of the pretty pageboys was engaged in bathing her forehead with what looked like goat's milk and water from a bowl. The other boy stood at the open window-space, which was large – exactly like the one in the next room – and was using a large feather fan to waft away the pungent smoke which was issuing from under the inner door. Nevertheless, the air was heavy with the smells of incense and burning herbs.

Fulvia stretched out a languid hand to me. 'Ah, you have come, citizen.' I bent over the hand, and she continued, 'I was beginning to wonder what had happened. I heard some sort of . . . commotion.'

'Eppaticus the Trinovantine,' I informed her. 'Come to demand his money. He claims that your husband owes him twenty thousand sesterces. That's five thousand *denarii*!'

I had hoped to provoke some sign of recognition at the name, but there was none. Fulvia wrinkled her pretty brow. 'Eppaticus,' she murmured. 'What an ugly name. I have never heard it, I am sure. I would have remembered it.'

'You would not forget *him* in hurry,' I said. I gave a brief description.

She shook her head. 'One of my husband's nasty business contacts, I imagine. I'm sorry, citizen, I cannot help you there.'

'And the money?' I enquired. 'Five thousand *denarii* is a lot of silver. You think your husband really owed him as much as that?'

She waved a careless hand. 'Oh, that is quite possible. Monnius was always striking deals.' She seemed more composed now, speaking about her husband, than she had done previously. She furrowed her pretty brow, and added, 'Did I not hear that money had been taken? About that amount, I think. Perhaps Eppaticus was right, and that was the money owed to him.'

'Twenty thousand sesterces?' I said in amazement. Pertinax had spoken of a 'substantial sum', but I had not imagined a small fortune like this. Even carrying away such a quantity of coins would be quite a feat in itself. 'Did Monnius regularly keep such large amounts in the house?'

Fulvia laughed. 'Oh yes, citizen. And larger sums than that. He had safe hiding places built especially – under the floorboards in his room, in his study, even in the walls. If you were to search this house from roof to soil I dare say you would find ten times that quantity in gold and silver, even now.'

'And could you lead me to these hiding places?'

She dazzled me with a smile 'Not I, citizen. I was never told his secrets. My husband did not trust females with money. Not even his mother. Of course, where I was concerned there was no problem. If I wished for anything, I had merely to ask. Monnius was always' – she smiled – 'a *susceptible* man.'

I let it pass, for the moment – though naturally there were

questions I would want to ask her later. I said, 'And the documents?'

'Documents?' She sounded astonished.

'I understand some scrolls have also disappeared.'

'Scrolls? I do not think so, citizen.' She frowned. 'At least . . . I had not heard of this. Documents? You are certain of that?'

'I report only what I heard,' I said. 'A sum of money and at least one document-scroll. Your husband would have had such things, I presume?'

'Indeed, citizen. His writing desk was always littered with them. I saw him take delivery of some new ones yesterday. Though they are only business contracts and copies of the imperial corn decrees, I think. Why should a sneak thief make away with those?'

'You have the advantage of me, lady. You have seen his "documents". Perhaps you could suggest a reason.'

Her pale cheeks coloured faintly. 'Perhaps I could have done, citizen, except that my father had firm views on educating women. He believed that girls should learn what he called "*useful* arts". Hence, I can play three types of instrument, sing you songs in Latin and in Greek, dance you most kinds of dance and tell you a hundred legends. I can dye wool, weave a length of cloth, mix you a remedy and oversee a household to perfection. But, though I can scratch my name on a wax tablet when required, in general reading is not among my skills. And I did not know that any scrolls were missing.'

She spoke with a kind of bitterness and I could only nod. Celtic girls have always received the same education as their brothers, so that these days, when so many richer Celtic men read Latin, one expects their educated womenfolk to do the same. I am inclined to forget that Roman families sometimes see matters differently. I changed the subject hastily. 'But, even if you could not read the scrolls, you can tell me something about what happened here last night?'

She had been waiting for that question, one could see it in her eyes. Proud of her skill at storytelling, perhaps, because she gestured me to a stool beside her, waved away the slave with the bowl, and, leaning up on her undamaged arm, arranged herself more carefully on the bed. It was a kind of art form, I could see that – every fold of drapery contrived to emphasise the muscular perfection of her form.

I dragged my thoughts back to what she was saying. '. . . I woke to hear a noise, in the next room. At least, I did not exactly waken, I was half awake already. I opened my eyes and there was a shadow beside the bed.' She was acting out the story as she spoke, and said the words with such feeling that I felt my own heart skip a beat.

'Go on.'

'There was a movement – I knew it was a knife, and I flung up my arm, like this, to shield my face.' She lifted her unbandaged limb to demonstrate. 'Next moment the knife was slicing my skin. Strange, I was aware of little pain – just something warm and sticky running down my arm.' She looked down at her fingers now, breathing hard.

'And then?' I prompted. She had closed her eyes and lapsed into silence, as if she were reliving the moment.

'I was terrified. I found myself screaming . . . screaming.' She paused. 'That must have frightened him, because he seemed to hesitate. I thought he was going to stab me again, but then there was a noise upstairs – thanks be to Mercury – and he rushed out of the room. I heard the knife clatter down – I think I'd closed my eyes again – and when I opened them . . . he was gone.' She opened them now and gave me that fluttering, uneven smile again. 'I am sorry, citizen, but that is all I know.'

'It *was* a man, however?'

58

'I am sure of that, citizen. A big, heavy man too, by the look of him – although of course I did not see his face.'

'But agile,' I said, 'since he seems to have escaped through the window-space in no time and scaled that ladder over the wall.'

She seemed to sense a challenge in that. She flushed. 'I may be mistaken, citizen. After all, it was very dark.'

I glanced at her. 'Of course. No doubt our murderer relied on that. And no one else in the household saw or heard anything?'

She shrugged. 'Annia Augusta and Lydia and her son have rooms in the other wing. As to the slaves who should have been on watch, I believe they were drugged. Given a sleeping potion to ensure that they *did* hear nothing. My old nurse thinks so, don't you, Prisca?'

The elderly slave-woman who had been folding garments ceased her task and nodded agreement. 'The mistress is right, citizen. There was something peculiar in the servants' wine last night, I knew it as soon as ever I tasted it. I said so to that pageboy at the master's door, but he wouldn't listen to me. He was half asleep before his head even touched the floor.'

Fulvia added helpfully, 'It would not be difficult to do it, citizen. Warmed water and strong herbs are added to the dregs of wine each evening, and the mixture is left in a large bowl at the kitchen door for the night-slaves, to warm them and help them keep awake. The whole household must know about it. If someone added a sleeping draught to that . . .'

'Perhaps,' I said. 'But would outsiders know about the wine? Or did the "shadow", whoever he might be, have someone in the household helping him? Someone who knew about that wine, for instance, and that there were thousands of sesterces in Monnius' study that night.'

Fulvia was staring at me aghast. 'But who . . .?'

'Oh,' I said, with careful carelessness, 'someone with a

friend or lover in the household. Someone like . . .' I paused, watching her intently, 'Lividius Fortunatus, for example?'

Chapter Seven

I had hoped for some reaction from Fulvia, but it was Prisca, the ageing slave-woman, who gave herself away. She turned the colour of a terracotta vase and dropped the folded garments in a fluster.

'Don't answer him, mistress!' she cried, before Fulvia's warning look could stop her. 'He can't know anything about Fortunatus. None of us would ever have said a word.'

That was as good as a confession. I looked at Fulvia. 'So I take it that Annia Augusta was correct? The name of Fortunatus does mean something to you?'

She looked from me to the maidservant and back again, then gave a helpless shrug. 'I see that it is useless to deny it now. Very well, citizen, I admit the truth. The name does mean something to me, and the owner of the name still more.'

'Good mistress . . .' The slave-woman stepped forward, twisting her hands in her tunic girdle and looking anguished. 'Don't tell him. Have a care . . .'

'Be silent, Prisca!' Fulvia motioned away her would-be counsellor. 'You have said too much already. However, since the truth is out, thanks to your runaway tongue, there is no longer any point in dissembling. Do not look so stricken. Perhaps it is as well the facts are known, and I should prefer the citizen to learn the story from my own lips, rather than hear a distorted version from someone else. Besides, Monnius is dead, and finding the man who killed him is of more

61

importance now than my reputation.'

That was prudent, I thought, especially since much more than her reputation was at stake here. I wondered if she realised how much circumstances contrived to make her seem a likely accomplice to murder.

It seemed not. She turned to look at me directly, white-faced but dignified. 'So I must throw myself on your discretion, citizen. I am a young woman, and my husband was old, ugly and . . . importunate. Violent sometimes. But he was rich and powerful, and, in his way, he loved me. He never would have let me go, alive.'

'He was a brute, citizen,' the maidservant burst out. 'I have known this poor lady pace the corridors for hours, weeping, when he'd done with her. She thinks I didn't know it but I did. Poor lady – no wonder she wanted a bit of tenderness now and then.'

'Be silent, Prisca,' Fulvia said. She looked at me, not dropping her eyes as modest Roman matrons do, but squarely and frankly as if inviting understanding. 'But she is right, citizen. I did, I confess it, once or twice seek consolation elsewhere.'

'So,' I said, still pursuing my own thoughts, 'Fortunatus did come to this house?'

She held my gaze. 'Many times, citizen. At my husband's invitation first – Monnius was a devotee of chariot racing – and then, increasingly, at mine.'

'Without your husband's knowledge?'

She did lower her eyes then. 'Sometimes, citizen.'

Again it was Prisca who rushed headlong into speech. 'Well, citizen, what if she did – who in the world could blame her? You do not know what a monster Monnius was. Always out gambling or drinking or making his hole-in-the-corner deals somewhere, coming home at all hours stinking of wine, women and garlic – reeling round the floor, sometimes, violent with drink – and then demanding his wife. I've stood by this bed with a lamp in one hand and a vomit bowl in the other – he always insisted on light when he came in here – and he would treat her so roughly. He'd summon her into his bed, sometimes, in the middle of the night, and do it all again. I have seen her covered in bruises from his so-called attentions. It brought tears to my eyes to watch it—'

'Prisca! Enough!'.

But the slave-woman was determined to defend her mistress, and she would not be silenced. 'Forgive me, lady, but the citizen should know.' She turned to me. 'I've served my mistress since she was a tiny girl, and no one ever cared for her like I do – but it was shameful, what Monnius did to her. And then the next day, in he'd come, with one of his gifts of silks and necklaces, trying to wheedle round her and promising the earth. And pawing her all over with his great hairy hands, ready to start again. What wonder if my poor mistress sought a bit of comfort with a young, good-looking man? Why, I could tell you . . .'

'Prisca!' Fulvia said again. 'Leave us. Now. At once. Wait in the corridor, and hold your tongue. How dare you speak of your master in this way? And in front of the pages too?'

For a moment I really thought the old maidservant was going to defy her mistress once again. But in the end she merely sighed, sniffed, and took herself off as instructed, still muttering beneath her breath, 'Well, the serving boys would only tell you the same thing.'

I saw the lads exchange glances. 'Would you tell me the same thing?' I asked them.

Again that uncomfortable exchange of looks. Then the older of the two said, unwillingly, 'There were rumours, citizen, in the servants' hall. That is all. If Lividius Fortunatus did come here when Caius Monnius was out, we never witnessed it ourselves.'

63

I understood the message perfectly. I have been a slave myself. Like all good servants, these two had seen nothing and heard nothing, and would have remained conveniently blind and deaf if the charioteer had burst in every night stark naked with a band of pipers. As to relations between Monnius and his wife, the boy had simply evaded the question. I wondered how much the pages really knew. If my patron, Marcus Septimus, had been here, no doubt he would have arranged to have the boys flogged to sharpen their memories. However, I let it pass. I have found the technique unreliable – Marcus has sometimes been misled when witnesses, in order to stop the torturer's lash, have suddenly remembered things that never happened at all.

The boys had told me something by their very silence, however. They were sympathetic to Fulvia, even when I was trying to find their master's murderer. That told me a good deal about Caius Monnius. I pressed my advantage.

'There are other rumours in the household, lady,' I said. 'Your mother-in-law blames Fortunatus for this murder, as I expect you know – and she seems at first sight to have reason on her side.'

Fulvia looked at me incredulously. Reason and Annia Augusta were obviously not often bracketed together in her mind.

I shrugged. 'Consider. Fortunatus wanted you – but you had a husband, so he could not have you. That is a common enough motive for murder. It would have been easy for you to let him in: over the wall, perhaps. I imagine a man of his physical prowess could scale it easily. You could have drugged the wine in advance – you told me that you have an under-standing of potions – and he strangles Monnius while the servants are asleep.'

'And tries to stab me, citizen? You think he would do that?'

'Perhaps he did it on purpose to divert suspicion. No one would suspect Fortunatus of attacking *you*.'

'I see!' She smiled wryly. 'You must think me very brave, citizen, to have permitted that. Suppose that he had lost his nerve, or stabbed me in the wrong place in the dark? None the less, I salute you. An ingenious explanation. But not true. Fortunatus did not kill my husband, citizen. Not even without my assistance – and certainly I did not help him or anyone else. Whoever killed Monnius, it cannot have been him.'

I raised my brows at her. 'You are very certain of that.'

'I am more than certain. It was a Roman feast-day yesterday, and there is a great five-day chariot-racing spectacular at Verulamium, in honour of the occasion. That is why Fortunatus did not attend my husband's banquet, as he often does. He was in Verulamium, driving for his colour.'

'In Verulamium?' I said, stupidly.

'All the Londinium *factiones* have gone there – one of the town authorities struck a bargain with the managers for the Londinium teams to come and race for their colours. He was promising huge sums in prize money besides. Do not look at me so doubtfully, citizen. There must have been a thousand witnesses – the last time Fortunatus appeared in Verulamium there was not a free seat in the stadium and people in the street outside were still fighting to get in.'

I sighed. The neat little mosaic of a theory I had carefully constructed had just shattered into a hundred pieces. If Fortunatus was racing in Verulamium, he could not have killed the *frumentarius*.

I know a little bit about chariot racing – it is thought of as a Roman institution, of course, but we were racing warcarts on this island before Julius Caesar ever set foot here, and, like every other Celt, I attend whenever my business makes it possible. Of course the races in Glevum are not professional affairs as they are in Londinium – the drivers there are simply

65

members of the college of youth, and the track is a makeshift affair with wooden stakes hammered in to mark the turning points – but the racing itself is no less exciting for that.

Of course it would be a little different in Verulamium. It is a large town – it was once the capital of the local tribes – but I doubted that it had a purpose-built stadium either. No doubt sponsoring a real spectacle, with professionals coming all the way from Londinium, was someone's way of impressing the populace and winning support for public office. Wealthy patrons of the *factiones* in every town do the same thing – queuing up for the honour of offering financial support to the colour of their choice, and even sometimes bringing teams from overseas. Presumably it works – entrance to these things is traditionally free, and there are always passionate crowds at even the smallest races.

In Verulamium probably half the town would have turned out, as Fulvia said. I could imagine it: scuffles for seats and fist-fights for the best vantage points in the standing spaces, while the visiting charioteers – with their whole retinue of stable boys, managers, guards and medical attendants – became the idols of the entire community, followed and cheered at wherever they went.

So how could Fortunatus simply have disappeared for the night? It was impossible. He would have been guarded to the hilt for one thing – people stake whole fortunes on the outcome of a chariot race, and there have been too many attempts in recent years to interfere with drivers and horses. Even in Glevum last year we had someone trying to dope the favourite, and stick a dagger between the driver's ribs. Fortunatus, the most famous charioteer of all, could no more have slipped off for an evening unobserved than the Emperor could have done so himself.

Besides, Verulamium is several hours away even on a good horse in broad daylight. Not even Fortunatus could possibly have raced all day – and it would have been all day, the organisers like to get value for their money – galloped to Londinium in the dark to strangle Monnius and then popped back to Verulamium again in time to start all over first thing in the morning.

So if it was not Fortunatus, who was it? He could have paid someone else to do it, of course – and invited blackmail for the rest of his days. The charioteer was a rich man and the penalties for conspiracy were fearful.

'In any case,' Fulvia was saying, breaking into my thoughts, 'I saw the man. The figure I saw at my bedside was taller and broader than Fortunatus. I assure you, citizen, I would have recognised *him*.' She gave me one of those sideways looks again, and sighed. She was delectable. No wonder they nicknamed the charioteer 'fortunatus'.

A renewed waft of smoke and incense from the next room reminded me of my duty. The undertakers had clearly lit the remaining candles. I said, 'Then I must thank you, lady, for your help, and apologise for having taken up your time. You must be anxious to prepare the lament.' To make the ritual washing of her hands and put the ashes on her head, I meant, but the words sounded unintentionally ironic.

She looked at me gravely. 'I will lament my husband, citizen, and sincerely too. Monnius was an uncouth bedfellow – I will not pretend otherwise – but he was good to me in his way. If he was suspicious about Fortunatus – and I'm sure his mother saw to that! – he was content to ignore it, provided that I was discreet in public and never showed a lack of compliance when he came to me. In fact, I think the notion sometimes excited him.'

I was on the point of leaving, but that stopped me. I tried to imagine feeling 'excited', when I was young, had someone made advances to my beloved wife. I failed. I forced the thought aside, and said, 'How so?'

She laughed, gaily. 'Fortunatus is young, rich, strong and famous. He could have any woman he wanted – and he wanted me. I think that made me seem more desirable to my husband.'

'Because you belonged to him?' I said slowly. It might be true. Jealousy, and a frenzied imagination, can lead to a kind of furious possession. Most Roman men would have their wives executed, or at least divorced and exiled to some barren island, if even a hint of infidelity had attached to them. Yet as Annia herself had told me, Monnius had brushed aside all his mother's warnings, and become even more fiercely besotted with his wife. And, I reminded myself, he permitted his first wife to live in the annexe.

'Exactly, citizen. You understand me, I think.' She smiled at me again, stirring a little on the bed and showing those uneven teeth. The effect was oddly provocative – like her words. No wonder Monnius and Fortunatus had fallen captive to her charms. I glanced uneasily at the two pageboys, but they just went on wafting the smoke away from under the door, their faces blank as stone.

'Well, I will leave you, lady,' I said again. 'If Fortunatus did not kill your husband, then I must discover who did. And who it was who drugged the slaves last night. If it was not you yourself?'

She laughed. 'I assure you, citizen, my expertise with herbs does not extend so far. A simple remedy for croup I might manage, or an ointment for bruising, but not a potent sleeping draught! I would never be certain it would work. Indeed, when I want one for my own use – on those occasions which Prisca was telling you of – I have Lydia make me one.'

'Lydia?' Monnius' former wife had not impressed me as a woman of many talents.

'Oh, indeed, citizen. It is one of the womanly skills in which Annia Augusta continues to encourage her – one of

the wifely virtues in which she outdoes me. Annia has taught
her everything she knows – only, of course, I could scarcely
ask Annia herself. You can imagine what she would say if I
requested a sleeping draught.'

I could imagine. 'And did you ever use one on your
husband? To ensure that he slept when Fortunatus came?' If
Monnius had been drugged the night before, I thought, it
would explain much about the manner of his death.

'I never entertained Fortunatus when my husband was in
the house, citizen. I have some notion of duty. I used the
sleeping potion for myself – when Monnius had been to my
bed I sometimes found it difficult to sleep.'

'And yet,' I said, struck by a sudden thought, 'you did not
take it last night?'

The playful smile vanished and she frowned. 'But I did,
citizen. I always do. Dear Jupiter, I had not thought of that.
The death of Monnius drove it from my mind. I took the
potion, yet I did not sleep. You think . . .?'

'That someone used your sleeping draught to drug the
servants? It seems a likely explanation. Could Monnius have
drunk any of it?'

'I don't think so. Why would he drink the watered dregs
left out for the servants?'

'There would not be sufficient in your draught, surely, to
drug a whole container full of that?'

She shook her head. 'There might well be, citizen. It is
only days since I took possession of a whole large jar of
sleeping potion. I have Lydia make a large amount, once
a month when Annia is not in the house, and I refill my
little phial every night. But how would anyone find it? I
keep it carefully hidden.' She clapped her hands, and the
two lads sprang instantly to life. 'In the large chest there,
under the clothing, you will find the container. Show it to the
citizen, boy.'

One of the pages scurried over and was already opening the great carved box for me, removing the garments which Prisca had so neatly stacked there. There it was: a glazed jar, about the size of a small water pitcher, neatly stoppered with a wooden insert. It was wedged firmly into place with folded underlinen, and a small drinking vessel had been packed beside it.

I motioned to the boy and he removed the jar from the chest. From the way he handled it and carried it carefully to me, I could see that it was heavy. I took it from him, and with difficulty removed the stopper. The jug was almost full.

I dipped an exploratory finger into the liquid, and sniffed. I could detect nothing. The faintest smell of herbs perhaps, but that was all.

I turned to Fulvia, who was frowning at me, perplexed. 'I think,' I said slowly, 'that someone has refilled the flask with water. If you drank only this, it would explain why you did not sleep last night.' I handed the container back to the page, and had him pour me some. I was about to take a very cautious sip – not without a certain trepidation – when Fulvia forestalled me.

'Drink that potion for him, boy. It may not be as harmless as he thinks.'

This was a brutally Roman way of resolving uncertainty. I had no time to protest, however. By the time I had exclaimed 'No, wait!' the page, with the dreadful resigned obedience of slave-boys everywhere, had already raised the drinking cup and emptied most of it down his throat.

I gave a heavy sigh. I have never become accustomed to watching a poison-taster at work. There was nothing to do now but wait to see if the draught had killed him.

Chapter Eight

To my relief – and certainly to his – whatever the pageboy had swallowed appeared to have done him no harm. After a few moments Fulvia gestured to him and, the colour returning slowly to his cheeks, he set down the cup again and returned to his station by the window.

Fulvia said, uneasily, 'It seems you were right, citizen. No wonder my slumbers were not very deep last night. Luckily the liquid was not poisoned. Perhaps I should be careful what I eat and drink – if someone tampered in the kitchens once, they might do it again. I must use a servant as taster. Although it seems our unknown visitor did me an unwitting service – if I had been as soundly drugged as my slaves last night, perhaps I would have suffered far more than a gashed arm.'

I nodded. 'So whoever did this must have known you had the sleeping draught. He steals it from your room, pours it into the servants' wine, and replaces the liquid with water from – where?'

She shrugged. 'There is always water in the kitchens, citizen. Barrels of it. We bought this house because it was convenient for the corn office but it is not connected to the city water supply. Monnius is . . . was . . . always talking of it. He made many other alterations, like building the annexe, but he decided it would be too expensive to bring water on to the property. I think Fortunatus put him off. He has bought himself a large house in the city for when he retires and is

71

having it rebuilt, but the price of joining it to the town supply has been enormous. He has even had to delay the building work while they lift the pavement and extend the pipes. Monnius could not live with such disruption. It is very little problem for the slaves to fetch water for us, and somehow it has never seemed worth the cost of laying the channels and paying the water charges.'

'Do you have a private well?'

'Of course. It fails sometimes, but even so we are close to the Wall Brook and the public cistern. There is even a rain barrel in the garden to catch the water off the roof gutter. Monnius used to say that if a property has piped water, it also has to have a drain, and that would cost us, too. We are a large household and he had arranged quite a lucrative contract with the local toga-weavers for the contents of the chamber pots.'

I understood that. Fine wool and leather is often softened and bleached by being soaked in urine – it improves the texture and the colour of the finished garment – and owners of the workshops often leave hopeful pots in public places on market day, or contract for collection of the commodity from private and communal sources. There is a tannery right next door to my little workshop in Glevum, and I have a similar arrangement with them – though it has never occurred to me to ask for money for my services.

'So,' I said, 'replacing the sleeping draught with water would present no difficulty at all – provided of course that our intruder was sure that the kitchen would be empty, and that you were not in your room?'

She flushed like a child. 'You are quite right, of course, citizen. I had not thought of that. It does rather suggest a knowledge of the household – or a close surveillance of our movements, at least.' She shifted on her pillows, making her long robes rustle. 'Though perhaps it might not have been so difficult, last night. Monnius held a banquet. Most of the servants were occupied with that, and for much of the time I was with him, playing the cithara and singing for the guests. My father's education again, you see. It would have been easy for anyone to slip into my room, open the chest and substitute one flagon for another.'

There seemed to me to be some objections to that, but I did not express them to Fulvia.

She noted my silence. 'You look thoughtful, citizen.'

I smiled. 'I was wondering why, in that case, this intruder did not steal your silver chain at the same time? I presume you do keep it in this room?'

Fulvia sat herself a little more upright and gestured to the page again. 'Bring me my casket, here.'

He took down a small gilded box from the shelf and gave it to Fulvia. She opened the clasp and passed it to me wordlessly. Inside were a number of fine jewelled pins and necklaces, including a triple-stranded silver chain exactly like the one I was carrying in the roll of cloth hidden in my belt.

'This casket was not locked?'

'No. There is a key, but it is cumbersome, and I do not often use it.'

'And yet your intruder did not steal your chain. I wonder why?' I said again.

'Simple, citizen. It was not here. I was wearing it last evening at the feast.'

I frowned. 'Then why not steal another of your necklets? You have a number here, equally strong and pliable. I still do not understand it. Why go to the trouble of finding another chain, of precisely the same pattern as yours, to strangle Caius Monnius with? It makes no sense unless the murderer wished to implicate you. That similarity of design is no coincidence.'

She laughed aloud. 'It is even less of a coincidence than

73

you suppose, citizen. A second chain of that pattern would not be hard to find. You can thank Annia Augusta for that. When Monnius first gave the ornament to me – a gift for Janus' feast last year – his mother first pretended to admire it, and then persuaded him that she must have one exactly like it made for her.'

One of Jove's thunderbolts could not have surprised me more. 'Great Jupiter! Monnius was murdered with his mother's chain?'

'Not necessarily. Annia, in turn, presented one to Lydia – so that she would not feel "excluded" from the family. It was done as an insult to me, of course. Monnius was a fool to agree to her demands in the first place.' A small flush of anger rose to her cheeks as she spoke, making her look more beautiful than ever. 'I was so furious that I almost insisted he bought one for the servant-girls – he had made the pattern so commonplace. I would not have Lydia and Annia Augusta preening themselves in copies of his presents to me, as if they stood equally in his esteem. I told him so. He blustered and squirmed, as he always did, but he admitted he was wrong in the end. He bought me a very pretty ring as an apology.'

Between his wife and Annia Augusta, I thought, Monnius sometimes had as little freedom as I did, for all his riches. I, at least, had only one patron to please. 'Then there were at least two other necklaces in the household exactly like your own?'

'They are not as fine as this one, but they are all of the same pattern.' With the help of one of the pages, she swung herself round so that she was sitting on the side of the bed facing away from me. She passed the casket to the slave, who put it on the shelf, while the other boy put down his fan and came hurrying over with a pair of embroidered slippers. 'That is one reason why I rarely wear my own version of the ornament.'

74

'But you were wearing it last night?'

'I was.' She extended one slim stockinged foot, and the page knelt down and reverently fitted a slipper on to it. Fulvia extended the other leg, and went on addressing me. 'The silversmith who made it was present at the banquet and Monnius felt it would be a compliment to him. If I was entertaining at his table, he always liked to choose the things I wore.'

I tore my mind away from the picture this created. 'The other women did not wear their necklaces?'

She waved the page away and got to her feet. 'If they did, citizen, then no one saw them do it. They were not invited to the feast. They had their meal in private, in Annia's annexe.' She smoothed down the folds of her stola and arranged the veil more neatly over her hair as she spoke, then took up the silken girdle and tied it deftly with her undamaged hand. 'Annia has a small *triclinium* of her own, there, where she can recline in comfort and take her meals – with Lydia if she wishes. Monnius prefers male company when he dines – or did prefer it, perhaps I should say. Though he was never averse to a little feminine entertainment.'

So, I thought, Fulvia Honoria had subtle ways of gaining her revenge. I could just imagine Annia Augusta's rage at being banished to her lonely annexe, with only whining Lydia for company, while her daughter-in-law attended the banquet among the wine, warmth and laughter, singing – and no doubt dancing – in a beguiling manner for her husband and his guests. I pictured Annia's outraged face and could not resist a smile.

Fulvia misinterpreted my amusement, and came round the bed to face me. 'Citizen, you must not think too harshly of my husband. My servant Prisca has a savage tongue, and she saw only the worst side of him. Monnius had many qualities.' She was standing close to me now, looking earnestly up into my face. 'He could be generous, when he was sober; he was shrewd and he was rich. I wanted for nothing, and although he could be bestial in bed he made few other demands on me – apart from being decorative, and singing and dancing for his friends at intervals. It was a small price to pay. He allowed me to visit friends, go the theatre and the public baths, and attend the chariot races too. How many other wives can say the same?'

She smelled of lavender and roses. I tried to ignore it, and concentrate on what she was saying. There was truth in that too. Many wealthy Roman matrons lead a pitiful life, at least to my Celtic eyes – largely shut away from friends and family, and subject to the whim of their husbands, who are also their legal guardians. Of course, within the household it may be different, and situations like this one, where women hold much power behind the scenes, cannot be as uncommon as they seem to outsiders. If I could find my Gwellia, I thought, I would allow my wife to do anything she desired, only to have her by my side again. Except, perhaps, to share her bed with chariot-drivers.

Thinking of Gwellia seemed to break the spell. I took a step backwards. 'I must not delay you longer, lady,' I said. 'The anointers will be finished with the body by this time.'

She extended one hand to me. 'Then farewell for the moment, citizen,' she said softly. 'Send Prisca to me as you go. I need her help to prepare myself for the lament.'

I bowed briefly over her fingers, and then took my leave. Prisca was waiting outside the room, and as I emerged she flashed me an outraged look. 'Your slaves are waiting for you in the *librarium*, citizen,' she said shortly, indicating the last room off the lobby with a wave of her hand. 'I sent them in there. They were getting in the way of the undertakers, and people coming in and out of my master's room.' Without waiting for a word from me she scuttled back to her mistress and closed the door.

The door of the study was half ajar, and Junio and Superbus were waiting for me. I glanced around the room. It was not unlike the *cubiculum* I had just left, except that it was smaller and there was no entry to the garden, only a small translucent window on the outer wall made of thin sheets of horn. It was sparsely furnished with a large writing table and a pair of stools, and a few shelves laden with all the paraphernalia of record-keeping: wax tablets, vellum scrolls, folded bark letter-forms and iron-nibbed sticks for writing, jars of soot, oil and octopus ink mixture; and a huge brass-bound chest, upon which Junio was perching.

He jumped up as soon as I approached. 'Ah, master, there you are at last. I have told Superbus that you wish him to go into the city and find Eppaticus. He is waiting for your orders.'

I guessed from Junio's tone that Superbus had not welcomed the news. He was looking more disdainful than ever, and without Junio I might have hesitated to send him on my errand after all. However, as Triumvir Pompey once famously said, the die was now cast. 'Splendid,' I said with a heartiness I did not feel. 'I'd like you to find out where Eppaticus lives, at least.'

Superbus gave me a stare as though I had invited him personally to deliver those chamber pots to the weavers. 'Citizen,' he said, with a slight bow, 'if those are your orders, I will do my best. Though I am not at all clear as to how I should proceed. Londinium is a very large city, and I do not know the man. I have few dealings with Celts.'

If I had been hesitating, the tone in which he pronounced the last word resolved my doubts. 'Oh, just go out and ask a few questions in the street, Superbus. This man was a giant with an unusual hairstyle, and he galloped away from here at high speed on a horse. Someone must have noticed him. You could begin by asking the two slaves who gave chase, for instance. They must have seen at least the direction he took.'

He seemed to think about that for a moment, and then he said ponderously, 'And perhaps I should speak to the door-keeper too, citizen?'

'Good idea, Superbus,' I said cheerfully. 'Of course, he wasn't at his post when Eppaticus left – the Celt had dragged him in here, and thrown him on the floor, very much where you are standing now – but no doubt the doorkeeper did notice where the visitor came from. If Eppaticus came and went in the same direction, that would give you a good indication of where to start asking.' I nodded at him encouragingly. 'Very good, Superbus. You are getting the idea of this already.'

The slave, who had turned very pale at the mention of physical violence, swallowed and said, 'As you wish, master,' in a much more humble tone.

Behind his back Junio, who had been enjoying the exchange immensely, gave me a gleeful wink. I almost regretted my sarcastic tone, and I softened it with an attempt at flattery. 'With your knowledge of the town, Superbus, you will have a much better idea than I would of where to look for him – where the corn markets are, and the Celtic quarter, for example.'

Superbus was still looking white-faced at the prospect of an encounter with the Trinovantine giant. 'And if I find this man, citizen, what am I to do with him?'

'Nothing,' I said. 'Simply find out what you can, and report back to me here. Or at the governor's palace, if I have left this house before you return.'

Superbus looked extremely relieved. 'At your service, citizen!' he said, and left hurriedly before I could change my mind.

I turned to Junio, who was still grinning like a fish. 'Well then, young man,' I said, clapping him on the shoulder, 'we have work to do. I want to talk to the other inhabitants of the house. But first you can tell me what news you have collected. I presume that you have been listening to the servant gossip as usual?'

Junio's grin broadened. 'You were the one who taught me to ask questions, master. It has become a habit with me.'

'I'm glad to hear it,' I said. 'So, sit down quickly, and tell me what you've learned.' It was not perhaps the most courteous of actions: I should have returned to the public rooms, but I was not anxious to meet Annia Augusta again before I knew what Junio had gleaned.

He perched on the chest again, and made a small grimace. 'Not a great deal, really. Except I do not believe the servants can be in it. Caius Monnius was terrified of plots and every other slave in the place was his paid informer, as far as I can see. No one could have managed this without someone seeing him and giving him away, for fear for their own skin. Caius Monnius would have insisted on the letter of the law and had the whole household of slaves executed for a plot against him. Even now they were falling over their tunics to tell me things, but they seemed to have no real information to give.'

'So they would have told Monnius if there'd been a slave plot against him. But would any of them have told him about his wife and Fortunatus?'

'I am not so certain about that, master. That would not be an executing matter, and the slaves all seem utterly loyal to Fulvia. She is a just mistress, they say, and although she can punish faults mercilessly, she is always fair. Things have improved since she arrived, they say. And they should know. Most of them have been owned by Caius Monnius for years: all of them, in fact, except Fulvia's nurse and pageboys – even Annia Augusta was not permitted to bring her own women with her when she came.'

'But none of them saw or heard anything last night?'

He shook his head. 'They were all sleeping like Morpheus until the screaming woke them – they had been working hard clearing away the banquet. And the slaves on duty downstairs were all asleep. That seemed to be unnatural in itself, with so many spies about – the staff seem to think that someone must have given them a sleeping potion. That is one piece of information that they gave me, by the way. Lydia has a way with herbs, did you know that? Apparently Annia Augusta taught her. Other people swore it couldn't have been Lydia who drugged the slaves, because she never left the annexe all day yesterday. There was quite an argument about it.'

I nodded. 'I think the servants' wine was drugged,' I said, and told him about my conversation with Fulvia. 'I even wondered if Monnius himself had been affected, but why would he be drinking the servants' dregs?'

'He hardly needed a sleeping draught last night, by all accounts,' Junio said. 'He had drunk enough to fell a giant. He was rather given to that, it seems – harsh when he was sober and bestial when he was drunk – though he could be surprisingly generous to his favourites at times. His mother is just as difficult in her own way, they tell me – demanding and hard to please. She is the same with everyone, even with Monnius, refusing to take his advice over her estates and declining to use his drying houses. One of the maidservants called her a human elephant, making a loud noise and trampling everything in her path.'

I have never seen an elephant, but I grinned at the description. From the tales I have heard, they are larger than life, with big noses, and have been known to stampede out of control in the amphitheatre and terrify the bystanders. The comparison with Annia Augusta seemed peculiarly apt. (Although one can never believe everything one hears. Some of the legends say that elephants wear their teeth outside, upside down on either side of their mouths.)

'And the lady Lydia?' I asked.

'Apart from her herbal skills, they think of her as a joke. She says, thinks and does whatever Annia Augusta tells her to, except where her child is concerned – she can be determined then, by all accounts. Apparently she was always the same. Completely indecisive. Some of the slaves can remember when Monnius married her – they did not live in this house then, of course. He built his career and fortune on her marriage portion. She could not find a husband, and her father gave her a rich dowry.'

'Of course,' I said. 'Monnius would have had the usufruct of that.'

'Exactly – but he had to give her back her estates when he divorced her. The servants say he tried to claim that there was a question over *her* fidelity, so he could keep the estates, but Lydia was so plain she was always above suspicion.' He grinned. 'The whisper is that when her father died, Monnius hoped to get control of her lands again, and that is why he let Annia Augusta bring her here, but Lydia's brother had been managing the money in the meantime, and most of it was lost in legal wrangles over the will.'

I nodded. 'Then . . .' I began, but I got no further.

From Monnius' bedchamber came the eerie sound of someone calling the dead man's name three times. Then a low tuneless wailing began, followed a moment later by the moaning of funereal pipes, and the dreadful keening of professional weepers. I looked at Junio. The lamentations had begun.

We scrambled to our feet like a pair of guilty schoolboys. It would hardly be acceptable to be found here, gossiping like a pair of equals. We went out into the lobby.

The moaning was louder there, and I glanced at Junio in

81

surprise. The voice that was doing the wailing did not sound like Fulvia's.

Chapter Nine

We had come out into the lobby not a moment too soon. An instant later there was a disturbance in the death chamber. A door slammed, there was the sound of raised voices – during which the wailing faltered – and finally one long last ululation before the tuneless moaning stopped abruptly, and a woman's voice took up the lamentation.

Junio and I stood back as the door to Monnius' chamber opened and the bier was carried out, borne high by some of the funeral attendants, and accompanied by others: some carrying the sacrificial herbs, some banging gongs and playing pipes, some simply wailing and beating their breasts. Behind them walked Fulvia, her brow now covered in ashes, her eyes lowered and her hands clasped, lamenting in a sweet, low, melancholy voice.

She did not glance towards us as she passed, and the noisy little procession moved away into the house. Monnius' bier would be laid down in the public space at the back of the atrium, where no doubt other civic officials and dignitaries would soon be calling to pay their respects, to leave their funeral gifts or even – if they had worked closely with him – to take their turn at the dirge.

A moment later the door to Monnius' chamber opened again and a sulky-looking young man in a black-edged toga came out, shepherded by a white-faced Lydia. She had been all in black before, but she had now added a shapeless long mourning cape to her attire, not unlike the one that Fulvia

83

had worn. Where Fulvia had looked a picture of elegance and grace, however, on Lydia the garment bunched in awkward folds, making her look scrawnier than ever – an impression she did nothing to dispel by clutching the garment to her with one arm, like a wounded bat. As soon as the door was shut behind them she began to talk to the boy, in a piercing undertone, with all the righteous outrage of an insulted Vestal virgin.

'Well Imagine that! Brushing you aside and following the corpse herself. Jove only knows what your father would have said. Still, never mind. You began the lament, that is all that matters. You closed his eyes and put the coin in his mouth, and so you should have done. You are his son – and you are legally a man, if only by a week or two.' She hitched her cloak a little closer round herself. 'And if that woman tries to contest the will, we'll see what the courts say about that!'

The young man pouted. From the set of his features that seemed to be his habitual expression. He looked a little younger than his fourteen years, although he must have been that age to have lost the childhood *bulla* round his neck and be wearing the plain white *toga virilis* which was the mark of legal manhood, and to which the mourning stripe had been hastily attached. His hair was short and curly, slightly reddish under the ashes with which he had adorned himself, and his plump, pale face was petulant.

'Oh, do not fuss so much, Mother. I don't know why you insisted on making such a spectacle of me in front of the undertakers. With Father's body lying there, too. His spirit won't even have left the house by this time. He'll think we have shown him disrespect, and then we shall be lucky if he doesn't come back to haunt us.' His lower jaw jutted defiantly. 'Don't blame me if the milk curdles and the slaves start dying. What else can you expect, making a scene in the funeral chamber?'

84

'I didn't make a scene!' his mother said, with more animation than I had thought she possessed. 'Monnius knows I would never offend his spirit. It was that woman, coming in and wanting to interrupt. Well, she can lament now all she wants. She didn't begin the ritual, you did, and nothing can ever alter that.'

Filius – this had to be the famous Filius – brightened slightly. 'There is one good thing about it, I suppose. I have done my duty now. I won't have to go in and do any more lamenting till the funeral.'

He seemed to be quite serious. It occurred to me that only Fulvia appeared to feel any real emotion at Monnius' death. I was about to step towards the pair, but at that moment Filius noticed me.

'Is this the fellow the governor sent?' he asked, looking me over from haircut to sandals, but addressing himself to Lydia, as though I had no ears.

'Yes, Filius dear,' his mother said. She had lost her animation suddenly, and was now speaking in the wheedling, apologetic tone I had heard her use before. 'Your grandmother sent for him. Don't scowl, dear. I expect the gentleman will want to talk to you. After all, you are your father's heir.'

'Well, I didn't send for him, and I don't want to talk to him,' Filius burst out, his voice suddenly emerging in a squeaking falsetto, which rather undermined his dignity. 'There's nothing to tell him anyway. I was sleeping in the annexe with you. I didn't hear about this rotten old murder till this morning – and then no one would let me come anywhere near the place. I didn't see anything until you took me in there, and then they had him covered up, so there wasn't anything to see.' He turned his back on me and would have walked away.

'So you are Monnius' heir?' I said, hastily taking Lydia's

lead. It occurred to me that if anything was going to capture this spoiled young man's attention, it was likely to be the mention of money.

I had guessed correctly. Filius stopped and half turned back, although he still did not favour me with another glance. 'There is no secret about that. It is all in the will, and that'll be read in the forum in a day or two,' he said, insolently twisting one of his chestnut curls in his fingers and looking pointedly at Junio. 'Father is leaving his country house to Fulvia and everything else to me.'

I wondered what Fulvia thought of that. She had talked of *this* being her house. 'Does your stepmother know of this?' I asked.

He shrugged. 'I don't know. I should think Fortunatus would have told her. He told me – he was a witness to my father's will. I suppose he might not have told Fulvia. She is only a woman, after all.' He pulled the curl out straight and looked at it with a smirk.

'Well, I shall have to find him and ask him,' I said. 'He's racing in Verulamium, I hear.'

For the first time Filius looked at me, with something like animation on the pudgy features. 'Not just Verulamium. They are going on to Camulodunum afterwards – there is another big exhibition there, in support of one of the magistrates. Fortunatus will win, of course. None of the others stand a chance against him – though lots of people back the Reds. They've been coming a good second for weeks and now they've bought Citus to appear for them – you know, the horse that won a hundred races. But Fortunatus says the Blues will win. You are an enthusiast for the chariots?'

'Not really. I prefer the games,' I said, untruthfully. In fact I much prefer a day at the circus, watching the races, to the more bloodthirsty diversions of the arena. 'I wished to speak to Fortunatus about Fulvia and the will.'

He lost interest then, and plucked at the curl again. 'Oh, that. Who cares? She's welcome to the stupid country house. I don't want it – it smells of pigs and sheep.'

'Filius!' his mother said. She turned to me. 'We may contest it, citizen. There is valuable property attached to that villa.'

'We won't contest it, Mother. I say so, and I'm the man of the family now, so you have to do what I want. And what I want . . .' he paused for a moment, as if trying to think of something truly dramatic, '. . . and what I want now is to lie down and have a servant bring me a goblet of warm milk and honey. I'm worn out with all this lamenting.'

So much, I thought, for observing a proper fast. In a house of mourning no hot food or drink should be prepared, except the grave-meats and the funeral feast, until the body is decently disposed of.

Filius, though, seemed oblivious of this. He turned on his heel and marched off down the corridor, giving every indication of being very pleased with himself.

'Well, make sure you have the servants strike a gong to keep away evil spirits, and make a little sacrifice to Vesta while you drink it,' his mother called after him. 'The rituals have already been disturbed, and you can't be too careful.' She flashed me an anguished look. 'Excuse him, citizen, he is not himself. But it is true what he tells you. All of us were asleep in the annexe, and the intervening door was bolted. It was impossible for us to hear anything. I can vouch for that. He would tell you more himself if he were not so shocked at losing his father. The poor boy is thoroughly cast down.'

If I had a son like Filius, I though sourly, I would have had him 'cast down' long ago, preferably from some very high place, like the Tarpeian rock. However, I could not say that to Lydia. I did say, civilly enough, 'I take it, lady, that since you were also in the annexe last night, you did not see or hear anything yourself?'

'Nothing at all, citizen.'

'And you have no idea who might have killed your husband?'

Her mouth hardened. 'You know what Annia Augusta thinks,' she said primly.

'I was asking you, madam citizen,' I said.

She flushed at this. 'I have no other suggestions to make. Annia may well be right, but I know no more about it than she does. I was with her all the evening, as I am sure she's told you.'

'And you noticed nothing unusual earlier in the day?' I was thinking about the sleeping potion in the servants' wine.

She shook her head. 'Monnius had a feast,' she said, as though that explained everything. 'So naturally Annia and I kept well away.'

'And Filius? He was not invited?'

She gave a sigh. 'I wanted his father to invite him, but Monnius refused. Banquets were for real men, he said, and Filius was still nothing but a spoiled child. He was always saying that, although Filius had his manhood ceremony almost a month ago. Monnius blamed me – said that I indulged the boy too much.' Two small red spots of colour touched her sallow cheeks, but – in contrast to Fulvia – the effect was disagreeable. 'Perhaps I did. I wish his father had taken more interest in his education.'

'Monnius had no hand in his upbringing?' I was surprised. After a divorce many fathers kept their male heirs – if not their daughters – in their own households, sometimes to be raised by their grandmothers. Of course! As soon as I thought of that, I knew what the answer would be.

'Annia Augusta insisted that the boy was best with me. Monnius paid for his schooling, of course, but Filius, poor lamb, was never a great scholar. He has had several tutors, but none of them really suited him. Filius has always had a delicate temperament.'

I nodded in what I hoped was an understanding manner, but inwardly all my sympathy was for the tutors. Young Filius' sulky, bovine face did not exactly suggest a lively intellect, much less a consuming interest in rhetoric and oratory. Any *paedogogus* engaged to teach him must have had an unenviable task.

I dragged the subject back to the night before. 'Filius knew Fortunatus?' I said.

Lydia's pale face lit up. 'Filius is like any boy of his age, citizen. He is a passionate supporter of chariot racing. My father used to take us to the circus, when the boy was young – of course it was a place where I could go with them. I never cared for it – the crowds, the danger and the speed – but Filius always loved it. I remember when he was quite small, he had a little wooden model of a horse, and he tied a blue ribbon round its neck and had a slave push it round the floor for hours. Filius would make him tip it over, and make it crash – just like the real thing. He would even lay little bets on it with stones. Of course there was only one horse in the race, so Filius always won.'

My tolerance for Filius anecdotes was limited. I said, 'And Fortunatus?'

'Filius supported the Blues, so Fortunatus was halfway to a god to him. When Annia brought us to this house to live, and Filius learned that Fortunatus sometimes came here to dine, naturally the poor boy wanted to meet his idol face to face. Monnius refused at first – I always suspected that Fulvia put him up to it – but poor little Filius begged and wept. He was so upset that he refused to eat, and even Monnius weakened in the end.'

So Filius had thrown temper tantrums till he got his way. I could imagine that. 'Did he see him often after that?'

Lydia's face softened. 'I will say this for Fortunatus, he was always kind to my boy. He made a point of talking to him whenever he saw him, and Filius used to lie in wait for him. He was a real fan. He even keeps one of Fortunatus' broken boots beside his bed. Though I don't think Fortunatus really welcomes it. I think he was more concerned with standing well in Monnius' eyes.'

'And in Fulvia's?' I said. It was cruel, but I needed to find out.

Lydia looked at me with such reproach that I quite regretted my words. 'On the contrary, citizen. She was impatient of the whole affair. She thought that Filius was "being indulged as usual". She made no secret of the fact. It is hardly surprising. Fulvia has always resented me and my poor boy.'

'Just as she resented your necklace,' I said. She looked a little startled and I added, 'You have one just like hers, I believe, that Annia Augusta gave you?'

She raised one hand inside her cloak and pulled aside the neck of it. 'This one, citizen?' She indicated a triple chain exactly like the one Fulvia had shown me, hidden by the folds of her dress.

I must have looked surprised. It is not usual for women to wear such adornments when they are in mourning. She let the cloak fall back and raised her bony chin defiantly, and for a fleeting second I saw a resemblance to Filius. 'Annia Augusta gave it to me, citizen, but Monnius chose the pattern. That is why I elect to wear it now. I have nothing else to remind me of my husband – everything that was not my dowry I had to leave behind when he divorced me. So I wear this. No one can see it, it is nearest to my heart, and I intend to wear it in his honour till I die. Not even Fulvia can take that from me.' Despite the whining, wheedling voice she spoke with so much feeling that I felt a fleeting sympathy for her.

'And yet you were a friend to her?' I said gently. 'Making a sleeping potion for her when she needed it?'

Lydia's sallow face turned the colour of brick. 'She has never been a friend of mine, citizen, and I have never knowingly sold to her outright. I have sold things to her old nurse once or twice – I didn't ask who they were for. Many people come here to buy remedies from me and her money was as good as anyone else's.'

Hardly how Fulvia had described matters, I thought. 'Did Monnius know about this trade in remedies?'

She looked affronted. 'Naturally, citizen – he laughed at me for it, sometimes, but he knew. And Annia Augusta too. She was rather proud of my skills – she taught me all I know. I have no money of my own, and naturally Monnius gives me – gave me – no allowance now . . .' She trailed off. 'My remedies earn me a few sesterces now and then, that's all, to buy bear's fat and lamp-black for my lashes, or white lead and Illyrian irises for my complexion. Not that it did me any good – Monnius said it was like trying to paint over crumbling plaster.' The red spots were burning in her cheeks again. 'And now, citizen, you really must excuse me. I must go to Filius. He is upset, and he could easily do something to disrupt the ritual again. We should have to begin the ceremonies all over from the beginning, and think what a dreadful omen that would be.'

She clasped her bat-like cloak about her, and flapped away in the direction of the atrium.

Junio watched her go. 'What will you do now, master?' he enquired. 'You wished to speak to the others in the household?'

I shook my head. 'I do not think we have the time. You have told me most of what I wanted to know. I have spoken to Lydia and to Filius now, and with all this in progress' – I gestured towards the inner rooms where we could still hear the lamentations rising – 'I doubt if we can achieve much more here at present. I might inspect the study, perhaps.'

Junio grinned. 'Lists of corn-dealers and suppliers, contracts for shipment and storage, and agreements for buying and selling grain. I had a quick look around the shelves while we were waiting for you.'

I smiled. 'What did Superbus make of that?'

The grin broadened. 'Not a great deal, master. He was reluctant to help, at first, and was blustering on about the law, but I reminded him that he was here on the governor's orders, and was supposed to do whatever you told him to. Of course, you hadn't actually asked us to look at the documents, but I didn't mention that. I knew you would want to know what they were. In any case, from the way he was holding one of the tax-scrolls upside down, I don't think he was making a great deal of sense of it. Though he would never admit he couldn't read it – especially when he saw that I could.'

I had taught Junio to read, after a fashion, and it was something of which he was extremely proud. Poor Superbus must have suffered yet another blow to his precious self-esteem. I said, briskly, to hide my inward amusement, 'So, nothing of any interest there?'

'Just one thing, master,' Junio said. 'The lists talk of six grain warehouses on the river in and around the city, but I can find inventories for only five. There are records for the sixth up to last season, but this year there is nothing at all. Of course, I have not had the time to search thoroughly – but all the other records are up there on the shelf, on scrolls, all carefully stored in order. It occurred to me, if documents are missing, perhaps that's what they were?'

'Well done, Junio,' I said.

My praise gave him confidence. He said, 'If Monnius really did have some deal with that Celt, perhaps the document was related to it in some way? Why else would it be locked away with the money, instead of on the shelf with the others?'

He was right again, but I was careful not to encourage him too much. I nodded. 'I will have a quick look and see if I can find those records anywhere – they might have been put away in the wrong place – but I'll lay a *sestertius* to a *quadrans* you are right. And,' I added, taking a quick decision, 'speaking of gambling, see if you can go out and hire me a litter. If the governor agrees, we may take a little journey to Verulamium.'

'But, master, the missing papers? The granary . . .?'

'We must look into it, of course, but that can wait. Something significant has just occurred to me. There is a five-day chariot-racing spectacular in Verulamium, I seem to recall, and then – if Filius is right – the team is moving on to Camulodunum. There is no time to lose. If we go at once we should just be there for the final day. Annia has an interesting theory about those missing documents. I think I should see this Fortunatus for myself.'

'A day at the races, master?' He couldn't keep the excitement from his voice.

'We are going there to investigate, not gamble,' I said sternly. Junio is even more of a racing enthusiast than I am, although for different reasons. He was born and bred in a Roman household, and learned to gamble almost as soon as he could walk. Junio would wager on the faster of two dead horses, as they say of the Romans.

His face fell at my words. The prospect of a day's racing without a single bet had clearly chastened him. 'If you are quick about your business now, I may give you a few coins to stake for me,' I said, relenting, and he set off with a grin.

It was not entirely indulgence on my part. As I had reason to know, Junio had also acquired at an early age an uncanny talent for winning his bets.

I looked through every document in the study, but Junio was right. Of the current contract and inventory for the missing corn-storage facility there was no sign whatever.

Chapter Ten

There was nothing more to be gleaned here, I thought, and I turned to leave, though my mind was full of a thousand questions. Why, for instance, had a man like Monnius – with all his expensive furniture, and the best tradesmen of Londinium at his bidding – chosen to lay such an appalling floor?

At first sight it was a simple mosaic design, very crudely fashioned, of interlocking shapes within a border: the sort of thing that Junio could have done within six months of joining the workshop. And even those shapes were not quite regular. There, under the carved Egyptian writing table, there was something very peculiar about the tiles. There was one segment of unusual regularity, with a wide gap between the tiles around the edge. Almost as though it had been done on purpose.

I stopped. Fulvia had spoken of hiding places. I moved aside the stool and knelt down to examine further. If I slipped my fingers into the crack, like this . . .

'Citizen!' A ringing voice from the doorway arrested me. I let go of the section of floor which had, indeed, moved slightly under my fingers, and backed out from under the table. Annia Augusta was standing in the lobby, staring at me in affronted disbelief. Two attendants were lurking at her side.

I scrambled to my feet and attempted to look as though crawling under the writing desk in another man's study was the kind of thing that I did every day. 'Forgive me, madam citizen. I am a pavement-maker by trade,' I said feebly. 'I was admiring . . .'

She looked at me stonily. 'I thought you were here to solve the mystery of my son's death, not to examine the pavements.' However, there was only disdain in her face, not a trace of anxiety, and her eyes did not flicker towards the hiding place. If Annia Augusta knew of its existence, she was an excellent actress.

'With regard to that,' I went on, brightly, ignoring the rebuke, 'those documents that were missing from the chest: I understand that you were the one who came in and found that they were gone. Can you give me any indication of what I'm looking for?'

Annia Augusta unfolded her ample arms, and said impatiently, 'There were some scrolls here yesterday and now they're not. That's all I know. And a great deal of money, besides.'

'Scrolls?' I said, refusing to be deflected. Only the most important records merited the permanence of documentation – storehouse records, for instance. 'Are you sure of that?'

'I am not accustomed to talk nonsense, citizen. They were scrolls. Two or three small ones, with seals on the end.'

More interesting news. If a document was sealed, the loss of it was doubly significant. A man's seal to a contract was binding under the law.

'And you have no idea what they were about?'

She was dismissive. 'Something to do with business, I imagine. You will have to ask the slaves. They were the ones who saw them locked away. Why are you so interested in these stupid scrolls? And how should I know what they were about? Do you suppose, citizen, that I opened them? Or that I could have read them if I did?'

In fact, I would not have been surprised on either count. Annia Augusta struck me as a woman of lively curiosity, and I could not imagine her as the product of an education concentrating exclusively on household skills. But I did not want her examining that piece of floor before I had a further chance to look at it myself. I murmured humbly, 'Perhaps not, lady. And the money that is missing, you saw that too?'

If there had been the slightest constraint and uneasiness before, it had completely disappeared. This time her answer was less grudging. 'Indeed I did, citizen. Thousands of sesterces there were – my son was counting them at the time. I saw him put them in that chest behind you. And lock it, as he always did. And this morning when I came in here, the chest was open – and it was empty, as you can see. No doubt when you find Fortunatus, you will find the money too.' She folded her arms again. 'Now, do you want to talk to the slaves? Try not to be too long with them – they are wanted for household duties, and there is a great deal to be done before the funeral.'

After what Junio had told me, I did not expect to learn anything more from questioning the household. 'I have a more pressing matter to attend to,' I explained. 'My slave will be back in a moment with a litter. I hope to visit the charioteers in Verulamium, before the festival is over and the teams go on elsewhere.'

She nodded grimly. 'So you are going to take my advice, at last. I am very glad to hear it. Perhaps now you will get on with it and search out that scoundrel who murdered my son.'

'Indeed, madam, I hope to speak to Fortunatus soon,' I said, and was rewarded with a grim smile as I moved towards the door. Instead of walking through it, however, I turned and looked at her. 'Though there is one more thing I wish to ask you before I leave. I believe you have a necklace like the one that was used to strangle Monnius. A triple-stranded silver chain?'

She frowned. 'I do. But surely that one was Fulvia's? What else would Fortunatus use?'

'It was not Fulvia's, madam citizen. She has it with her. And Lydia is wearing hers – I noted it a moment ago. Can you produce yours?'

Annia Augusta flushed. 'I can. At least, I can account for where it is. I lost one of the small stones set into the chain, and Monnius sent it to the jewel merchant to have the gem replaced. I suppose it is still in the workshop. It would be easy to check.' She looked at me suddenly. 'You are surely not suggesting, citizen, that I strangled my son? I would have more wit than to do it with my own necklace if I did.'

And that, I thought, as I followed her meekly back through the house, was certainly true. Unless she had done it with her own necklace hoping that everyone would reason in that way.

As with many town houses, there was no way to the entrance except via the atrium, and I was obliged to sidle my way round the edge though the funeral bier was now laid out in the open space at the back of it, and the extravagant rituals of official grief were being observed. Fulvia was still there, tunefully lamenting, while the pipers wailed and the professional keeners beat their breasts and wept. Pine cones had been added to the braziers, to disguise the smell of human corruption, and the air was heavy with the scent of candles, incense and herbs.

I went into the entrance passage and the doorkeeper nodded at me from his niche as I passed. 'Water and fire in those pots, citizen. On the lady Lydia's orders. She said to tell you they were there, so you could purify yourself properly.' I must have looked startled – this formality was not usually observed by mere visitors to a house. He winked. 'Always a stickler for fulfilling observances, the lady Lydia.'

I obliged, and was stepping obediently over the 'fire' (a

small metal bowl with a few coals burning in it) when a thought occurred to me.

'Last night,' I said, rinsing my hands solemnly in the perfumed water, and drying them on the small towel provided, thereby 'washing my hands of death' in the approved Roman fashion, 'did you see *all* the feasters leave the house?'

He was suddenly sober. 'Oh yes, citizen. And their slaves. The master was always terrified of plots against him, and I was always most careful to see that everyone had gone.' He looked anxious now. 'The other servants will bear me out. You will tell the governor that, won't you? Annia Augusta will have me whipped as it is, for falling asleep at my post, and if they think I allowed one of the feasters to hide in the house . . . dear Jupiter! I shall be lucky to come out of it alive. And then I let that Eppaticus in this morning – oh, merciful gods!' He began to pluck at my toga in agitation.

I handed him the towel to occupy his hands, and hastened past him out of the door. What a household of tensions, I thought. It was quite a relief to get out into the open air again. Junio was there, with the same litter which had carried me to the house earlier – it was at my disposal for the day, I learned, and had been standing by for further instructions, on the orders of the governor. Junio helped me in, and we set off again at a brisk pace.

In no time at all we were back at the palace. We swept in through the gates, and the crowds of people who had business with the governor and were jostling in the courtyards stood back to let us pass. There were dozens of them, of every age and class, dressed in everything from tunics to togas. I realised for the first time what an immense administrative burden Pertinax must bear, in addition to his military duties – no wonder he had a household of scribes and secretaries at his disposal, as well as guards and sentries, though of course even the clerks were officers seconded from the army.

99

The governor was in council when we arrived, so a long-nosed secretary told us as we were ushered into the palace. Nevertheless, the man condescended to carry a message when he discovered who I was. He provided a wax tablet, on which I scratched a few words, and bore it off importantly, leaving me standing in the colonnaded entrance. I felt rather foolish and conspicuous, especially as other appellants (some of them important people, judging by the wide patrician stripes on their togas) were being turned away or briskly told to come back tomorrow when the governor would receive them. People were gazing at me curiously, and whispering behind their hands.

After what seemed an eternity the long-nosed clerk returned, his manner now entirely respectful. 'The governor's apologies,' he murmured abjectly, 'but he was unable to leave the meeting. However, your requests are being dealt with, and a carriage-driver is being found to take you to Verulamium without delay. His Excellence has given you this' – he handed me a letter-scroll of bark, sealed with the governor's personal seal – 'which will ensure you lodging at any military post. He is sending you a small purse to defray expenses, and if you like to go to the *triclinium* he has ordered a light repast for you before you undertake the journey. There is a meal awaiting your slave, too, in the servants' quarters.'

I blessed Pertinax for his swift and generous response, and went to partake of the 'light repast' as suggested, a good, simple meal of cold meat and fruits. I was in the process of washing it down with a large jug of cool, clean water when the serving boy sidled up to me and murmured apologetically in my ear.

'I am sorry to disturb you, citizen, but there is someone wishing to see you. Urgently, he says, before you leave.'

I glanced towards the doorway indicated. Superbus stood there, although there was no longer anything superb about him. He looked shocked and ruffled, his immaculate tunic crumpled and torn at the neck, and as he came towards me in answer to my signal I saw that he was hobbling a little. One of his smart sandals was broken, although he still approached with as much formality as he could muster. It gave him a kind of touching dignity.

'Superbus,' I said in greeting. 'What has happened to you?'

He bowed gravely. 'I was attempting to fulfil your orders, citizen, when I had an altercation in the market.'

'I am sorry to hear that,' I said. 'What happened?'

Superbus heaved a reproachful sigh. 'I had been asking questions, citizen, as you directed, trying to find out about Eppaticus – though contrary to your expectations, no one seemed to know anything, at least not anything that they were willing to tell me. The moment I so much as mentioned his name, everyone suddenly became secretive. No one would admit to having dealings with him. He trades in this and that, was all I could discover. Wine two months ago, slaves last month, anything – it differs from month to month.'

That in itself was interesting. I had already suspected that some of Eppaticus' activities were on the outskirts of the law. If his customers were less than helpful, it was almost certainly because they were afraid of the *aediles*, the market police – or of what Eppaticus himself would do to them if they betrayed him to the authorities.

But Superbus had not become dishevelled simply by questioning people who were too frightened to talk. 'And then?' I prompted.

'And then,' he said, in an affronted tone, 'when I was just about to give up and come away, a big fat Celt in plaid trousers and a tunic came up behind me in an alley. Grabbed me by the shoulder, pushed me against the wall, and wanted to know why one of the governor's slaves was hanging around asking questions about Eppaticus.' He looked at me resignedly. 'I imagine that he recognised my tunic borders. The palace servants are well known in the market.'

I nodded, rather guiltily. I had guessed something of the kind. 'And what did you tell him?'

A strange expression crossed Superbus' face, a mixture of self-congratulation and defensiveness. 'I told him I was interested in buying one of the slaves.'

'Well done, Superbus!' I said, with more surprise than was altogether tactful. It was a more quick-witted strategy than I'd expected from him. It was entirely plausible for one thing – senior slaves in important households sometimes did have slaves of their own. It was more for status than anything, and in that case buying from someone like Eppaticus – selling old and worn-out slaves at a knock-down price – might well look like a better proposition than paying full price at the slave auction. 'What did the man say?'

Superbus looked uncomfortable. 'He wanted to know how much I was willing to pay. I didn't want to offer a price, but he insisted, and in the end I suggested a figure. A very low one, of course.'

I winced. Under Roman law agreeing a price is tantamount to fixing a bargain, and Superbus seemed to have bought himself a slave, sight unseen. I could only imagine what kind of broken-down, or even diseased, individual he would find himself in possession of, and how he would provide for such a creature here in the palace. Most slave-owning slaves are very senior in the household hierarchy.

'So you have acquired a slave?'

He swallowed. 'Not yet, citizen. That is what enraged the Celtic gentleman. I didn't have the money with me.'

'Even though he picked you up by your tunic and shook you till your teeth rattled?' I suggested.

Superbus nodded.

'Then you have had a lucky escape,' I said. 'Now he will have to provide the goods in order to demand the money, and you will be able to escape from the bargain.' I grinned. 'Unless of course you want to buy a slave.'

I meant it as a jest but Superbus coloured, and I realised that his quick response had not been due entirely to cunning.

'In any case,' I went on, 'you wouldn't want one of those Eppaticus was selling. They were last month's commodity, you said, so by this time he'll only have the leftovers that no one else wanted to buy.' Superbus looked so chastened at this observation that I hurried to change the subject. 'Did you discover, by the way, whether he ever dealt in grain?'

Superbus' face fell still further. 'I am sorry, citizen. It did not occur to me to ask.'

I smiled. 'Perhaps that is just as well. If Eppaticus is edgy about questions, as it seems that he is, asking about the grain trade might have been distinctly dangerous.'

'You think my assailant was Eppaticus, citizen?'

'I don't think so, from your description,' I said. 'The most striking thing about Eppaticus is his height. And he did not wear trousers. More likely one of his attendants. But not a man to trifle with, all the same. Fortunately he won't come looking for you here – the palace guard would soon see him off. Just make sure you keep away from the market for a while – in fact, it might be better if you did not leave the palace at all. A pity. I had hoped to send you to find the jeweller who made this necklace for Annia Augusta.' I took out the bloodstained article from my pouch, still wrapped in its piece of protective linen. 'Never mind, I will send it to Pertinax and ask him to despatch someone else to make enquiries.'

Superbus nodded, and withdrew, still hobbling. I finished my meal, and entrusted the necklace to the table-slave, who promised to deliver it to the governor with my request. When

I joined Junio on the steps of the palace, he had already collected my few possessions for the journey.

The next few hours passed in a dreadful dream. Pertinax had been as good as his word, and an imperial gig was waiting to transport us. Gigs are a light, swift, open form of transport, and can rattle along the cobbled roads quicker than any closed carriage ever invented. On the other hand, any open carriage is at best a draughty affair, even if there is not a stiff breeze blowing, and 'rattle' is the operative word. We bounced and lurched northwards the whole long afternoon, through a countryside busy with agriculture. None of the wild lands that surrounded Glevum, here. Little hamlets had sprung up around the road for miles, and even when these had been left behind, much of the woodland had been cleared, and every valley seemed to have its little farm – sometimes a Roman villa, sometimes a Celtic roundhouse – each with its own assortment of animals, crops and fields of next year's grain.

On we plunged, terrifying ox carts and mule waggons as we passed, swaying wildly up hills and still more wildly down them, while I clutched my narrow wooden bench with both hands and Junio crouched miserably at my feet.

And then, just when I thought that I could endure it no longer, we stopped at little *mansio*, an official staging post. But not for long. Time enough to change the horses and swallow a welcome drink of watered wine, and off we went, to repeat the whole bone-juddering experience again.

Even so, it was dark before we got to Verulamium. There was a brief argument at the gatehouse before they would admit us, but a glimpse of the governor's seal and warrant, even by the uncertain light of a flaming torch, was enough to have the guards change their minds in a panic, and not only let us in, but organise stabling for the horses and have Junio and me escorted personally, and with fulsome apologies, to the commander.

Verulamium, like the capital, has maintained a small garrison-fort inside the town ever since the Boudicca uprising more than a century ago, and it was there that we were taken. The commander was in the *praetorium* having a supper party in the privacy of his home, but the official seal worked its charms again, and he did his best to offer hospitality at the garrison. I have a dim memory of being seated on a wooden stool beside a fire, and given a hearty meal of warm army bean-stew and coarse brown bread, before I was shown to a small, sparsely furnished chamber in the barracks, usually reserved for passing messengers.

A small brazier and an oil-lamp were promised, but I stretched out on the clean bunk bedding at once, pulled a blanket over me, and, with my young slave lying in another bunk at my feet, had closed my eyes and was fast asleep before anyone had time to return with the expected items. It had been an exhausting day.

Even so, one image haunted my sleep. The floor in Caius Monnius' study had been lifted, and in my dreams I could see clearly what I had only glimpsed in those few moments before I had been interrupted. The secret hiding place beneath the floor was crammed almost to bursting with bags of silver coins. I did a rapid calculation. There must have been five thousand *denarii* at least: that is to say, at current market rates, roughly twenty thousand sesterces.

'What was it doing there?' I murmured as I slept. 'And what becomes of Annia's theory now?' But my lost Gwellia, who always stalked my dreams, only smiled mysteriously and vanished like smoke before I could touch her with my hand.

Chapter Eleven

The next morning we were woken by a soldier, a double-pay officer in full uniform, who brought us a breakfast of hard wheaten biscuits and thin wine.

'Standard army rations,' he told me, with a smile, 'though the commander has sent you some fruit in too, seeing that you come from the governor. Oh, and I am to give you his apologies, citizen. He didn't want to rouse you early, but I think you said you wanted to attend the chariot racing? It is already an hour after dawn, and if you and your servant want to be sure of a seat . . .?'

We did. Junio was on his feet almost before the *optio* had finished speaking, and was already splashing cold water enthusiastically from the jug beside the door into a large bowl which he had found on the stone bench. Very cold water, I suspected, since the promised brazier had never arrived, and I eyed these preparations rather reluctantly from the comfortable warmth of my bed, while the *optio* bowed himself out with promises to return as soon as I was ready to leave. He would personally escort us to the stadium – on the commander's express instructions.

I was dressed only in my tunic, but I rose and stood shivering on the stone floor while Junio rinsed my hands and face. Then I gnawed my way through some breakfast and allowed myself to be dressed once more in my toga, though Junio was so excited by the prospect of the day ahead that he had to make two attempts at draping the cloth. He was so eager and anxious to be gone that I took pity on him in the end and fastened my own sandals, while he crammed food into his mouth. When I looked up he was standing ready at the door, before he had really finished swallowing. Army biscuits are said to breed hard men – certainly they exercise the jaws.

I clapped Junio on the shoulder and we set off together.

The *optio*, true to his word, was waiting outside the door, and as soon as we made an appearance he took up a place beside me, gesturing for two other members of his company to bring up front and rear. Junio had naturally stepped deferentially behind me, so I found myself forming the central part of a little procession as we walked out of the barracks. The guards at the gate of the fort moved smartly to let us through, and in the streets outside, the townsfolk stood even more hastily aside, abandoning their business to whisper and goggle at us as we went by.

I am not used to being stared at, and I found myself falling into step with the soldiers and marching along rather importantly, the townsfolk in the busy streets parting before us like cheese under a cook's cleaver.

'Wonder what he's done, poor fellow,' I heard a trader mutter, as he and his laden donkey tried to squeeze themselves into a doorway to let us pass. I suppose I did look as if I were under some kind of military arrest. I walked the rest of the way to the stadium in a more chastened frame of mind, and my feet deliberately out of time with those of my marching escort.

The stadium had been set up just outside the town walls, at the foot of a small hillock, and was obviously large. A high wicker fence surrounded the enclosure, with an impressive entrance gate at one end through which the public were currently pouring.

As we made our way to the head of the jostling mob, I

noticed a large and heavily built guard using a cudgel on an unfortunate youth in an ochre tunic who was trying to scale the fence, although entry to the stadium was free. I grimaced in sympathy, but the boy had been taking an obvious risk. The organisers of race meets always take a dim view of visitors who attempt to get in without running the gauntlet of fast-food sellers, wine and water vendors, souvenir stalls, soothsayers and official betting booths which have been granted expensive licences to operate inside the fence.

If the people in the streets had not known who we were, here we were certainly expected. The same cudgel-bearing guard appeared, and wielded his weapon – rather indiscriminately I thought – to open a path for us among the throng. People do not argue with a cudgel, and we were soon inside.

My patron, Marcus, would doubtless have thought it nothing, after the Circus Maximus in Rome, but compared to the races I had seen in Glevum this was a revelation. The stadium was huge. The slope of the hill itself formed a natural grandstand on one side of the track; a wooden framework had been erected on the other side, with tiered benches on top of it, while at the further end, behind the turning post, was a covered viewing box for town officials and any visiting dignitaries.

The track was impressive, too. There was a purpose-built central reservation, with a wide track around it – sand laid on hammered clay, by the look of it – and a dozen slaves were already raking the surface flat. Proper hurdle fences separated the spectators from the action and there were portable wicker starting-stalls provided for the horses. A pair of wide wooden gates under the civic box led from the stadium into the stables and changing yard beyond. At the turning point, six rocking dolphins, made of gilded wood, were permanently displayed on poles, ready for the circuit-slaves to tip them forward one at a time, as the horses passed, and so help the crowd keep count of the laps.

The *optio* was right about obtaining a seat. Already the far bank was packed with spectators, many of them waving red, white or blue scarves in anticipation. I was surprised how few Green supporters there appeared to be. In Glevum there are always hundreds of them, not least because the Green faction is notoriously 'for the people' and against the governing classes, and supporting them is one of the few ways in which ordinary citizens can safely demonstrate their lack of sympathy with the Emperor.

(In fact, as I discovered later, support for the Greens was very strong in Verulamium. The absence of scarves was on my account – rumour of my imperial warrant had spread, and upon my arrival at the racecourse all the Green colours had been hastily hidden. Even in this outpost of Empire, it is sometimes dangerous to be seen cheering for the wrong people.)

Perhaps because of the presence of my escort, finding ourselves somewhere to sit was not a problem. Spectators melted away at our approach, and we were able to commandeer an excellent vantage point on the hill, near the turning point. We had hardly settled ourselves there before a slave arrived to invite us to join the civic dignitaries in the box over the stands, but I (very politely) declined on the grounds that I was acting on the governor's instructions and wished to have a closer view of the horses. I did not want to be part of the civic party – people in the official box become almost as much of a spectacle as the chariots themselves and I wanted to observe Fortunatus without half the town knowing I was doing so.

I know from experience that the best view is always obtained from a point just before the apex of the corner, where one can see the horses turning at the other end and the whole of the straight – where the speed is greatest – and obtain a wonderful view of the entry to the bend, where the skill of the horsemen is most in evidence, and – as Junio could tell you – most of the spectacular crashes occur.

Pertinax's bounty as we left permitted me the unaccustomed luxury of buying a handful of 'hot nuts and crispy pork pieces' from one of the itinerant vendors who moved among the crowd. They were not very warm and not remotely crispy, but as we sat back upon the bank and joined the rippling anticipation of the crowd I began to share something of Junio's excitement. I handed him the little container made of twisted bark, and he helped himself to a piece of greasy pork with a sigh of pure happiness. The soldiers were all three staring into the distance with an expression of loftiest disdain, so I did not offer them any. I gave Junio a few coins to stake on one of the teams, and he set off to find someone to bet with, while I huddled the rest of my purchase to myself and settled back to wait for the spectacle.

I did not have long to wait. First the donor of the games entered, a candidate for local office in a gleaming white toga, heralded by a flourish of trumpets. He was warmly greeted by the assembled company, and made his way to the official box. Then came the old priest of Jupiter, who had doubtless performed the morning's sacrifice for a successful day. He was shaky and senile, but he too was politely applauded. So were the traditional tumblers, dancers and pipers who followed him.

I was smiling at the antics of one of the acrobats when Junio came struggling back through the crowd, looking rather pleased with himself.

'Did you bet on Fortunatus?' I said, leaning forward to speak to him – he had settled himself on the far side of the *optio*. 'I hope you got good odds?'

Junio grinned a little sheepishly, but before there was time

111

to say another word a sudden surge of anticipation ran through the crowd. A moment later there was the thundering noise of hooves as the horsemen cantered down the road outside and wheeled through the gates. Urchins danced daringly at their wheels, to be seen off in no uncertain fashion by the cudgelled guard, and a moment later the whole stadium was on its feet, cheering, stamping, whistling and waving. Even the occasional green scarf made an appearance.

It was a spectacular and unexpected entry. Even a non-enthusiast could scarcely fail to be impressed. The magnificent horses (the first race was clearly to be a four-in-hand) were obviously the finest money could buy: wonderful creatures, coats gleaming, heads tossing, their harness decorated with the colour of their *factio*. The drivers, too, were dressed in coloured tunics, under the leather bandages which covered chest and legs, with coloured plumes on their helmets; and the little lightweight wicker chariots, shaped like upturned shells, were painted in the same hues of blue, green, red or white. The four professional teams were followed by their local counterparts, to the more muted delight of their supporters. Three times they trotted in procession round the course, while the crowd cheered and roared, and women threw garlands at their feet.

Then the local teams withdrew through the inner gates, the stalls were moved into position, and the four professional charioteers drew up to await the start. The cheering had ceased now, and the crowd waited with a kind of hushed anticipation. Then the donor of the games came to the front of the civic box and threw down a handkerchief as a signal, the slaves whisked away the wicker stalls and in an instant the race had begun.

What followed was almost too quick to see. Hooves thundered, whips cracked, wheels leapt and drivers cursed. I felt my own pulse racing as the speed increased, and the murmur of the crowd became a growl and then a roar. I have seen good racing in Glevum, but the Londinium teams were in a class of their own. As they turned, almost in front of us, I could see the chariots bouncing off the ground with the speed of it, the drivers using their own weight to balance their fragile vehicles, and urging the horses on as though Cerberus himself was after them. Then they were gone, around the turning point in a cloud of dust, and there was only the drumming of the hooves to mark their progress up the other side of the central barrier.

Around the further turn they came, the horses snorting and straining. White's driver barged the Green's, and the crowd went wild. One of Green's wheels left the ground, and the chariot almost overturned, but the man was skilled and with supreme effort threw his whole body over the upper rim as it toppled and brought the vehicle juddering back to earth. He had lost time, as the other teams swerved past him: yet a moment later he was thundering down the course in pursuit.

The gods were evidently watching, for at the next corner the White driver glanced backwards at his rival, and in that instant lost the race. He took the bend too sharply and too fast, and lost control of his chariot. It leapt into the air and he was catapulted forward, losing the reins. He pulled his knife out to cut the chariot free from the leather traces, but he was not quick enough. Driver, chariot, broken wheels – all came tumbling down together in an untidy heap to be swept remorselessly onwards by the charging horses. I saw him try to struggle upright, bruised and wounded, and then he was thrown clear, almost unseating the driver of the Reds. He lay on the track motionless, blood seeping from under his helmet, until the circuit-slaves came running out to seize his legs and pull him off the course before the horses came round again.

His horses streamed on, dragging the chariot with them.

Three dolphins down. Four. Five. The rogue horses made it difficult for the remaining drivers, who had to keep their wits about them. On the sixth lap the driverless chariot whipped about on its traces and threatened to entangle itself under Red's wheels but the pace scarcely seemed to slacken. The crowd gasped, hoping for another 'shipwreck', but the driver steered himself clear, overtook Green on the apex of the bend and thundered home to victory. Blue came in a disappointing third.

I glanced at Junio. His face was glowing with excitement. 'So much for the famous Fortunatus,' I said. 'I hope you didn't stake all my money on him.'

He took on that sheepish look again. 'Fortunatus isn't here,' he said.

I rounded on him. 'What?'

'That is what they told me, master, when I went to bet.'

'It is true, citizen,' the *optio* put in, clearly sensing my irritation with my slave. 'Fortunatus was thrown from his chariot in the very first race, on the first day, and he has not competed since. He didn't break anything, so the team surgeon says, but he hit his head. They took him back to the team inn on a shutter, but it took him hours to come to himself and even then he was complaining of headaches and – worse – of not being able to see. He won't be racing again in this tournament, though the *medicus* says he may recover, in time. People were very disappointed. It was quite the talk of the town.'

I was angry. 'Why didn't someone tell me this before?'

The *optio* shrugged. 'You merely asked to attend the chariot racing, citizen. I did not know it was only Fortunatus that you wanted to watch.'

There was justice in that. I had not explained to the commander why I wanted to come to the racing, just in case any rumours reached Fortunatus. I muttered crossly, 'And

114

after I have travelled from Londinium expressly to talk to him. Where is this inn they have taken him to?'

The *optio* shook his head. 'I am afraid, citizen, that Fortunatus has already returned to Londinium, under the care of one of the team guards. Or so the rumour goes. They say the *medicus* decided that the only cure was rest, and that Fortunatus could do that better in his own quarters. If I had only known that you wished to speak to him in particular, citizen, I could have saved you a wasted journey to the circuit.'

But Junio knew, I thought to myself, and he had not seen fit to tell me, though he discovered the truth before the race began. I whirled to face him. 'Why—'

He was already looking contrite. 'I did not know that he was not in the town. I merely heard that he'd had a fall, and naturally I assumed that he was being tended by the *medicus* at the team inn. And then the horses were coming, and since you could hardly leave in the middle of a race . . .' He gave me an uncertain glance.

I scowled. 'I suppose so,' I said ungraciously. 'But we have wasted time as a result of your silence.'

He gave me a sideways look. 'I'm sorry, master. Truly I am. But you have gained *something* by the delay.'

'Which is?'

'That *denarius* you gave me. When I heard that Fortunatus was not racing after all, I bet it on the Reds. You have doubled your money. And you did enjoy the racing.'

There are times when I find it very difficult to be angry with my servant for long. Under the incredulous eyes of the *optio*, though, I did my best.

Chapter Twelve

Junio was clearly disappointed at being dragged away from the excitement so soon, and perhaps the soldiers were too, but if so they were too well trained to show it. The *optio* himself was a real racing enthusiast, however, and he proved a positive well of information on the subject.

'The Blues are staying at a lodging house close to the west gate of the town,' he told me importantly, as his soldiers forced a way down the thronged hill for us, a violent but highly effective procedure – people were treading on each other to allow us through. Behind us, there was a scuffle as small groups of supporters, all sporting different colours, scrambled frantically for our seats. 'I could take you there if you wish. Or if you would prefer to go round to the stable enclosure . . .?'

That was the obvious choice to me, since that was where the team would be, in preparation for their next race. I was afraid that we might have trouble getting in – members of the public are not usually permitted behind the scenes – but the *optio* was confident. He led the way unhesitatingly, straight across the circuit, where the slaves were hastily raking the sand back over the clay track. They waited, blank-faced, till we passed and then raked out our footsteps with their own, walking backwards as they worked.

Even so, nobody shouted at us. One or two urchins in the crowd gave us an ironic cheer, but the civic officials in the box ignored us, and when we reached the inner gates they

117

were thrown open for us without question. An armed escort has its uses.

The gates led to a short, dark passageway which opened out into a huge yard, surrounded by stalls and makeshift stabling for horses, and at first sight it appeared to be almost as thronged with people as the stadium itself.

As we came in the eight local chariots were lining up, two-in-hand this time, to take their turn at the racing. Their drivers, resplendent in their uniforms, balanced their precarious vehicles and waited for the signal to enter the stadium. Some were nervously adjusting their helmets or their harness, others steadying their restless horses, while some were trying to dissipate the tension by exchanging jibes and insults.

'Call yourself a racing driver, Gaius Flaminius? I could overtake you on a pregnant mule!'

The victim of the taunts, a tall thin youth in Green colours, turned as red as his tormentor's chariot. 'Is that so, Paulus Fatface? Well, I'll tell you something. The only reason your horse gallops so fast is to get away from the smell of your feet!'

We left them to their battle of words and went on into the yard beyond.

It was alive with activity. Stable-slaves hurried everywhere: leading horses, carrying buckets, polishing harness, sweeping straw, tripping over their sandals in their haste while their masters shouted and cursed.

In the stalls beyond, the horses that had completed the earlier race were being cared for. A man who was clearly an animal *medicus* was bandaging the leg of a handsome chestnut with white ribands in its mane, while a nervous-looking slave hovered nearby with salves, just out of reach of the creature's hooves. You did not have to be a racing man to see what was happening: they were treating one of the horses that had been damaged by pulling the overturned chariot.

118

I glanced around for the unfortunate driver, and saw him laid out on a shutter in the corner. His face and body were battered and bloody and he was evidently dead. No one paid any attention to him. Nearby, his substitute was already donning his cloak and helmet under the critical eye of a stout man whom I took to be the coach, who was waving his arms in a last-minute demonstration of tactics. The young man was a reserve driver, by the look of it, and nervous at his sudden elevation – his face was so white that he scarcely needed the plume on his headgear to identify his colour.

Each *factio* clearly had its own quarter of the yard, and, in the nature of these things, Blue was inevitably in the furthest corner. I nodded to the *optio*, and he led the way. No one questioned us, or even paused in their activity, but I was uncomfortably aware of curious stares following us as soon as our backs were turned. The moment I looked around, however, every man was engaged in his work, eyes fixed firmly ahead of him. These were people who preferred not to meddle with soldiers.

The driver of the Blues, presumably Fortunatus' replacement, was busily lashing out at a stable-slave as we approached, both with his tongue and with his whip, for giving a hot horse cold water, but on our arrival he stopped his tirade and turned to greet us. 'You were looking for me, citizen?' He was a lightly built young man, but strong – the perfect build for a driver – with muscles like whipcord. He was clearly no coward, but at my approach he ran his tongue round his lips like a schoolboy who has failed to prepare his homework.

'I came,' I told him, as a murmur from the stadium crowd and the sound of flying hoofbeats told us that the next race had begun, 'to ask about Lividius Fortunatus. I understand he had an accident?'

I had meant it as the simplest overture, but the effect was

dramatic. The tongue flicked out again, and his voice almost failed him. 'I should be honoured, naturally,' he managed at last, 'if in my humble way I could render the remotest service to His Excellence the Governor, but I know nothing about it. I did not see the race at all, so I do not see how I can assist you, citizen.' There was so much sweat on his face, he looked as if he had been drinking from a street fountain.

When a man grovels like that it usually means, in my experience, that he has something to hide. Also, he is often easy to bully. He had mentioned the governor, and that gave me an advantage. I assumed my most menacing expression.

'Nonetheless, on behalf of His Excellence Helvius Pertinax, I would like to know . . .' I began, but the words died on my lips. From the recesses of the stall another man had appeared.

This was the Blue team coach, that much was clear from his manner and his dress, and he was as hefty as his driver was slight. He was muscular enough, under his colourful tunic, and had no doubt once been athletic, but now the body was running to fat. Wine and good living had etched the face almost as much as the ugly scar which ran across it from eyebrow to chin – the relic of some ancient shipwreck on the chariots, no doubt. Most trainers have been drivers in their time, some of them ex-slaves from other provinces, and this man had the swarthy skin and dark eyes of a Greek. He hurried towards us courteously enough, but there was no trace of welcome in his eyes.

'Perhaps I can be of help to you, gentlemen?' He was having to speak loudly and deliberately to make himself heard. 'As he told you, our replacement driver did not witness the race. I did. A most unfortunate incident, and terrible for Fortunatus. A tragedy for our *factio*. I am the team manager, by the way. My name is Calyx.' He smiled. The corners of his mouth moved reluctantly, as if they were pulled up by strings, and were not used to the exercise. 'Yes, a tragedy. If it had not been for that, the Blues would almost certainly have won.'

I glanced at the substitute driver. He was mopping his face with the back of his hand, and looking as relieved as any man can look who is about to risk life and limb in a flimsy cockleshell amidst the hooves of thundering horses. The unfortunate slave he had been lambasting, I noticed, had picked up his water bucket and escaped.

I turned back to Calyx. 'What exactly caused the accident?' I asked, raising my own voice over the enthusiastic sounds of the crowd. 'It was not like Fortunatus, by all accounts, to be shipwrecked.'

It was more a comment than a question. In fact I thought I knew the answer. Almost certainly Fortunatus had been caught at an unguarded moment and barged by the chariot of another colour while he was off-balance – that happens all the time, as we had seen earlier, and is regarded as part of the contest. The only surprise was that an experienced charioteer like Fortunatus should have allowed himself to be caught out like that.

The carefully sculpted smile hardened on Calyx's face, as if it had been suddenly set in wax. 'Most unfortunate,' he said loudly. 'Some fault with the chariot perhaps, or one of the horses skittish. Perhaps we shall never know for sure. No other chariot was involved and Fortunatus himself can remember nothing of the accident.' He spread out his hands and moved forward as if to usher us physically from the scene. 'So perhaps you will excuse me, citizen. I don't think I can be of further help to you, and I have a race to supervise.'

I can be stubborn when I wish. 'But you saw the fall yourself?' I said. Or rather I hollered. The hubbub from the track was increasing every moment.

He shrugged. 'It was all over so quickly. One moment Fortunatus was galloping away from the start and the next

121

moment he was lying on the track. Luckily it was near the starting stalls or he might have gone under the wheels of another colour, and then what would have happened to the team?'

It was hard to keep up a conversation in the circumstances, but I pressed him again. 'You did not see what caused it?' I shouted over the din.

The wax smile was slipping little by little, but he kept his manner civil. 'There must have been some problem with the chariot, citizen. I did not see what, exactly; my attention was elsewhere for a moment. When I glanced back I was simply in time to see him fall.'

In that case, I thought, Fortunatus might have staged the accident. It seemed a desperate expedient – the last driver to feign a fall in Rome was put to death for his presumption. His *factio* had dragged him before the courts, furious that he had taken bribes and lost the rest of the team their share of the purse. Too risky, surely? Or perhaps the accident was not of Fortunatus' making.

'Was there damage to the horse, or chariot? You must have seen them, after the race . . .' I stopped. The roaring of the crowd had risen to a climax, and a moment later the gates burst open and the local teams came trotting in, the victor (it seemed to be Paulus Fatface) brandishing his garland. The others came behind him, most of them looking dazed and dishevelled, although they were all still aboard their cars. They streamed past us in a whirlwind of leather and dust.

Calyx held up his hand, and spoke for the first time in a normal voice. Even the pretence of a smile had left him now. 'I tell you, citizen, I know nothing about it. It was an accident, is all. These things happen in chariot racing. Even the best drivers have mishaps, often when they are trying hardest. As for the chariot, I could not say. After the race I was more concerned for Fortunatus than for his racing car.' He was still moving us away from the Blue quarter.

I was almost walking backwards. 'But surely one of the stable-team . . .?' I protested. 'Someone must have looked at the chariot?'

'I will ask them, since you require it, citizen. When the day is over. I cannot interrupt them now. Our next race will begin in a moment. Now, if you will excuse me, I have work to do. I'm sorry to be unhelpful, but I've told you all I know.' He nodded, turned on his heel and hurried back to his team.

The *optio* turned to me. 'You want me to arrest him, citizen? I am sure a short session at the guardroom would assist his memory.'

I shook my head. 'It is too late. No doubt he and his friends are already preparing a plausible account of the event, in case we should ask again.' I nodded towards the stables where Calyx was already in deep conversation with two men in tunics, whom I had not noticed earlier, who had now emerged from the shadows. An ugly-looking pair too: one was short and fat, with shoulders like an ox, grizzled hair, and a face like a discontented bull, presently lowering in my direction. The other was taller, thinner, greyer and possibly more sinister. The most disconcerting thing about him was not his narrow face, with its long crooked nose and cruel thin slit of a mouth, but the dreadful, casual strength of the long supple fingers which were even now twisting and testing a strip of narrow leather. As I glanced towards him I saw that he had fixed his eyes on me: cold, grey, close-set eyes with a dead, expressionless stare which chilled my blood. He saw me looking and turned swiftly away.

'You think that Calyx was lying, citizen?' The officer sounded shocked, as if the idea of lying to an *optio* was the height of civil disobedience.

'I don't *think* that he was lying,' I said. 'I know that he was.'

123

I turned to my young slave. 'Isn't that right, Junio?'

Junio grinned. This was a game we often played. I was trying to instruct him in my skills, and he was delighted by the opportunity to show off his abilities in front of strangers. 'I think so, master. Obviously he was lying when he said he wasn't watching Fortunatus,' he said. 'The race had just begun, he said so himself, and that is the very moment when the whole event can be won or lost by someone getting into a good position. Calyx is the coach and manager, and there were hundreds of *denarii* hanging on that race, yet he tells us that his "attention was elsewhere". Of course he was watching. Or if he wasn't, that is still more odd. Fortunatus was his most successful driver.'

It was exactly what I had reasoned myself, and I rewarded the boy with a smile. Junio preened.

One of the soldiers looked admiring, too, but the *optio* said, 'Oh,' in the tone of someone who felt he should have thought of it himself. 'He isn't watching now,' he added, as an afterthought.

'Exactly,' I said. 'You would expect him to be out here in the preparation area during a race. If he was in the stadium, it must be because that particular race was important to him. And yet, as Junio points out, he wasn't even looking at a crucial moment. Or says he wasn't. Very curious, to say the least. And he seems oddly unmoved by the whole event. Not that he would weep for Fortunatus, but he strikes me as a man who would become very angry if his financial expectations were crossed. Yet he appears to have taken his losses like a stoic.' I signed. 'I'd give a great deal to know exactly what happened to cause that shipwreck.'

A small hand tugged at my toga. 'Citizen?'

I looked down. It was the cold-water slave with his bucket, his arms and shoulders already turning blue from the blows he had received. Around him, the four-in-hands were begin-

124

ning to assemble again. The drivers seemed twice as lofty
and assured after the amateurs of the last race. Even the new
driver for the Whites looked perfectly at home in his flimsy
car.

'Citizen?' the boy said again, more urgently.

'Well?'

'I can tell you a little bit. The slave who shares my sleeping
space was on duty in the circuit at the time. There really
wasn't anything to see, he says. Fortunatus simply seemed to
let go and topple out of his chariot – nobody was near him
and there was nothing the matter with his car or horses. He
thought perhaps Fortunatus had been ill.'

I stepped aside to let a stable-hand pass with the bandaged
chestnut before I asked, 'And had he?'

The boy glanced nervously towards Calyx and his companions, but they were still conferring earnestly, their backs
now turned to us. 'Not at all, citizen. That is the strange
thing. He had been in the very best of spirits. And afterwards,
when he was brought back to the inn on a shutter, the team
coach cursed and ranted, but he did not seem really upset, if
you know what I mean. I know what he is like when he is
genuinely angry.'

'I imagine you do.' I looked at him suspiciously. 'And you
are in danger of enraging him now, if he sees us together.
Why are you telling me all this?'

The boy shrugged his bruised shoulders. 'You saved me
from a flogging, citizen. Besides, I heard what you were saying
just now, about how you would give a great deal for information. Fortunatus promised me a *sestertius* if I looked after his
horse after the event, only of course, as it was . . .'

I could take a hint. I did not have a great deal to give but
I gestured to Junio, and he produced the extra *denarius* which
we had won on the horses. The boy was delighted with it. His
eyes opened as wide as oyster shells, and he took it reverently

and slipped it into his tunic folds at once. Then with a murmur of gratitude he disappeared about his business. Not a moment too soon. The four-in-hands were assembling again, and already Calyx had left his companions and was glaring around the courtyard, thundering, 'We are ready for the arena. Where is that wretched bucket-boy!'

We left him to it, and went back through the gates. We only just had time to get off the course and out of the stadium before the trumpets blew again, and the professional drivers came cantering in. As we walked away from the enclosure we could hear the cheering that told us the next race had begun.

Chapter Thirteen

'Well then,' the *optio* said briskly. 'What is your next step, citizen? Do you wish us to accompany you to the inn where the Blue team is staying?'

I thought about that for a moment. 'We might send a messenger,' I said at last. 'Just to be quite certain that Fortunatus really did go back to Londinium.'

The *optio* nodded. He muttered an order and one of the escorting soldiers set off at a lumbering run, his armour creaking and clanking as he went. 'You suspect that he did not return to the city after all?'

'On the contrary, I am almost certain that he did exactly that. If he did, then I should go back there myself at once. In the light of everything I've learned, I am particularly anxious to talk to him as soon as possible. I presume the governor's gig is still at my disposal?'

'It is standing by in the stables, waiting for you,' the *optio* said. 'The horses and the driver will have been fed and rested by this time. But are you sure there is nothing further that I can show you here?'

There was something rather plaintive in his tone, and it occurred to me that the officer was mildly disappointed. He had been looking forward to a day at the racing as my escort, and no doubt when he returned to normal duty in the barracks the duties awaiting him would be much less agreeable.

I hardened my heart. 'I would love to see more of the city, but like you I have official business to perform. Perhaps we could return to the garrison, and wait for the return of our messenger? I will have a better idea of what I want to do when I find out for sure where Fortunatus is.'

'As you wish, citizen!' He seemed to take my words as a rebuke, and we made our way back, along the route by which we had come, at a brisk pace and without a word exchanged. No wonder the stares of the passers-by were more goggle-eyed than ever.

At the gate the *optio* gave the password of the day – 'Mighty Saturn, chosen of the planets' – and we were admitted, to make our way back across the little gravelled parade ground, where a group of men were now training noisily with swords and spears against wooden stakes hammered into the earth, under the shouts and curses of their officers.

Through the inner gate we went and into the headquarters building, where the *optio* went off to announce our presence and I was shown to a bench in an ante-room to wait.

The commander was unfortunately occupied, I was informed, but his resources were at my disposal. The *optio* delivered this message breathlessly and then retired, while my remaining escort took up a post outside the door – through whether this was to guard me against the army, or vice versa, it was hard to determine.

'So the garrison is at my disposal, eh?' I grumbled to Junio. 'I suppose the commander is obliged to say that, since Pertinax is commander-in-chief of all the British legions, but from where I'm sitting I can't see much sign of it.' I craned my neck to look through the open door of the ante-room to the main street of the fort, and the lines of identical barrack-rooms opposite. 'The legion is far too busy with its own business.'

'At least it gives us something to look at while we are waiting, master,' Junio said.

He was right. There was constant activity: working parties

with waggons bringing in supplies, messengers coming and going with sealed orders, even fatigue detachments marching to the latrines with buckets and brooms. The entertainment of watching them palled quite quickly as the morning wore on, however. I sat on my bench and kicked my heels, while Junio hovered helpfully beside me.

We waited. After what seemed at least a decade, a silent soldier brought us more hard biscuits and watered wine and disappeared again without a word.

'How do legionaries manage to live on these things?' I said.

'Lots of them *prefer* wheatcakes,' Junio said. 'They think that meat is decadent and makes a fellow soft.'

I was about to make some scornful comment when the *optio* appeared again. He was looking important and at his heels came our so-called 'messenger', red-faced and panting as if he had run all the way from the town.

I waved aside the usual civilities, and once he had recovered his breath the man delivered his message in that singularly toneless voice that *nuncios* use when reporting to a senior officer. 'I beg to report, citizen, that the rumours all appear to be true. Fortunatus was observed to leave for Londinium just before noon on the *Nones*.'

'The very first morning of the games!' I exclaimed. That was exactly what I had wanted to know. If he left Verulamium before midday, then Fortunatus could indeed have been in Londinium on the evening of the murder, despite what Fulvia had told us to the contrary.

The soldier, who had been staring straight ahead, dutifully waited until I had finished my interruption and then resumed his sing-song narrative. 'He was carried back to the team inn about the third hour. It was a fine day and this same time is estimated by three other witnesses.'

I nodded. The time, of course, could only be approximate.

The army has calibrated candles to ensure that guard watches are changed at regular intervals, but most mere civilians can only estimate things by the sun. 'About mid-morning, then. Go on.'

'He was visited by the *medicus* soon after – there are two more people ready to swear to that – and permission was granted for him to return to Londinium. That was arranged at once. I interviewed the slave who hired the carriage.'

He paused, and I asked – as I was clearly expected to do – 'What did he say?'

The soldier cleared his throat and quoted the slave in a curious high-pitched voice, as if to underline that this was not part of his own recital. ' "Fortunatus said he would be more comfortable in his own quarters and the team surgeon agreed. Of course the charioteer is a wealthy man and he hired his own carriage." Those were his words, citizen. The carriage left the town before midday – the slave says so and the guard on duty agrees. That is all I could discover, citizen.' He touched his helmet in salute and brought his heels together so sharply that his plate mail rattled.

That was not quite as I had heard the story earlier. 'Fortunatus himself suggested the return to Londinium?'

'So I understand, citizen.'

That was interesting, too. I said, 'And the team coach let him go? It seems to me that if he was well enough to travel, let alone to make his own arrangements, his manager would have thought him well enough to race.'

I was half talking to myself, but the soldier obviously felt that having delivered his information he had done all that could be required of him. Still standing stiffly to attention, he rapped out, 'That is all I know, citizen.'

It was the *optio* who said, 'Fortunatus is said to have been blinded by the blow to his head, citizen. He could hardly race in that condition and in that case the team would have no further interest in him. I should think that Calyx was glad to see him go, and have one less billet to pay for.'

I said nothing.

The *optio* paused, and then said in a different tone, 'Although, of course, they say he will recover – and in that case you'd expect Calyx to keep him here, wouldn't you, if there was any sign of improvement? If only so that the team doctors could keep an eye on him and make sure that he could get back in a chariot again as soon as possible. Great Jupiter, Greatest and Best. I do believe you are right, citizen! It *is* odd, when you stop to consider it. What do you suppose the motive is?'

I shook my head. 'I don't know. Fortunatus may have had his own reasons for wanting to return to the city at that time, and perhaps he bribed Calyx to let him do it without disappointing the racegoers.' It was logically possible. Fortunatus could have bribed Calyx to look the other way, staged an accident and so contrived to return to Londinium in time to strangle Monnius. Even if his return was noted, those feigned head injuries would be an alibi. It was difficult and dangerous, but possible – and if anyone had cool nerve, Fortunatus did.

Perhaps it was not even as dangerous as all that – if I had not arrived asking questions, no one would have thought about it twice. I wondered how big a bribe would be needed to corrupt Calyx. Though I must not jump to conclusions, of course: there might be some other explanation altogether.

I did not explain any of this to the *optio*. I said, 'I wish I knew how seriously Fortunatus really hurt his head, and how and why that shipwreck happened when it did.'

'Permission to speak, citizen?' the soldier put in.

'Go on,' I said. 'Have you thought of something else?'

The soldier continued to gaze at the painted plaster above my head, but he had lost his official monotone as he said,

131

'Forgive me, citizen, it may not be important. I thought nothing of it at the time. But the slave who hired the carriage did tell me that Fortunatus was very suspicious of the inn servants. Insisted on keeping his purse in his own hand and counting out his money to pay the driver. The boy was thinking only that the man mistrusted him, and I suppose one might count out money from the shape of the coins, but . . .' He tailed off.

I grinned. 'You mean, it rather sounds as if Fortunatus could see, at that stage? Well done, soldier. I suppose the inn-slave didn't let slip anything else?'

He glanced at me in an embarrassed fashion. 'He did say that when the slaves came in to take Fortunatus to the carriage, the charioteer seemed so impatient that he got up from his couch and lay down on the shutter himself. Then a moment later he was back to moaning and holding his head as if he couldn't do a thing unaided. Of course, I have no other witnesses to this. I promised the boy I wouldn't mention it – he seemed to think that it might earn him a flogging – but in the circumstances . . .' He seemed to recall himself, and with a muttered 'Citizen!' he stood to attention again and resumed his contemplation of the wall.

The *optio* puffed up like a fighting cock and seemed about to speak to him severely, but I cut in quickly, 'You have done well, soldier, and I promise you that no action will be taken against the slave in question. You have my word as represent-ative of the governor.'

The *optio* turned as red as a Druid's apron, but he could hardly gainsay that authority. 'Very well. Dismissed. Back to your detachment,' he barked, and the soldier, with a muttered, 'Thank you, citizen,' prepared to obey.

He laid one hand upon his sword hilt and raised the other to heaven. 'I will do all that may be ordered, and am ready to obey every command. May Jove and all the gods bless our

Lord the Emperor, the Divine and Immortal Commodus Britannicus Caesar,' he intoned, then swivelled smartly on his heel and marched away.

The *optio* turned to me. 'So, citizen, you wish to return to Londinium? Your gig is ready and waiting – the garrison commander has given the order. He wishes me to ask if you are sure that there is no further assistance he can give.'

'There is,' I said. 'I would be very grateful if he could arrange for someone to keep an eye on Calyx while he is in the town. Whatever Fortunatus is up to, I suspect that the Blues manager is in it too, and that there is money in it for him. Quite large amounts of money, since he takes the loss of the prize purse so calmly.'

'I see.' A gleam appeared in the *optio*'s eye. 'Certainly, citizen. I'm sure that something could be arranged, although it may mean sparing someone from the garrison to return to the races for the rest of the day. Myself, perhaps, since I know what he looks like, and I was detailed to accompany you there in any case.'

'I think that would be most appropriate,' I said. I had rather guessed that he would volunteer himself, if it was a question of attending the races again. But I did want him to remember what he was there for. 'It is important to send someone in authority – someone who will not become so interested in the racing that he forgets to keep track of Calyx – and of those two men whom we saw with him, too, if possible.'

The *optio* understood my meaning. He coughed and then said, 'Of course, citizen.'

'In that case,' I said, 'I will leave it in your hands. What hour is it? A little past midday?'

He looked uncomfortable, and I realised for the first time that perhaps he had left me waiting a little longer than necessary. 'A little after that, citizen. I heard the *apparitor* sound the trumpet at the courthouse as I was coming through the town.'

I nodded. We had not heard it at the garrison, but the noonday trumpet was not meant for us, it was meant for those summoned before the day's courts at the town *curia* – they were obliged to be present before noon, and if they missed the noon fanfare they were officially too late. Of course, on an overcast day like this one, it was not easy to judge the exact moment when the sun was at its highest, but that trumpet marks the legal end of morning, and that was good enough for me.

'Then I leave here later than Fortunatus,' I said. 'Let's see if it is possible to arrive back in the capital before the city gates are closed. If I can do it, he certainly could have done.'

The *optio* nodded. 'You wish to try that, citizen? I will explain it to the gig-driver. He is awaiting you now. If you and your attendant would like to follow me . . .'

He must have explained to good effect because we fairly flew along the road, changed horses at the *mansio* and still reached Londinium comfortably before nightfall. Comfortably in the metaphorical sense. I have never been more pleased to see a warm bath-house and a massage in my life. I was blue in unexpected places – and for days afterwards Junio walked with care, like a newcomer to the cavalry.

Chapter Fourteen

'Citizen Libertus,' the governor was saying, 'I am extremely glad to see you.' He had made a point of having me summoned to his rooms, as soon as he heard that I was in the building, so he could speak to me in person. He was being prepared for an official engagement, and a slave was helping him into his *synthesis* – that light and useful combination of toga and tunic which men of substance often wear to formal banquets. 'I am sorry I am not able to entertain you myself. I was not expecting you back so soon, and this is one of a series of civic banquets to mark the end of my period in office. However, I have made arrangements for a meal to be prepared for you. You may eat in the *triclinium*, or have it served in your room if you prefer.'

The thought of rattling around in the empty dining room of the palace did not appeal to me, so I accepted his latter offer with alacrity, and then, at his urging, told him the events of the day. He listened gravely, while slaves placed rings upon his hands, cleaned his ears with ear scoops and rubbed perfumed oil into his hair.

He was visibly startled when I told him about Fortunatus. 'You say he has returned to Londinium, hurt?' He shook his head. 'He must have entered the city very quietly, otherwise I should have heard of it. He is famous among the soldiers and that kind of news travels very quickly.'

This had not occurred to me, although now that Pertinax had mentioned it, it seemed obvious enough. Of course, wheeled transport was not permitted on urban streets in daylight, and Fortunatus would presumably have had to transfer to a litter to get back to his quarters. That would certainly have drawn attention to his arrival. 'Unless, of course, he was well enough to walk,' I said.

In that case, as we both knew, he might well have managed to slip past the town guard unremarked. Even in a place like Glevum, a well-known man could pass the gates unnoticed in a crowd, provided he wore a simple hooded tunic, kept his head down, and there was nothing to connect him to his background. In a city of this size it would be easier still.

Pertinax thought about this for a moment. 'You think that this charioteer is the killer?' he said at last.

'I don't know, Excellence. I only know that he *was* here in the city that night, after all, and therefore it would have been possible. Unless of course that fall from the chariot has really affected his sight, and he is confined to his bed. I hope to discover that tomorrow. I want to confront Fortunatus in person, if I can.'

The commander-in-chief of all the Britannic legions nodded his head. 'And if you wish to pay a visit to the grain stores, as you were suggesting, I will arrange to have you taken there. It would be quite convenient. The Blues have their headquarters very close to one of the granaries.'

I began to thank him but he waved my words aside. 'By the bye, mosaic-maker, those enquiries you requested yesterday. I sent a slave down to the market to ask at all the jewellers', and we found the fellow easily. It was exactly as you thought. The necklace belonging to Annia Augusta was repaired, and returned to Monnius' house. On the very evening of the murder, in fact. The jeweller delivered it himself, at the feast, and he confirms that it is indeed the one you brought away from the house and left with me. He recognised the replacement stone, he said, though I couldn't detect any difference between them.'

I murmured my thanks.

Pertinax smiled and extended one hand for a slave to clean his fingernails and buff them with scented oil. 'I am sorry, Libertus, to have given you all these duties and then left you to dine alone when you are supposed to be my guest. However, I have tried to make amends. I asked your slave what foods would please you most. I have ordered what he suggested – fresh trout baked in cabbage leaves, a dish of leeks and peas with oil, and a plate of peppered plums to end with. And no *liquifrumen* or *garum* with it. That meets with your approval?'

It certainly did. I stammered that I was honoured that the governor should concern himself so much with my welfare. I hoped that, in turning down the *garum*, Junio had managed to convey my dislike for all varieties of the Romans' beloved fermented fish-entrail sauce without giving offence.

Pertinax smiled broadly. 'Oh, and at his suggestion there also will be some spiced mead for you – he assures me that he can prepare it. My kitchens will arrange the rest – they will bring it to you shortly.'

He bent forward to allow an attendant to fasten the brooch-pin on his shoulder, and made a gesture of farewell. 'Goodnight, pavement-maker. I wish you well in your enquiries. Bring this to a quick conclusion, and we shall soon be on that progress to Eboracum.' He held out the perfumed hand for me to kiss the seal ring, and I bowed myself out of his presence backwards.

The province of Britannia, I thought to myself as I followed the attendant back to my bedchamber, would do well to find another governor as good as this austere and kindly man.

When I got to my room I found Junio waiting for me, with the promised supper on a tray already set waiting on the

137

table. I was surprised, and a little irritated. I had expected
Superbus to attend me, and I wanted to hear more about
Eppaticus.

'Master?' Junio said in an introductory tone as he stripped
off my toga and helped me make a swift libation to the gods.

I frowned. I knew that gambit; it meant that he was dying
to tell me something.

'Well then,' I said, settling myself on a stool and preparing
to make short work of the trout. 'What is it? Come on, I
know you have heard something in the servants' hall.' I put
down my spoon suddenly. 'Don't tell me that the Trinovantine
came here after all, and tried to hold Superbus to his bargain?'

'Not quite that, master,' Junio said. 'Someone did come
here this morning. A well-dressed slave, according to the
doorkeepers, with a message, apparently for you. Superbus
took it.'

'A message!' I frowned. 'Who would be sending me a
message? My patron Marcus, perhaps?'

'I don't know, master.' Junio paused. 'But that is not really
the problem. Apparently a little later Superbus went out . . .'
Another pause.

'And?'

'And he hasn't come back,' Junio finished dismally.

I gaped like the trout. 'Then where is he? Where did he
go?'

'I don't know, master. That is what all the other servants
have been asking me. He claimed that he was going out to do
something for you. Something very confidential.'

I almost groaned aloud. 'For me?'

'Yes. That is why no one in the household questioned it.
Everyone knew that His Excellence had put him at your
service. Only, of course, they were expecting Superbus back
– especially now that we have come ourselves. The chief
slave sent for me on purpose to ask about it.'

This time I did groan. 'And does Pertinax know that one of his valuable slaves is missing?'

'Not yet, master – though he will have to be told. Of course, if Superbus does *not* come back there'll be a slave-hunt for him.'

I buried my head in my hands. In a household this size, a single slave might be gone for hours before he was missed, and even then it would not be by his master. But once a slave-hunt was in progress, every soldier in the town would be alerted, and there would be a price on Superbus' head, dead or alive. If it was supposed that I had helped him to escape, I could be under arrest myself.

Though I doubted that he had run away. More likely he was the victim of attack. Eppaticus, for instance. If so, I was legally responsible. I had borrowed Superbus, and if anything had happened to him in my service, which I might have prevented, the law would require me to replace him – just as I would have to replace a horse or any other possession that I could not return in good working order. And after the earlier attack, I should have prevented this. I found myself trying to calculate what Superbus' market price might be.

'Of course, he may turn up safely yet,' I said, as though by voicing the idea I could persuade myself.

'Yes, master.'

'Pertinax is a fair man. If Superbus was attacked, he would never hold me responsible. In any case, it may have nothing to do with Eppaticus at all. Or with Superbus breaking his bargain.'

'No, master.'

I pushed away the platter. Junio knew as well as I did that, if I could not afford to pay for Superbus, my own servant might be taken in 'noxal recompense'. Suddenly I was no longer hungry. I would simply have to throw myself on

Pertinax's mercy, I thought. I was not looking forward to it. Losing an expensive slave is a poor way to repay hospitality.

'Where in the world do you think he went?' I demanded, as much of myself as of Junio. 'What was he up to, for Mars' sake? Putting himself in a position where Eppaticus could find him? Surely he didn't go down to the market enquiring at the jeweller's himself? I distinctly told him not to. In fact, I told him very particularly to stay in the palace.'

'I know you did, master.' Junio was doing his best to be comforting. 'Perhaps Superbus decided to buy himself a slave from Eppaticus after all. Unless,' he added with a sudden flash of insight, 'he went off to try to redeem himself a bit? Ask the questions that he didn't ask the first time, and find out if Eppaticus ever dealt in grain?'

Once he had suggested it, I had to admit that it seemed extremely likely. It would be just like Superbus, from what I'd seen of him, to try to rectify what he saw as an error of judgement. It was hardly comforting, however.

'Great Mars! In that case, anything might have happened to him.'

Junio had turned pale – he didn't need me to spell out the possibilities.

'Especially if there is a lot of money at stake. And I think there is. Five thousand *denarii*, at least.'

Junio said nothing for a moment. Then, 'So, what are you going to do tomorrow, master? Go to the granaries, look for Fortunatus, or try to find Superbus before someone else does?'

I had been asking myself the same question. Previously I had planned to send Superbus to Monnius' house, overtly to ask more questions of the slaves, but in fact to keep discreet guard over the coins that I had found. But now that was obviously impossible. I said, after a little thought, 'Perhaps the granaries. The governor says that the Blues live near one, and talking to the traders may lead us to Eppaticus too. Oh, Mercury! I hardly know what to do first.'

Junio went over to the brazier, where something was bubbling gently in a metal pot. 'I suggest,' he said with the shadow of a grin, 'that what you do first is drink this spiced mead I've prepared for you, and then take some rest. Then, perhaps, if you have finished with those plums . . .? We shan't make matters any better by wasting good food tonight, and it will be impossible to do anything in a strange city in the dark. We should merely end up being missing ourselves.'

Trust a slave to take a practical view. I reclined on my pillows and did my best to think aloud as I applied myself to the mead and Junio made a hearty meal of the scraps. 'What happened at the chariot race?' I said. 'Was Fortunatus really injured as he said, or did he take the opportunity to come back here, scale the garden wall and throttle his rival? But if so, how did he know where to find the necklace? It only came back to the house that night.'

Junio looked up, his mouth full of vegetables. 'And how did he let Fulvia know in time to drug the wine?'

I shook my head. 'And even if he did, why hide the money under the floorboards? Even if Annia is right, and he was trying to make us think that Monnius was killed for money, surely he would take away the cash? And why steal the scroll? This case is full of mysteries. And another thing – what was the message Superbus took for me? Where did he go? And most of all, where has he got to now?'

Whether it was the mead, the comfortable bed, or just the exertions of the last few days, I don't know, but somehow I felt that I would think more clearly if I closed my eyes a moment.

When I opened them again, it was morning, and Junio was bending over me again. 'Wake up, master. The governor has

141

arranged for you to visit the grain warehouses this morning. I have breakfast for you here.'

I struggled upright on my pillows. 'Superbus?'

'Still missing, I'm afraid, although his master knows it now. The town guards have been alerted, and soldiers are searching the city for him. His Excellence is not blaming you – he seems to feel that this is somehow related to the death of Monnius, and that it is lucky you and I escaped.'

I wasn't sure I shared that interpretation, but I was duly grateful for it. I eyed the bread and fruit with more enthusiasm. 'And he has arranged for us to go to the granaries?'

'There has not been time to alert the warehouses, but you still have that official letter with his seal on it. That should gain you entry anywhere. He gave orders for special transport for you, as soon as he had made the morning sacrifice. They should be waiting now. I have been given directions, master, and I am to take you down there as soon as you are ready.'

Chapter Fifteen

What happened next was a surprise to me. Instead of leading me down into the courtyard to a waiting litter, or even to one of the town gates to take a carriage, Junio took me to the back of the palace, turned left at the gate, and down a short path to the river bank.

'Your transport, master,' he said, with a gesture and a grin.

I found myself confronted with a barge.

I do not care for water travel. I was captured once by pirates from the sea, and after being hauled aboard their filthy craft I was held in chains in a stinking hold for days until they dragged me blinking into the daylight at a distant port and sold me into slavery. That was an experience I never want to repeat – although it still haunts my nightmares – and I have kept away from water ever since, except when it is necessary to cross a river by a rope-ferry, and even then I scramble off as soon as possible.

I have seen more peaceful water-traffic of course, many times: the docks in Glevum near my home are constantly busy with ships of all descriptions. But I had never voluntarily been aboard a boat since my captivity, and my chief sensation as I was helped up the plank to this one was something very akin to panic. I was sure that it was about to start rocking dangerously, although the water was calm, and I was very glad to sit down on the wooden seat that was provided for me at the stern.

The bargemaster, a squat dark fellow with a bushy beard,

hurried up to bow before me and ensure that I was comfortable – so far from my previous experience that I began to feel
a little more secure. Junio, though, was delighted by the
whole event. When I recovered myself sufficiently to glance
in his direction, he was squatting on the deck at my feet, and
grinning with careless satisfaction.

'What a splendid notion, master,' he murmured. 'I asked
one of the household about it this morning, and it seems that
all the grain stores are by the river. This is much the fastest
way of visiting them, even if you do not care for boats.'

I hadn't realised that Junio knew about my fears, and in
the interests of dignity I did not reply. Instead I took a feigned
interest in the preparations around me. The governor's
personal standard was run up on a small post at the back,
and the slave-crew settled into position. It was a dual-purpose
barge, designed to be towed by horses when required, or
rowed by a bank of oarsmen, one oar on either side. A man
with a drum appeared from the quay and took up a position
at the bow.

'They've let go the ropes, master! We are off!'

Junio hardly had time to frame the words before the
bargemaster barked a command and two rows of oars were
lowered into the water, like so many long white teeth. They
could row, those men. I would not have believed that anything
so bulky could move with such apparent ease. Out we went,
leaving the riverbank behind, and joined the traffic on the
water.

It was a whole other world out on the river. Great ships
from distant provinces, some of them sixty feet or more,
filled the waterway, their huge square sails filled or furled.
Small boats, punts and cockles wound their way between
them, carrying everything from fish to hempen rope. A barge
filled with horses rocked at anchor as we passed, and
Londinium towered above us in the morning sunshine. And

still we ploughed onwards. The oars splashed in time to the drummer's beat, men strained and grunted, and once I swear I saw an eel slither through the depths beneath us. I was beginning to enjoy myself.

The bargemaster sidled up again. 'You wish to see the corn stores, citizen? You will see the first one in a little while, on the right – the steer-board side.' He grinned, showing a gap where his front teeth had once been, and indicated the slave manning the steering oar at the back. 'Not that they will be expecting you at the granary. We travel faster than any messenger.'

I thought to myself that if I hoped to learn anything at all, the fact that nobody was expecting me might prove to be an advantage. I was about to say so to him, but by that time we had reached the bend in the river and I caught my first sight of one of the Londinium grain stores.

There are grain stores in Glevum, of course – any large city has a need for bread and flour – but nothing I had seen before prepared me for the scale of this. It was an enormous building, as of course it would have to be: the lands around Londinium are not suitable for growing corn, and every grain of it has to be imported and stored somewhere. The warehouse stood on its own wharf, where a contingent of slaves under the supervision of a bad-tempered soldier with a lash were struggling to move heavy sacks of grain on to a wide, flat-bottomed boat alongside. Further along, another lesser boat was being loaded with smaller sacks.

'Army rations,' the bargemaster said, with the air of one long familiar with the river and its ways. 'One and a half thousand troops in the Londinium fort.' He spat contemptuously into the water. 'Most of them the governor's personal guard. But there's another section – town watch they call themselves – and they've got their beaks in everything, mostly on behalf of the army *procurator*, so naturally the best of the grain crop goes to them. Not like the likes of us. Won't find *them* having to pay three times the proper price for a sack of corn, and then finding when they get it home it's full of weevils, or so damp that it is half rotted before they open it.'

I looked at him questioningly. Bargemasters are famously experts on any subject you care to mention – even I had heard that – but this man seemed to speak with personal feeling.

'Haven't there been edicts to control the price of corn?'

'Oh, there are supposed to be. But only up to a certain quantity. If you need more than that, you have to pay whatever they are asking. The official price is a waste of time – first sign of a wet season, and it goes shooting up like a ballista.' He spat again. 'My sister's husband has a baker's shop, a very up-to-date affair, with two ovens, three boys to help him and his own donkey-mill as well. In a good place too, just east of Government House – just where all the minor officials have their accommodation. You would suppose, wouldn't you, that a man like that would do a splendid trade?'

He barely waited for my agreement.

'My father thought so anyway, when he arranged the match for her. But with the price of grain – wheat, barley, rye, it's all the same – the family has been close to starving more than once. Men will only pay so much for a loaf of bread, whatever the price of grain, and when half of *that* turns out to be useless, there's no room for profit.'

He turned away and began barking orders to his men. As if by magic half the blades stopped beating and instead dropped, like a single wounded insect, into the water, the steering slave strained at his oar, and the barge moved smoothly up beside the wharf. The soldier with the lash came belligerently over, and then, seeing the governor's pennant flying behind us, clearly thought better of it and hurried off to find somebody official to welcome us ashore.

The man who did so was a small, pale individual, thin as a blade of corn himself, with a fringe of faded sandy hair around his balding head. He was dressed in an amber-coloured tunic of fine wool, with a good cloak and leather leggings, and was clearly a man of some substance; possibly even a citizen, despite the dress. There was a *pilleus*, a freeman's cap, tucked into his belt, and freeborn men in any substantial city these days earn the distinction of citizenship simply by being born within the walls. He came towards us bowing frantically and looked (as he must have been) astonished when he found that the only occupant of the imperial barge was an elderly Celt in a travel-stained toga.

He recovered hastily. 'Citizen, to what do we owe the honour?' He had a habit of pressing the ends of his long thin fingers together as he spoke, and bowing over them like a temple priest. 'I am the chief clerk of stores and civil overseer for this granary. The governor has sent you here today? Is there some problem with the imperial stores? If so . . .' His pale eyes flickered nervously to the official pennant as he spoke.

'Nothing of that kind at all,' I murmured soothingly. 'It is merely that I should like to see over the granary. There are one or two unresolved enquiries as a result of Caius Monnius' death.'

I tried to keep my reply deliberately vague, while sounding as efficient as possible. If the truth were told, I had very little idea myself what I hoped to learn from this visit – except perhaps to understand the office of *frumentarius* a little better, and discover what kind of service Eppaticus might have provided, for Monnius to owe him five thousand *denarii*. Or, to put it another way, what kind of underhand activity it was that had sent him bolting like a startled carriage horse at the mere mention of Monnius' murder.

147

If I had intended to reassure the overseer, I had not succeeded. The pale eyes were flickering like candles in a gale, and he pressed his thin fingers so hard together that the tips went white. Nonetheless he went through the motions of welcome. 'Of course, of course. A terrible business, the death of Monnius. We were all most shocked to hear it. Now, Mightiness, if you wish to look over the granary . . .?' He waited while I made my way ashore, with the assistance of Junio and the bargemaster, and then added, 'Where, exactly, would you care to begin?'

As I know rather less about Roman granaries than I know about boats, this was a difficult question to answer. At my *oppidum* when I was young, we simply dried the rye on wooden racks, threshed it, and kept the resultant grain in a pit, with prickled branches set around it to keep off the mice. I said, with as much authority as I could muster, 'Let us start from the beginning. Show me where the corn comes in, and what you do with it.'

That seemed to worry him still more, but he began to gabble a description, leading the way as he did so. 'This is the main quay – at harvest it is full of grain barges. They bring it down from some of the shallower rivers by canoe, and offload it into barges when they meet the main waterway. Cheaper than road transport, and besides, Caius Monnius arranged for drying houses to be built on the riverbank, so that even if the weather is bad or the corn is green it can be dried out and used.'

I nodded. 'I had heard that.'

The warehouse manager pressed his fingers together again. 'They have proved their worth, this year alone. Some of the harvests in the east would have been wholly spoiled by the rains. And once the corn is dried, of course, it keeps much better too. Then, even out of season, people can come here and buy from us. With the kilns we have grain all year round.

Much more efficient than it used to be. But still half the cost is transport, as I expect you know.'

I was thinking about that five thousand *denarii*. 'Do farmers transport the goods at their own cost?'

For the first time, he smiled. A thin little ghost of a smile, as if the idea pleased him. 'It all depends. Some of this grain is tax corn, collected by the government – that's used for the army, in general. Then on some large estates we have an outright option on the whole crop every year, and of course the *procurator* owns many farms himself, and in those cases, obviously, there is no charge for transport and drying. If it is a smaller man with just a field or two, then he will bring the corn here at his own expense, and pay to put it in the drying kilns.'

'Or apply for a compulsory loan to build his own?'

'As you say, citizen.'

'It is a wonder he chooses to sell his corn at all,' I said.

He smiled again. 'But of course, citizen, he has to pay his land taxes. In coin. So he is forced to bring his goods to market to earn the money.'

'Very well,' I said, impressed by the ruthlessness of his logic. 'So the grain arrives here. What happens to it then?'

He led the way, up and down ladders and in and out of rooms heavy with grain dust, showing us how the grain was barrowed into large storage areas, and raked constantly to keep it dry and turned.

'Here you are, you see, citizen,' he said proudly, as we reached a central court. 'This is the loading area.' A number of wooden channels, with hatches, stood around the walls, and at one of them two slaves were holding a wide-mouthed bag. The shutter opened and a waterfall of golden grain streamed down the chute and into the sack. One of them shouted something, there was a sound of hand-wheels turning and the shutter closed again, cutting off the stream of corn

149

just as the top of the bag was reached. The two slaves dragged the sack away, another began sewing up the top with a bronze needle, and the whole operation began again. An overseer with an abacus was counting off the sacks as they were completed.

'About five *mobius*-fuls to fill a sack that size,' our guide announced, indicating one of the corn measures hanging on the wall. 'Worth about twenty *denarii* at this time of year, though the price seems to be going up all the time. That's good news for us, of course. Some people want less than a sackful, and others more. We sell to bakers, market traders, large city households – and to the army, too, of course. It is shipped out again by river, or loaded on to waggons at the back. We are just inside the town defences here, but we have our own entrance through the eastern wall.'

'This is important business then?' I said, impressed by the idea of a private gate.

He preened. 'One of the most important in the city. Some of our grain is even exported to Rome. Now, I don't think there is anything else I can show you, gentlemen?'

I bent down to pick up a few seeds of scattered grain. They were different in size and shape, and one of them was spongy to the touch. 'Why are there several different chutes?' I asked, looking at the wooden channel through which the corn was pouring again.

'Each grain comes down from a different storage area,' he explained. 'This one is spelt and rye, that one is barley, and so on. Spelt is the easiest to store – it has to be roasted before it can be threshed, and so it never rots. Of course that's less of a problem now, thanks to Monnius' drying floors.'

He led the way outside, and waved a hand. 'Oh, and Monnius recently began a scheme to deal in hay – there is quite a market for it as winter fodder for horses. That is stored in the warehouse over there. It has been a good investment – we are quite close to one of the racing stables here, and they are pleased to have it, as well as their usual grain. We have even sold hay back once or twice to some of the farmers we bought it from. At a profit, of course.' He gave me that thin smile again. 'That is all, citizen, unless you wish to see my office? It is through this door, although there is nothing to see.'

There might, of course, have been much to learn if I'd had time to examine in detail all the documents stacked, or stored in pots, around the walls. Invoices, lists, records, orders – scribbled on bark, scratched on wax or inscribed with elaborate care on vellum scrolls – the office was a mass of documents. There was another abacus, and a steelyard, too, with a series of little weights beside it.

'For corn?' I asked, surprised. The weigh pans looked too small.

He gave me a pitying glance. 'For weighing money, citizen. In a city this size there are always lots of strange coins in circulation. Egyptian, Greek – all sorts of things. People even take shavings off imperial coins and melt them down. I always have my banker weigh the coins we receive to make sure they contain the right quantity of silver. Or of gold, of course. Sometimes the sums involved are very large.'

As much as five thousand *denarii*, I wondered. That decided me. I asked the question that had been on my lips all morning. 'Do you ever have dealings with a man called Eppaticus?'

He did not start, or blush, or falter. Instead he became unnaturally still. The only movement was in the narrow fingers, pressing on each other harder than ever. At last he said, 'I believe I have heard the name, citizen. Though I myself have never had the pleasure . . . I will glance through my records for you, if you wish.'

'If you would be so kind,' I said, but knew that it was

useless. There were so many records in that office, a man could search there for a year and find nothing – especially if it was something he did not want to find. But there was nothing else to be gained here, and there were several other warehouses. I allowed myself to be guided back towards the barge, where my boatman was waiting for me. The smaller boat had loaded up and gone, I noticed, and the larger one was almost ready to leave as well. I would have to hurry if we were to clear the quay without hindering commerce.

The warehouse official watched me teeter up the plank and take my place on the seat, his face wreathed in smiles now. 'Farewell, citizen. I hope we have been of service. And now, if you will excuse me, I have a customer.' He hurried off in the direction of a tall man in a long cloak who had just strolled on to the quay, and a moment later they were walking off together, deep in conversation.

As we pulled away from the quay I glanced at the cloaked figure, and in the same instant he glanced back at me. We both reacted together. He turned abruptly and began to walk away. Boat or no boat, I jumped to my feet.

'Back!' I shouted to the bargemaster. 'Take me back there at once!'

He raised a shaggy eyebrow, but he barked out the order. The oarsmen backed their oars, and slowly – infinitely slowly it seemed to me – the boat slowed, then turned about on itself and began to inch back towards the shore. The barge-master looked at me quizzically. 'You know that fellow, citizen?'

'I don't know him exactly. I have never spoken to him, but I have seen him before. I wonder what he is doing here so soon. He must have made great efforts to get here.'

I glanced at Junio. He was gazing at the shore with a kind of rapt excitement. 'It *is* him, isn't it, master?'

'That's him,' I said. A tall, thin, greying man with a crooked nose and thin cruel slit of a smile. The last time I had seen him he was talking to the trainer of the Blues – yesterday morning in Verulamium.

Chapter Sixteen

I am not a young man, and I was stiff from my battering journey of the day before, but as soon as the barge touched the quay I was on my feet, and I was down the plank almost before the bargemaster had time to lay it for me.

The warehouse official was still standing there, pressing his fingers together and looking bewildered. I did not waste time on civilities.

'That man,' I demanded. 'Who is he? What was he doing here?'

The official blinked. 'Glaucus, citizen? He came to buy some grain, naturally.' The pinched face was suddenly flushed with concern. 'There is nothing unusual about it. He comes here very often. He buys the corn stores for the Blue *factio* – for both the men and the horses. Their quarters are very close to here. Is there some kind of trouble, citizen? I do hope not. The *factio* are good customers of ours.'

So crook-nose was nicknamed Glaucus, I thought. The grey. It was a name more usually given to horses, but with his long face and close-set eyes it suited him perfectly.

The controller of the warehouse was still bobbing along beside me, firing questions like an archer loosing arrows. I ignored them, and asked one of my own. 'The Blue quarters are close by, I think you said?'

'Indeed, citizen.' He was bending his fingers almost backwards in his desire to help. 'Go out of the back gate . . .' He gave me the directions: it did not seem to be far.

'Right,' I said to Junio, who was at my heels as usual. 'Let the bargemaster know where I am going. If I am lucky I may catch two sparrows with a single slingshot and find Fortunatus at the same time. You can catch me up at the Blue quarters.'

Junio grinned his understanding and scampered off on his errand.

I did not wait for him. Looking back, perhaps that was a foolish decision – wandering around the back streets of a city I did not know, without even the protection of a slave – but I had become careless under Pertinax's protection, and besides I was anxious to catch up with Glaucus.

As soon as I left the warehouse, I looked up and down the road for him, but he had disappeared like a bubble, so I set off for the Blue headquarters, following the directions which had been given me.

It was not far, and I found it easily. It occupied most of a block in a little alley close to the main street, hemmed in by the blank outer walls of a run-down house on one side and a carpet-maker's on the other. It might have been an ordinary inn, from its general appearance: a wide gate led to a large stable yard surrounded on three sides by a colonnaded building, with – judging by the window-spaces visible – large rooms on the lower floor and a cluster of tiny attics under the rooftiles. Another gateway at the side led to further stabling beyond. I took a few steps through the entrance arch, but instead of a welcoming innkeeper anxious to take my money, I found a burly slave blocking my way.

'Your business, citizen?' He was dressed in a uniform-style tunic of a delicate cerulean blue – presumably in honour of the *factio* – but it accorded very oddly with the solid leather breastplate, helmet and groin-protector which he also were.

'Is Glaucus here yet?' I enquired briskly. 'I saw him at the granary earlier.' I did not actually say that I had spoken to him, but I thought the implication might get me through the gate.

The burly slave did not move an eyelash. 'Glaucus is not expected back today, citizen.'

I tried another gambit. 'Then perhaps I could have a word with Fortunatus? I heard that he was hurt in Verulamium. I was speaking to the lady Fulvia . . .'

At the mention of her name the guard relaxed. 'I am sorry, citizen,' he said, in an altered tone. He was friendly now, almost conspiratorial. 'Fortunatus is not well enough for visitors. He is in his quarters, resting.' He glanced over his shoulder as he spoke, in the direction of one of the rooms on the upper floor.

I made a desperate calculation. The doorkeeper could scarcely leave his post, and once I was beyond him there was nobody about to challenge me. I doubted there were many people in the building. There would be a few servants and stable-boys about, of course, but most of the *factio* was in Verulamium.

I wagered everything, like Junio at the races. 'Fortunatus will see me, I'm certain,' I said airily, pressing a coin into the man's hand, and walking confidently past him before he could prevent me.

'Citizen, wait . . .' He was calling after me, but I gave him a breezy wave and strolled away in the general direction of that backward glance. I reasoned that he must have been looking at Fortunatus' chamber, and in any case an air of assurance was my best defence. I had no idea where the staircase was, but I went through the largest door I could find, and sure enough there was a narrow flagstoned entrance hall with rickety wooden steps leading up to the rooms beyond.

A bored slave-boy was dozing on the topmost step, but he struggled to his feet as I came up, a look of incredulity spreading over his face. He was a small, wiry creature, perhaps twelve years old, and he wore a tunic of that same cerulean blue.

'Citizen?' His voice had not yet broken.

'I have come to see Fortunatus,' I said again.

Now it was panic which raced across the boy's features. He was half my size, but he stationed himself firmly outside the nearest door, his arms and legs spread out as though physically to prevent my reaching it. 'My master is resting,' he said breathlessly. 'I have orders not to admit anyone.'

'What is going on up there?' To my surprise, the gatekeeper had abandoned his post and lumbered over to the stairwell.

'He is demanding to see Fortunatus,' the boy said. 'I've told him . . .'

'I told him, too,' the burly slave replied, starting menacingly up the stairs. All affability had disappeared from his manner now.

I was more than a match for the slave-boy, but this guard was a different matter. I was beginning to fear for my safety when I remembered something that I should have thought of before. I was still carrying the governor's warrant in my belt. I produced it now, with a flourish.

'I am on official business,' I said, brandishing the seal. 'In the name of His Excellency, the Governor Pertinax, I demand to speak to Fortunatus.'

The two men looked at one another. Then the guard shrugged. 'Well,' he said to the slave-boy, 'it is over to you. This is none of my business.' He trudged away down the stairs and back to his gate.

The boy looked at me helplessly, but a warrant was a warrant. In any case, I was bigger than he was. With obvious reluctance he pushed open the door and stood back to let me pass. I went into Fortunatus' chamber.

It was not a grand room, for such a wealthy man. Of

course, Fortunatus, like others of his profession, had purchased himself private quarters elsewhere. When his contract expired – or he could buy himself out of it – he would doubtless retire there in luxury. In the meantime, it seemed that these simple quarters provided by the team sufficed. The window-space was still half shuttered, but there was enough light to make out the main features of the room. There was a wooden chest for his possessions, a chipped pottery bowl and jug, a battered stool beside the window and a cot, of sorts, on which I could dimly make out a huddled form, completely hidden under a pile of woven blankets.

'He is resting, citizen, as you see,' the slave muttered, indicating the bed.

I found myself nodding reluctantly. Perhaps my suspicions had been ill founded, and Fortunatus really had sustained a dreadful injury. Certainly the figure on the bed was horribly motionless – like a man in one of those deep swoons that lasts for days. I was about to mutter my apologies and make a rather embarrassed retreat when the attendant spoke again.

'He shouldn't be disturbed, citizen, so if you have quite finished here . . .'

He was so agitated in his manner that a horrible misgiving dawned on me. Suppose Fortunatus was not merely sleeping, but dead? Was that why the slave was so anxious to get rid of me? The more I looked, the more suspicious I became. I moved a little closer, but I could detect no sound of breathing. The huddled blankets did not rise or fall.

With a sudden movement I seized the bed coverings and pulled them clear. It was a risk, I knew. I was prepared for almost anything – a bloodied corpse, a headless trunk, the horrible contortions of a poison victim. What I found was a bundle of loose straw, tied roughly in the proportions of a man.

Fortunatus was not there at all.

159

I rounded on the slave, but he was already bolting towards the door. I started after him, as fast as my ageing bones would permit, and managed to seize the shoulder of his blue tunic as he made off down the stairs.

'Stay there!' I panted – he was trying to tear himself free. 'Or I'll have the governor's guard come for you and take you in charge.'

It was an empty threat, but it halted him, and he permitted himself to be hauled back to the landing, where he stood before me literally quivering with fear, his eyes fixed abjectly on his sandal straps.

'Well?' I demanded. 'What have you to say for yourself?'

For a moment there was no sound but whimpering, and when he raised his eyes at last they were brimming with tears. He took one terrified and sobbing breath, and then to my consternation he flung himself full-length at my feet. 'Have mercy, citizen,' he begged, clutching at my toga hem. 'You don't know what they are like! They would have beaten me to death if I had simply let you in!'

I began to murmur that the law did not permit it, but that only made him sob the more.

'Never mind the law! I've seen them do it before, with people who have crossed them. Terrible accidents happen around horses – something would have happened to me. They would have seen to that.' He gave a despairing wail as the full horror dawned on him. 'They'll probably do it anyway, if the governor doesn't have me executed first, for trying to deceive you! And you carrying his warrant, too! Oh, dear Mercury! What am I to do?'

I took him by the shoulder of his tunic and hoisted him upright. I had some sympathy, naturally – I have been a slave myself and I know what it is to be frightened – but if what he said was true, I was dealing with peculiarly ruthless and dangerous men. This was not a moment to show weakness.

I gave him a little shake – if he did not fear me just as much as he feared his masters I would get nothing out of him – and said brusquely, 'Tell me the truth, and you may just save your miserable skin. Where is Fortunatus? I heard that he was injured in Verulamium.'

'He f-f-fell from his ch-chariot, citizen. That is . . . all I know.' The boy's voice was shaking, and I realised with horror that he was urinating with fear.

'So, what has happened to him now? Is he dead? What have they done with him?'

He raised his head and looked at me, and for the first time I read surprise in his expression – and what looked strangely like relief.

'They haven't done anything with him, citizen. He's only . . .' He trailed off again.

I seized the tunic roughly and shook him again. 'Only what?' I bellowed. 'Tell me, or I'll have you dragged in the arena for the dogs to eat.' I sounded in my own ears like a villain in a fable. Of course I had no authority to do anything of the kind, even if I'd wanted to, but the slave-boy did not know that. You could almost see him imagining the horror of that death.

He looked at me helplessly a moment and then said, 'He has gone to see a lady, citizen.'

'A lady?' I had not expected that. Suddenly a hundred new possibilities were racing through my head. 'You mean the lady Fulvia?'

The boy shook his head, and for the first time a sort of smile hovered round his lips. 'Not that sort of lady, citizen. This one is called Pulchrissima and she is a sort of acrobatic dancer in a tavern just outside the town. She is a friend of Fortunatus'.'

He did not need to say more. I didn't know the local taverns, of course, but I knew enough about Roman bars in

161

general to know what kind of acrobatic dancing Pulchrissima was likely to engage in. Her very name, 'most beautiful', would have been enough to tell me that, although of course if she was 'a friend of Fortunatus'' it was possible that he enjoyed sole rights over her performances. For a substantial fee, of course. That would hardly be a problem for a man of Fortunatus' wealth.

I found that I was still gently shaking the slave-boy. 'Where is this tavern then?' I said, letting go of him, but speaking more severely than ever.

He swallowed hard. 'It is just outside the east wall, citizen – by the gate.'

'You're sure that he is there? I don't want another wasted journey.'

The boy looked wretched now. 'I am almost certain of it, citizen.'

I remembered something Fulvia had said. 'Hasn't he bought himself a town house recently? Surely he would go there? It would be much more private than the inn. Fortunatus is well-known in the town.'

'You are quite right, citizen. Fortunatus does not like going into the inn – too many carters and carriers use it, he says. But he is having the house rebuilt, and joined to the city water supply. The alterations are not half finished yet, so I am sure he will have gone to the tavern.'

'Very well,' I said, and turned to leave, but he came running after me.

'Don't go away and leave me here, citizen. They'll kill me if they know I've talked to you.'

'I'll have to leave you here,' I said, sounding more brutal than I meant. 'I can't take you with me – you'd only be captured and brought back to them anyway, and then they *would* have grounds for putting you to death. Better to stay here – let them think that I was satisfied by seeing that lump of hay.' I stopped, struck by a sudden thought. 'Why did you do that anyway? Easy enough, surely, just to claim that Fortunatus was out?'

'Fortunatus instructed me to do it, in case the lady Ful— in case somebody sent for him.'

'The lady Fulvia?' I said. That was interesting. 'She sometimes sent a message to him here?'

The boy looked overcome by confusion. He hesitated. 'You didn't come from her, did you, citizen? You obviously know her, since you mentioned her name.'

I shook my head. 'She has no idea I've come,' I said reassuringly. "I wanted to speak to Fortunatus on my own account. But it seems I shall have to look for him in the tavern. I am glad to know that he was not badly hurt by his shipwreck in the stadium.'

My words were intended to allay his fears a little, but they seemed to have the opposite effect. He let out a kind of despairing groan, and then, with no thought for custom or civility, he rushed past me and down the stairs, and had disappeared from sight before I had fairly recovered from the surprise.

Chapter Seventeen

I followed the slave-boy down the stairs, but by the time I got out into the yard he'd disappeared. I asked the gatekeeper where he had gone, but the man had clearly decided that his best protection was to have become suddenly blind and deaf. He offered a dozen alternative solutions, all equally implausible, but I could get no sensible information out of him, although I was sure that he could have told me where the boy had really gone, if he wished.

This was disconcerting, but, I reminded myself, the internal affairs of the *factio* were not my immediate concern. My task was to confront Fortunatus, not to chase after errant slaves. I nodded a curt farewell to the guard and went out of the gate with the intention of going straight to the tavern I had been told about. I would send Junio, who was doubtless waiting in the street, back with a further message to my bargemaster to explain where I had gone. Knowing Junio, in fact, I was rather surprised that he hadn't managed to talk his way into the *factio* headquarters, as I had done: but perhaps the guard had tried to reassert a little of his authority by deliberately keeping my servant outside the gate.

'Junio,' I began, but there was no sign of him.

I looked in all directions, but the alleyway was empty.

For the first time I felt a stirring of alarm. I had told Junio to come here, and it was not like him to delay in carrying out my orders. I hurried back to the guard, but if he had been unhelpful earlier he was doubly so now. To listen to his account, one would suppose that he had never seen a strange slave in the alleyway in his entire life. His manner had changed too. He delivered his information in a toneless voice, and with a marked reluctance to meet my eyes. In fact, he gave me the impression of being increasingly worried about something and I soon realised that no amount of questioning, governor's warrant or no governor's warrant, was going to make him change his story.

I was seriously anxious now. Had something happened to Junio? There was something mysterious about this *factio*, and I was disturbed by the way my attendants kept disappearing. First Superbus, and now this. There was only one thing to be done. I abandoned all thought of finding Fortunatus and set off towards the warehouse and the barge as fast as my aged legs would carry me.

I was halfway down the alley when I heard a hissing whisper. 'Citizen?'

I looked around, but for a moment could see nothing, only the blank walls and the empty alley. Even the gatekeeper from the *factio* had gone back to his guardroom under the arch, and was nowhere to be seen. I felt a little prickle at the nape of my neck. At the far end of the narrow street, where it met the major thoroughfare, the life of the town went on. Pedestrians with bundles, men on donkeys, traders with handcarts jostled by, but few of them spared a glance for the little alley, and certainly none of them had spoken. In any case that voice had surely been behind me?

'Over here, citizen!' I realised uneasily that the sound was coming from a tiny alleyway, scarcely wider than a man, that ran down beside the carpet-maker's shop – one of those narrow passages that are used in most big cities for the disposal of waste: stinking refuse which is piled there until the rains and rats take it away, or the farmers come with night carts and carry it off – for a small fee – to fertilise the fields. The entrance to this one was so heaped up with rubbish – an accumulation of building rubble as well as damp scraps of wool, food, and human excrement – that I had scarcely noticed it was there.

'Citizen!' I saw him at last, lurking behind a pile of broken stones, and let out an audible sigh of relief. It was not Glaucus, or an enraged Eppaticus, merely an aged slave, dressed in the distinctive blue of Fortunatus' *factio*, who was gesturing urgently to me as though speed and secrecy were a matter of life and death.

I moved over to him, frowning. 'What . . .?'

He was old and frail, much older than I was by the look of him, and a few white wisps of hair hung round his ashen face. He was so thin and pale that he might have been a fugitive, apart from the smartness of his tunic. There was something almost pathetic about him. Perhaps that is why I felt suddenly more confident, and went towards him, instinctively lowering my voice to match his own.

'What do you want?'

'You are looking for someone, citizen?'

I nodded. It was not a difficult deduction, perhaps, but I did not think to question it. 'Have you seen Junio? My servant?' I said anxiously.

He reached out then and seized my arm. 'This way, citizen. At once. There is no time to be lost.' He let go of my wrist, and turned away down the narrow passage, threading his way through the filthy rubbish heaps. I hesitated a moment, but he stopped and beckoned me again, more pressingly than ever.

I clambered over the slag pile at the entrance to the lane and followed him. I could hear my heart thumping with anxiety. What had they done to Junio? Where had they taken him? And who were 'they'?

The old man turned a corner and stopped beside a narrow

door. It was neglected and unpainted but stout enough, and the building it led to seemed in reasonable repair. He slid back the bolt, taking care to make no noise, eased the door quietly open and stood aside. His voice was no more than a conspiratorial murmur. 'In there, citizen, quickly. Before it is too late.'

He sounded urgent and almost without thinking I plunged past him into the passageway. A flight of stone steps opened at my feet, and in the semi-darkness I almost tumbled down them, but I recovered myself in time.

My guide, still standing at the doorway, waved me on. 'Do not make a noise, citizen!' he hissed. 'Down there! Make haste! Be quiet – and be quick.'

I was beginning to share his agitation, and I obeyed as quickly as I could. The only light was from the open door, and the steps were steep, but I groped my way downwards into the dark below. The wall beside me was cold and damp – there seemed to be rotting vegetation under my fingertips – but the thought of what they might be doing to Junio spurred me on. I looked up. The old slave was still at the door, watching my progress anxiously. 'Tell me when you are safely down.'

I almost stumbled a dozen times, but I reached the bottom at last. I felt cautiously forward with my foot – then, with increasing confidence, my hands. I seemed to be in some sort of unlit passageway, the floor uneven and littered with stones as if the building was abandoned. Not that I expected furniture.

'I'm here!' I called up softly to my erstwhile guide.

For a moment I thought he had not heard me. Then with a faint click the outer door closed to, and I found myself in blackness so total that I could not make out my hand before my eyes. The old slave had set himself a problem, if he hoped to come down those steps in the dark, I thought. I waited, expecting to see a flintstone strike and the sudden glow of tinder in the dark. Nothing happened.

I waited. I could hear my own breath now, and smell the dank smell of vegetation and decay. Still there was no sound from above me. The thumping of my heart seemed fit to burst my ribs. Then, faintly but distinctly, I heard a noise – the unmistakable scrape and clunk of the bolt being pushed across.

Even then I could hardly bring myself to believe what I had done. I had walked – without coercion, of my own accord – headfirst into a trap. Of course, when I came to consider it, I should have known better. Following an unknown slave down an unused alley in an unfamiliar city – the merest child would have known better. The man had not offered me a single piece of information or identification – he had simply preyed upon my fears and I had followed him. It was as simple as that.

And now I was a prisoner. In what seemed to be a disused building, too. The outer door was bolted behind me, and even if I could grope my way up the steps again there was no way of getting out. It was shaming as well as frightening. I felt my way back to the bottom step and sat down heavily.

I tried to think. Rather too late, as I was well aware, but better now than never. Even so, I could come to no conclusion. I had been deliberately led away and locked into a cellar by a man I had never seen before. It seemed to make no sense at all. Perhaps I had merely fallen prey to one of the gangs of thieves who doubtless operate in London, as they do in every big town. Considering how easy it had been, I was lucky not to have been set upon and robbed earlier.

Except, of course, that there had been no attempt to rob me. Kidnap me then, and demand money for my return? Perhaps these were slave-traders, and I was to be sold back into servitude. I hoped that I had been merely seized for ransom. In that case someone would come and talk to me, if only to find out where to send demands. Anything was better than being left here to rot, or die of thirst and hunger. Already the morning was drawing on, and – because I was alarmed and there was no possibility of obtaining water – my mouth was already desperately dry.

I hardly dared to contemplate the obvious – that my investigations had brought me too close to the murderer for comfort, and someone – in the Blue *factio* presumably – had wanted me locked up and out of action, perhaps for good. If that was the case, there was no certainty that anyone would ever come. For who would think of looking for me here?

Perhaps it was that which spurred me into action. At least I could explore the place I was in. It would not be easy. I had expected my eyes to become accustomed to the gloom, but there was little sign of that. There was not a chink of light from anywhere, and the blackness seemed more impenetrable than ever. I got up and tried a few tentative steps with my arms outstretched, but the floor was so uneven that I almost fell. My hands, however, had touched nothing but a void – the basement, whatever it was, seemed bigger than I'd thought. I wished I had made some attempt to measure distances – as a pavement-maker I should have thought of that.

I got down on all fours. The loose stones on the floor dug into my knees, but I was more confident like this and by sweeping the ground with one hand I was able to clear the worst of the obstructions. I was anxious about finding my way back to the steps – ridiculous if I was to be left here to die, but at least it gave me a point of reference – so I found the wall and edged my way forward, feeling my way by that.

A very few shuffles brought me to a corner, and finally to another. This was not a corridor at all, then, but a room – built as some kind of storage space perhaps. That must be it.

I was in a *cella* – a sort of underground storage room sometimes found in larger houses built on rising ground. I began to feel around for any sign that something might once have been kept here, and almost at once my guess was confirmed. One of my hands discovered a large circular space set in the floor a little further from the wall – the remains of one of those huge sunken *amphorae* which one sometimes finds in larger houses or in villa courtyards for storing oil or, occasionally, wine.

I pushed up my toga sleeve (the gods alone knew what state my proud new garment was in by now) and reached my arm down to its full extent, but whatever had been stored in there had long since disappeared. A sniff of my fingers suggested that it had once been wine – turned to vapour for the gods, perhaps, since the container had been left without a lid. Certainly, it was not about to slake my thirst.

Further groping told me that there was another buried amphora a little further off, and then a third – all equally empty. The discovery had lent me hope, however. This place had once been used by a living household. Although it clearly was deserted now, it was unlikely the only exit was the door I had come in by. A household needs to reach its storage space. I felt my way back to the wall and began my blind exploration again, with renewed energy.

The second wall was so much longer than the first that I was beginning to imagine that I had lost my bearings altogether in the dark. I could hear my own breath, unnaturally loud, rasping like a harried horse. Panic was beginning to overcome me. I fought it down, forcing myself to think rationally – telling my tortured brain that, at the very worst, the wall I was following would eventually bring me to the steps I'd started from.

Why that should have seemed like an improvement, I do not know – I can only report that in that black, dank, foul-smelling pit of obscurity any certainty was better than none. I groped my way onwards with increasing desperation, until my questing fingers found an alteration in the wall. Wood instead of stone? It might be so. A frame. A hollow. A door, then? I dragged myself upright and ran my hands all over the area, almost crying with relief.

It was a door – I could feel the planks of wood. My hands could find no fastening – presumably it was bolted from within – but I located what felt like the edge of a plank and pushed with all my might. The thick wood did not yield an inch. I tried again, thumping against it with all my strength, using my arm, my foot, my whole body. I even took a few steps back and made a run at it. This time I thought it did shudder a fraction at the top, but it was my frame rather than the door's which was taking the brunt of the damage. Perhaps I could lever one of the planks away? I still had my eating knife in my belt.

With a strength born of desperation I reached upwards, feeling for the corner of the outside plank. Ugh – my fingers sank into a nest of something soft which yielded under my touch and sent little scuttling somethings up my arm and into my tunic, so that my skin and hairs crawled with them. In the oppressive dark that was the final horror, and I found myself sobbing aloud and slapping at myself in a frenzy. Only spiders, I tried to tell myself; but my voice and body seemed briefly to have taken on a life of their own, and I could hear myself moaning as I flapped and stamped, rather as I have heard criminals do on their way to face the beasts. I tried to control myself, but I seemed to have lost the power – as if I were witnessing someone else's panic and the frenzied noises I emitted were not of my own making.

It was not my most heroic moment.

But the worst was yet to come. My frenzied stamping had taken me away from the friendly comfort of the wall, and when I had at last managed to regain command of myself – my fingers damp and gritty with what felt like a thousand tiny arachnid corpses – I found that I had completely lost my sense of direction. I reached out my hands again, tentatively this time, but they met nothing but blackness. Mercifully the floor seemed rather clearer here.

I took a step forward, and stumbled over something at my feet. Something large and heavy: soft but stiff, and very, very cold. It appeared to be lying in a pool of moisture. I bent down to investigate. Something, when I explored it further, that seemed to be man-shaped. Something that was not breathing. Something . . . dead.

I was fumbling desperately by this stage. 'Junio?'

I traced the feet. Sandals – just like the ones my slave had worn. The body was lying on its front and there seemed to be loose rope around the ankles. My hands moved up. A servant's tunic and a leather belt. Wrists, cruelly bound together with a length of rope. I could hardly bear to go on, but I had to know. My fingers reached the neck, and found the chain and name disc that every slave must wear. Short, wet, matted curly hair. Sickened, I turned the body over and reached out for the face – dreading that my hands would trace the boyish features I knew so well.

What I found was a soft and shattered mess. I leapt back as though stung by a million spiders. I could almost see the hideous mosaic of splintered flesh and bone. This time I did not shout or sob. I opened my mouth, but I could make no sound at all.

Some emotions are too terrible, even for grief.

173

Chapter Eighteen

I do not know how long I remained there in the dark beside the body. It might have been an hour or two, perhaps less, but to me, shivering with shock, despair and grief, it seemed a lifetime. My desolation at least spared me one misery. After the discovery of the corpse all sense of thirst and hunger left me. I simply squatted there beside the lifeless form, as incapable of action as if I had been drugged by one of Lydia's potions.

I was roused at last by a noise from the street above. Faint at first – so faint that I half thought I had imagined it. Then it came again, more loudly now, and this time there could be no mistake. I got to my feet, listening intently. Footsteps and muted voices in that unfrequented alley. I was debating whether whistling or shouting was more likely to penetrate the outer walls and so attract attention to my plight when suddenly the noises stopped again and another sound, even more unexpected, reached my ears.

Someone was sliding the bolt.

For a moment a wild irrational hope possessed me and I was ready to shout 'Here!' and throw myself on my deliverers, but then whatever intelligence I possessed reasserted itself. Of course, this was not likely to be rescue. Quite the contrary – anyone who had come to this place on purpose was much more likely to be my executioner.

The door upstairs flew open, and although when I had first come in the light from the aperture had hardly seemed enough to grope my way down the steps by, after the long period of captivity in total darkness the sudden daylight almost dazzled me. I closed my eyes for a moment against the light, and when I opened them once more I realised that the outer door had been pushed to again, and someone was standing at the top of the stairs lighting a taper from the embers in one of those portable braziers.

My brain seemed to stir into life again, with my eyes, and I realised that for a moment I had the advantage. The incomers – and there were clearly several of them – would find themselves in darkness, even with the taper, whereas I had unaccustomed light. I could already see the dark outline of the steps – to my surprise I was only a few feet from them – the black circles in the floor which marked the tops of the sunken pots and the sinister dark outline of the corpse. The room was smaller than I imagined: it had seemed endless in the groping dark. I could see the wooden door set in the further corner, and behind the steps there seemed to be some kind of darker space, a sort of alcove probably used for storage once. All this I took in at a single glance, and I looked around for something sensible to do.

There was no method of escape, that much was obvious, but I reasoned that if I could reach the alcove I would have, at least, the advantage of surprise. What use that was to me, I was not sure. Perhaps it is merely an instinct with captives. I had no hope of overpowering them; I am no longer a young man and I was only one against several. I think I had some dim idea of slipping past the men as they came down the steps, though realistically there was never the slightest hope of that.

The taper was well alight by now, and I could distinguish the outline of at least four men in the sudden light of its flames, and then the gentler glow of embers dimmed, as someone put the lid on to the pot of coals. Another taper was lit, and then another – three in all. To me it seemed as if the sun had risen. I had to remind myself again that, to the men accustomed to daylight, those brilliant flames offered only a minimum of illumination.

Someone lifted his torch aloft and held it over the stairwell, illuminating the uneven stone of the steps. That served my purpose, however, since it meant that the darkness beyond would seem denser than ever. Now that I knew where I was going, I scuttled as silently as I could in the direction of the alcove. It was a kind of doorless cupboard – one or two high shelves still remained in it – but there was just room for me to huddle there and listen to the approaching slap of leather sandals on the steps beside me. I heard the clunk as the brazier was set down against the wall.

'Where is he?' a dry, sharp voice enquired. 'You told me he was here. If you've let him escape I'll have you flayed.' They were all four down the stairs by now, and the speaker moved into the ring of light. I was appalled – though not surprised – to see the face and recognise the man. It was Glaucus, the Grey, his crooked nose and pitiless mouth looking crueller than ever in the flickering shadows.

He looked towards the dark heap on the floor, and his expression hardened. 'Great Mithras! You haven't killed him, have you? You useless son of a sow, I told you that I wanted him questioned first.' One casual but savage backhand blow, and one of the other figures was grovelling on his knees, dropping his taper as he fell. By its light I could make out his face – it was the old slave who had lured me here.

I should perhaps have revelled in his fall, but Glaucus had signalled for the fallen taper, seized the man by the hair, and was now holding the flame viciously close to the man's neck. 'Well, what have you to say for yourself?'

'Most merciful one,' the slave was stammering with fear and pain, 'that is not the man. That's just the slave we captured earlier. I told you about him, Mightiness – he was asking too many questions.'

So that poor battered shape was 'just' a slave, and therefore of no importance. It made me more furious than ever – although the gibbering speaker was 'just' a slave himself.

Glaucus sent him sprawling to the floor. 'Fool! You bring him here, and then you let him die.'

The old man grovelled. 'It was an accident, Mightiness.'

Glaucus aimed a kick at him. 'So you say. So where is this other fellow now? That infernal spy of the government? I suppose he *is* here somewhere? The door into the rest of the building is still blocked? If he has got away I'll have you fed to the dogs.' He seized the taper and began to peer around the room.

The fate of my poor slave made me despair, but the instinct for self-preservation is strong. It was only a matter of time before they reached me, and I had no doubt of their intentions. I could see their shadows, larger than life-size, flickering on the wall, and hear the scuffling of their sandals on the stones.

Stones! What an idiot I was. I bent down and scooped up one or two. They were not large, but they afforded me some sort of weapon, and I still had the knife at my belt. Too late. The movement of picking up the pebbles had drawn the attention of Glaucus to my corner. He strode towards me, the taper in his hand. By its light I could see an unpleasant smile playing on his lips.

'Well,' he said, coming to a halt in front of me. 'What have we here? A little rat hiding in a hole.' He gestured brusquely to the two men at his side. 'Fetch him out of there.'

They were big men, both of them. I remembered, irrationally, that Fulvia had talked of her attacker's being large.

They seized me by the upper arms and it was pointless to resist. I did, though, clench my hands around the stones which I still carried. If I waited long enough perhaps I could find a chance to use them. I had no hope of escaping now, I could see that well enough, but I was always a fair shot with a slingstone and if I was to be killed in any case there was nothing to be lost. If I could get a clear aim, at least I might find an opportunity to take one of the men with me when I died – Glaucus for preference. Revenge for the death of 'just a slave'.

My two captors dragged me out to stand in front of Glaucus. They hauled me upright, keeping my arms behind me, so that I was forced to bend forward in a painful stoop. I stole a sideways look. Both men were armed with large swords at their sides, but, since each guard was holding me with one hand and carrying a taper with the other, the weapons would not be easy to draw. I stood rigid but unprotesting, like a subjugated slave, and dropped my gaze submissively. My best chance would come if my captors were unprepared for any kind of resistance.

Glaucus was gratified to find me cowering. I could detect it in the way in which he said, 'So, citizen' – the word was mocking now – 'we meet at last. You have been following me, I think.'

'I have been looking for Fortunatus,' I said, still looking at the floor. My voice was quavering, and not through any acting skills on my part. 'I need to talk to him about a crime.' I felt my listeners stiffen. 'On the provincial governor's orders. I am carrying his warrant. I have it here, at my belt.' It was a faint hope, but the governor was the representative of Rome, and defiance of his warrant was tantamount to defying the Emperor.

Even Glaucus, it seemed, was not immune to the implication. He seemed to hesitate a little, although he did not signal to the guards to let me go. He placed a hand under my chin, lifted my head so I was forced to look at him, and moved his face to within an inch or two of mine. It was menacing.

'A palace slave came here yesterday, spying around this house. We know he was from the palace by his uniform, and we know you sent him. He mentioned you by name. And the day before he was asking questions in the marketplace about our grain supply. Be good enough to explain this, citizen. Why did you send him here?' The thin smile was colder than a winter pond.

The arrival of the tapers seemed to have cleared my brain. It suddenly occurred to me whose house this must be. Surely it was Fortunatus' – the one that Fulvia and the team-slave had talked about. He was having it rebuilt, they'd said – that would explain the piles of rubble outside. And, of course, why the place was empty and disused. And it made sense of what Glaucus had implied – that Superbus had been here yesterday. If my guess about the house was right, I thought I knew what he'd been doing here.

'I didn't send him here,' I said, with as much dignity as a man can summon when he's being held painfully captive in a cellar. 'In fact, I particularly told him to stay in the palace and wait, but he received a message from somewhere in my absence, and he went out in answer to that. If he came here to Fortunatus' house, I believe I can tell you where that message came from. It came from Fulvia – Fortunatus' lover.'

Glaucus sneered, but he drew back a little. 'Nonsense. The charioteer's woman is called Pulchrissima. He is with her now. She has, shall we say, peculiar skills, and since Fortunatus has found her he talks of nothing else. He plans to marry her when he retires.' I noticed that he did not deny that Fortunatus owned the house.

'All the same,' I said, 'I believe that slave was carrying a message from Fulvia. The woman whose husband was murdered.'

Glaucus sounded mystified. 'You are telling me that you came here simply to investigate a murder? That is why the governor sent you here?' He lifted up my face again, and stared at me. Then he spat contemptuously at my feet. 'I don't believe a word of it.'

'This was no ordinary man. The chief corn official of the city was found strangled in his bed two days ago. The news must be all round Londinium by now. A man called Caius Monnius.'

I felt, rather than saw, the four men round me stiffen.

One of the guards said, 'Mightiness . . .?' but Glaucus silenced him.

'Go on!'

'At first I thought that Fortunatus might have done it. The man's wife was his lover, as I say. That gave him a motive. If he was in Londinium at the time, he might have had the opportunity, though increasingly I think it is unlikely. That is what I wanted to talk to him about.'

Glaucus stared at me. 'Fortunatus and Caius Monnius' wife? You think that I would not have known of that? These are more of your lies, citizen!' For a moment I thought he was going to strike me.

The old slave piped up. 'Most noble Glaucus – there may be truth in it. I've heard Fortunatus laughing with the other drivers about some rich woman who was courting him. She couldn't get enough of him, he said. In fact she was becoming indiscreet and he was sure her husband was beginning to suspect. And yesterday when that palace minion came poking round here he did say he had a personal message for Fortunatus. Perhaps the citizen is telling us the truth.'

Glaucus turned away from me and looked at him a moment. 'You told me that a slave from the governor's palace had come here to spy. Did he ask anything about the gambling or the race?'

The old man shook his head.

'So he might have been bringing a love message for Fortunatus? From Caius Monnius' wife?'

The old man nodded excitedly. 'Exactly so, most mighty one. He asked if Fortunatus had been badly hurt – he said there had been rumours of an accident and wanted urgent news. Demanded to know where Fortunatus was, in fact, which was extremely worrying. But if she was his lover, and had heard the gossip, perhaps she really wanted to know about Fortunatus' health and where he was for her own purposes.'

I hurried to offer my support for this. My only hope lay in convincing Glaucus that he was making a terrible mistake. I tried to struggle free but the guards still held me tight, so I made my contribution bent forward like a frog. 'That could certainly be true,' I said. 'Fulvia is a wealthy widow now, and no doubt she has hopes of Fortunatus. She doesn't know about Pulchrissima. Once she'd heard rumours of the accident, of course she would enquire about his health.'

Glaucus ignored me. He seemed unnaturally patient now. He turned to the slave. 'But you didn't ask the messenger who'd sent him? You simply took him prisoner?'

'According to your orders, noble one. Better to be safe than to regret, you said, and promised us a bounty if we found a spy. Besides, I didn't have a chance to ask him anything, though I intended to. I brought him here and had the team guards tie him up, but as soon as I turned my back he tripped over his bonds in the darkness and fell down the steps.'

Oh, great gods of stone and stream! The corpse! It all made sense. I almost cried aloud. It was not Junio lying there, it was Superbus. Why had I not seen the likelihood of that? I regretted it instantly – it was unkind to poor Superbus – but I could have wept with the joy and the relief of it.

'And you have a warrant, citizen?' Glaucus was looking at me thoughtfully. For the first time since they had seized me, I felt a glimmer of hope. Junio was alive, and Glaucus seemed subdued. The news of Monnius' murder had clearly startled him. Perhaps I would after all escape from here alive.

I wondered what my captors would do, in that case. They had defied the governor's warrant, and killed one of his slaves. They would hardly wait around to be arrested. Perhaps they would leave the *factio* and melt away into Londinium, where one would never find them – since, of course, if one cannot produce the accused in person, there is no case in Roman law. At the very least, I thought, they would rob me before they went.

Glaucus seemed to read my thoughts. He nodded to the slave. 'Very well. Take that knife from his belt. We cannot leave him armed.'

The old man bobbed forward and did as he was told. Glaucus took it from him and examined it. 'A fine blade, citizen. I shall see it is not wasted, never fear.' He gestured to the slave. 'And you, come here. You took that palace slave prisoner. This knife shall be part of your reward.' He handed his taper to one of the guards – who necessarily let go of me to take it – and put one long hand on the purse pouch at his waist.

The old man quavered into a smile and stepped forward hopefully. But his reward was not to be in coin. Glaucus reached out and seized the fellow's hair, forcing back his head. Then with his other hand he plunged my knife savagely into the scrawny neck, almost before the fawning smile had died. The old slave fell with a gurgle. Glaucus withdrew the knife and wiped it carelessly on the tunic of the dying man. 'Useless swine!'

He put the knife into his belt and turned to me. 'Your warrant, citizen.' He leaned forward and removed it from the

183

pouch where it hung and, taking a taper from the guard, examined it a moment. He gave me that mirthless smile of his, then, very carefully, held my precious document in the flame until the seal melted and the bark-paper smouldered and curled. Then he shook out the flames, seized me by the scruff of the neck and stuffed the charred remains inside my tunic. I felt the bite of heat against my skin. 'So much for your warrant, citizen. Tomorrow, when I throw your body in the river, you may show it to the fishes. Perhaps they'll be impressed by it. I'm not.'

The sudden blow which caught me on the cheek was so violent and so unexpected that I almost buckled at the knees. If it were not for the two henchmen holding me so firmly by the arms, I think I would have found myself grovelling on the stone floor as the slave had done.

Glaucus smiled. 'Now, little songbird,' he said softly, 'we shall see how you can sing.' Almost before I realised his intention, he had drawn the knife again. The two guards held me pinioned while he slashed the toga from my shoulder, then deliberately raised the taper and held the naked flame against my skin.

I cried out and tried to struggle free.

'Bind him!' Glaucus barked. 'Use that dead fool's belt.'

He held the light while the two guards dealt with me. One held me while the other undid the rope tie from the dead slave's waist and bound my elbows firmly to my sides. I tried to take a deep breath and brace against the rope – an old trick, known to slave-boys everywhere, to make the bonds less tight – but there was little I could do. I fingered the stones I held, but the guards seized me and forced me back into that excruciating position. I was doubly helpless now.

Glaucus applied the flame again. Despite myself I gave a yelp of pain. 'You sing already, cagebird? That is just a touch of what is to come. You will answer my questions, citizen spy, or you will feel the scorch of my taper on every inch of your body. And I have your knife. There are things that can be done with a blade that make a man beg for the mercy of death.' He smiled. 'So you will tell me, citizen, how much you know. What have you been blabbing to the governor? Tell me the truth and I'll be merciful. A quick clean end.'

'Like poor Superbus there?' I heard myself say, and wondered at my own foolhardiness.

Glaucus glanced without interest at the lifeless form. 'That palace informer? That was not my doing, citizen. This fool here' – he flicked at the old slave's body with his foot – 'let him fall down the steps and kill himself, before I had time to question him. If I had dealt with him, believe me, he would have died more artistically – and he would have told me everything he knew.' He lifted the taper again. 'As you will tell me, also, in the end. So make it easy for yourself. Spare yourself suffering and tell me now. How much have you learnt?'

I tried to sound casual and self-controlled. 'About Fortunatus? Nothing much at all. I knew he was the lady Fulvia's friend. I went to Verulamium to speak to him, but he wasn't there, so I came back to look for him. That's all.'

The flame touched my skin again, for longer this time. I could smell, as well as feel, the burning flesh.

'You lie.' Glaucus' tone was patient, reasonable – like a merchant disappointed in a bargain. The effect was much more chilling than anger. 'You were at the stadium asking questions about the race. So I ask you again, citizen. How much do you know?'

'About the accident?' I said foolishly. 'Only that Fortunatus fell at the first corner, and had to be sent home by the *medicus*.'

This time the pain was sharper still. I felt the hairs singe on my chest.

If I did know anything, I thought, I would cheerfully tell him. I was not sure how long I could go on enduring this. It was clear that Glaucus was involved in something – something so dangerous that men would kill for it – but I still had no real idea of what it was. His taper was burning low by now, and he reached out a languid hand to take a replacement from one of the guards, who lit another from the brazier. That left a single guard restraining me. If there was to be a moment for me to make a move, this had to be it.

I expelled my breath and relaxed my arms at last, to create as much slack as possible in my bonds. It was not much, and the second guard still had a firm hold on one arm, but there was just enough room to wriggle the other one a bit so that I could move it from the elbow. It was my left hand, which was not ideal. I was in pain and my movement was terribly constricted, but it was all the opportunity I had. Glaucus already had the fresh taper in his hand, and the guard was turning back to pinion me.

It was now or never.

I flicked the stone out of my hand, hoping to hit the guard. But with my upper arms bound to my sides my aim was poor. I missed. The stone flew harmlessly past him and fell against the wall with a clatter.

All the same everyone jumped and looked in that direction. The remaining guard let go of my arm, and I made a bolt towards the steps, still bound at the elbows, flicking my other missile as I went.

It was hopeless, of course. The guards were after me at once, and I was pushed roughly to the ground. I lay sprawled wretchedly against the steps while Glaucus came up with his guttering taper in his hand, and looked down at me with a kind of mocking sigh.

'You are a fool, citizen. You might have spared yourself

186

this. But since you have not yet learned who is the master here, you force me to teach you.'

One long, strong hand drew out the blade and he bent down towards me. 'First the steel, then the flame,' he said. 'Until you tell me what I want to know. Now, about this murdered man. How much have you learned?'

I went through my account again. Glaucus was unimpressed. I felt the prick of the blade against my neck.

'Why were you at the *factio* today?'

I said, desperately, 'Looking for Fortunatus. He was not there – he was pretending to be ill, but he was with this dancing girl of his.'

The taper licked my flesh. 'And why the interest in our grain supply? Trying to discover how many horses we are running?'

'I don't know anything about your grain.'

The knife again. 'Then why were you at the granary this morning?'

It went on and on. The same questions, over and over. But there was nothing I could add. Through misting eyes I could still see that cold smile on Glaucus' face as patiently, with horrible precision, he traced his patterns of torment on my flesh.

Chapter Nineteen

Time passed.

I was moaning now. I could hear myself. I had fought it down for as long as I could, knowing that it would just give Glaucus pleasure, but by this time I could bear the pain no longer. Already my head and sight were swimming. Passing out would have been a kind of mercy, but Glaucus seemed to know how to keep a man just this side of unconsciousness.

Before I quite blacked out he let me come round, but every time I drifted back to my senses the torture began again: another little jab of agony on flesh already screaming with cuts and fire. I was beyond speech now – I tried to form words but only gurgling sounds escaped my lips.

Then suddenly it stopped. For a moment I was too foolish and battered even to take that in, but it was true. My damaged skin still throbbed like fire, but there were no new torments. I tried to force open my unwilling eyes, but everything seemed uniformly grey. I could hear Glaucus cursing and stamping.

'Great Mithras curse him! He is passing out on me – that is no use. And he has made me burn myself. Give me another taper, now – at once!' So that was it. His wax-light had burned down and he had thrown it on the floor to extinguish it when it had scorched his fingers. From a dim red haze of pain I hoped that it had hurt.

When I swam to consciousness again, I heard Glaucus' voice. 'Well, it is a waste of time going on – he'll tell us nothing in this state. I'll have to wait till he recovers a little, and then we'll see what whips and hooks can do. I will be back, so don't you start on him. I don't want him dying before he begins to talk. Mars knows what he has already told the governor. I never trust these governmental spies.'

Whips and hooks! Agony already flowed through me like a hot red tide, but fear forced me to listen.

'Will you be gone long, Mightiness?'

'Not long. I'm going to find Fortunatus and bring him in. I want to talk to him, too. Bedding Monnius' wife, of all people! Monnius – one of our biggest sponsors! I'll have the fellow taken under guard and locked up until the race. Pluto and all the Furies take the man! He's endangered the whole system with his womanising. If I could find another driver of his quality I'd strangle him with my own hands and use someone else.'

'You want him got rid of, Mightiness? It would be a pleasure.'

I heard Glaucus give a dry bark of laughter. 'Not now. There's still Camulodunum to come. That should be a very profitable day. Who is going to back an unknown driver, and against Citus too? Too bad the poor creature will be lame. Never fear. Fortunatus will do as I tell him. He wants his share of the money – and there should be plenty. Thousands for us all. In the meantime, you look after this interfering wretch. Don't touch him unless he tries to escape. However, if I haven't come by sundown, then he's yours. Do what you like with him. You can dump all three bodies in the river after dark – put them in a sack and make sure you weight them well. I'll see that extra rations are waiting for you at the barracks.'

He was gone. Whether it was pain or fear or hunger I don't know, but I was at the end of myself. A sort of shivering terror seized me, and I lay there semi-conscious, though whether for minutes or hours I could not tell. At last I was aware of one of the guards stirring me with his boot.

'Here, Rupius! Leave him alone. You heard what Glaucus said. He's coming back— What's that?'

A sudden blinding flash of light – was that the door? – and then there was a roaring in my ears. My heart seemed to contract with fright, and the world misted over. I dimly knew I was hallucinating – I had known the same thing in a fever. Strange shadows danced before my eyes and there were indistinct and distant noises, dull thumps and shouts. One long, thin scream, then silence. Utter blackness fell.

This must be death, I thought, and closed my eyes.

When the soul leaves the body, so the Romans say, it travels to the nether world, transported by the ferryman across the Styx. I had never been sure that I believed the tale – we Celts have our own explanation of demise – but I was dully comforted to find that it was true. I found myself rising up, without any conscious effort on my part, as if I was being borne upwards and outwards into a place of sweet air and glorious blinding light.

I expected the agony in my chest to cease, but that did not happen. Instead I appeared to be floating in a kind of welcoming green haze which swallowed me from time to time and eased the pain. I abandoned myself to it and allowed myself to be carried along. Literally carried, it occurred to me after a while. Not in a litter. Pairs of strong arms were bearing me along. Lots of arms, supporting my back, my head, my legs – all of them gentle and considerate, and carrying me as though I were a feather.

Blackness descended again, heavy and palpable, like a blanket shrouding my face and limbs. I concentrated on opening my eyes but everything was dark. Perhaps it was always so, in the other world. I seemed to feel the weight of darkness on my skin. I tried to raise a feeble hand to touch it, but it was useless. It seemed my elbows were still bound, and I could scarcely move my limbs in any case.

But the effort was enough. The blackness lifted of its own accord, the floating feeling stopped and I was aware of many forms around me and a strong, dark, bearded shape at my side, although the whole scene dissolved at once when I tried to focus on any part of it.

'Libertus? Citizen? Can you hear me?' Someone was calling me by name.

I moved my lips, but no sound came out. 'Who . . .?' I managed finally.

A deep and reassuring voice. 'It is the boatman.'

I nodded inwardly. The Styx. That seemed fitting.

'Lie still and do not worry, citizen. We'll soon have you aboard. My crew have got you now. Praise be to Jupiter you are still alive. A little longer and we might have been too late.'

Alive? I had begun to think that I was dead. I tried to make sense of it in my fuddled brain. It took me a little time to work it out, but of course! This was the boatman who had brought me here. Somehow I had been rescued. I struggled to raise myself a little, but a firm hand pushed me gently back.

'Only a short distance now, citizen, and we'll have you on the barge. The governor has a *medicus* at the palace, and once we get you there he'll have those wounds bathed and salved in no time. For now, the most important thing is rest.'

'What happened?' I tried to ask. It was no use. My voice was no more than a quaver. No one heard.

The crew – I could see now that it was the crew – had made a sort of cradle of their arms and were carrying me between them. At a signal from the bargemaster they set off again at a smooth trot. Down past the warehouse, through the gate and out on to the waiting vessel. Only there did they set me gently down, with one cloak folded up beneath my head, and another – which had served as the blanket covering my face – tucked over me to keep me warm.

I needed it. I found that I was shivering, all at once, and the pot of cold water which someone was holding to my lips was the sweetest drink I ever tasted.

'He's drinking!' It was Junio's voice. 'I thought those devils had killed him.' He lifted the container to my lips again.

I drank, and spluttered. Water trickled into me like life itself. 'And I thought they'd . . . killed you.' The words came with a struggle but I was making myself heard.

'Master! You are awake!' He was bathing my face now, holding a wet cloth to my temples. I felt the mist recede and the pain in my chest, which had been ebbing as the mist increased, stabbed me again.

I winced. But my mind was clearer now and I opened my eyes more fully. Junio saw it. At once he dropped to his knees beside me and began to kiss my hand urgently.

'Oh, master!' he said. 'Thank the gods! This is all my fault. I should never have left you unattended.'

I shook my head. I was the one who had gone off on my own, without waiting for Junio to return. And I had walked unaided into a trap. 'What . . .?'

He clasped my hand so fiercely that it hurt. 'I brought your message to the boat, dear master, but as I was delivering it, who should come creeping out of the warehouse but Eppaticus.'

I had closed my eyes to listen, but at the mention of that name they flew open again. 'Epp—?'

'I was sure that it was him from your description. There cannot be two Celts in the city of that gigantic size, although I could not see his pigtail; he had pulled the hood of his cloak over him. I got the impression that he had been hiding in the grain store, waiting for you to leave.'

That would not surprise me. I tried to nod.

193

'I knew that you would want him followed. I thought I stood least chance of being recognised – the bargemaster is bearded and conspicuous – so I asked *him* to find you and tell you where I was, while I set out after the Celt.' His voice was wretched with remorse. 'I was trying to be clever, master. I should never have done it. I should have come straight back to you.'

'I tried to find you, citizen,' the boatman said, swimming hazily back into my view. I had been dimly aware of him barking orders in the background, and now I could detect the splash of oars and the gentle movement of the barge.

The bargemaster crouched down beside me, his dark beard very close so that I was sure to hear. He spoke very slowly. 'I went back to where he said he'd left you, but there was no sign of you. I even found my way to the *factio*, in case you had gone there, but the fellow at the gate told me they hadn't seen you.'

Liars, I thought. No doubt Glaucus had put them up to that. 'Go on,' I murmured through thick lips.

'I didn't know what to do, citizen. I wandered around all the streets, and then I caught sight of that fellow you were chasing when you left. He was marching along with a thin slave and pair of big uniformed Blue guards wearing swords.'

He looked at me to make sure I had followed this account. I signalled encouragement as best I could. My brain seemed to be functioning again, but I was having trouble forming words.

It seemed the bargemaster had followed at a distance, reasoning that Glaucus might lead him to me. 'I kept them in sight, and in the end I saw him turn down into a most unlikely lane. Not the sort of place you would expect a man to go. Nothing but midden heaps and piles of builder's waste. When I got there he had disappeared, but there was only one place he could have gone, a storage entrance into a deserted house. I didn't like the look of that at all, but I was no match for four of them, especially since two of them were armed. I came back and got the boys. We had no swords but oarsmen are stout fellows. A broken oar, some grapples and some rope . . . we hurried back, and found you just in time.'

'Glaucus,' I managed to say, 'did he escape?'

'We didn't see him.' The bargeman shook his head. 'Only the two team guards. Like tigers, they were, when they came for us and there was a bit of a struggle. One of my fellows cracked one with the oar and laid him out at once. The other one put up a fight, but he was outnumbered ten to one: someone hit him with a grapple-hook, and he went down screaming like a pig. We had no idea what we would find. We almost fell over your body on the stairs. When we saw what those brutes had done to you, my boys were none too gentle, I can tell you. It will be some little time before those two wake up, if they ever do. We've left them in the cellar under guard. We'll go back and see if they're alive or dead when we've got you to a *medicus* – and we might as well pick up those slaves as well. We'll have to return them to their owners some time.'

Beside me I had heard Junio catch his breath. 'Slaves?'

'Two of them down there in the cellar,' said the boatman. 'Both dead.'

'Eppaticus has got slaves for sale,' Junio said. 'I saw them. I did find out where he was going – he has a big barn just outside the walls. A sort of warehouse. He seems to sell everything in there, from pots to pageboys – though there was no grain that I could see. Were these slaves some of his?'

'No chance of that,' the boatman said. 'We brought them up into the light to have a look at them. One of them was the Blue *factio* slave I'd seen before. Fallen out with his masters, by the look of it. The other, I'm very much afraid, belonged to Pertinax. He was wearing palace uniform. The governor won't be very pleased by that.'

'A palace uniform?' Junio looked at me. 'Superbus?'

I tried to explain that I hadn't actually seen him, but that I was sure it was. What came croaking from my lips was something else. 'I thought it was you, at first.' I was shaking again. 'Lying there.'

Junio squeezed my hand. 'You did?'

'All stiff and dead. I almost fell over it. The body. In the dark.'

There was a little pause. Then Junio said, 'If it was stiff, master, you weren't thinking straight. You have seen dead bodies many times. If it was already stiff, it could not have been me. I was talking to you only a short time before.'

He was right. I should have worked that out. It would have saved me a lot of anguish, though it made me feel no better now to realise that.

Junio was grinning at me cheerfully, pleased with his deduction.

'Impudent wretch!' I muttered, but he only grinned the more. All at once I felt a little more human. 'More water,' I commanded, and he brought it to me, supporting my head tenderly while I drank.

I was hurt, shocked and exhausted, but I was alive and so was he. Life was not wholly cruel. I lay back and let the barge take me to the governor's palace.

Chapter Twenty

The reception that awaited me when I arrived could not have been more gracious and concerned if I had been the Emperor Commodus himself. As soon as Junio got ashore and the events of the day were told, a whole army of slaves, carrying beds, cushions, blankets and reviving cordials, was sent to bring me home. There was even a priest in my room when I arrived, scattering libations to every god in the pantheon, and I heard later that an ox was sacrificed – to the delight of the barge crew, who were invited to eat the parts of it not wanted by the deities.

Junio and the retinue of slaves half carried me to my bed, where I was soon visited by a *medicus*. He eased and bathed away my bloodstained clothes – a process which almost made me pass out again – and chewed up soothing herbs to treat my cuts. His salves and ointments made me sweat and swear, but once the initial sting had passed I could feel the heat subsiding from my burns. Then he bound up my wounds, dressed me in a spare slave's tunic from the palace and gave me a strong potion to drink which ushered me into instant oblivion.

When I dreamed, it was of furnaces. I was in a dark cavern full of crawling things, but when I opened my mouth to scream, blessed cool water trickled through my lips – and somehow I knew that it was Junio, giving me a welcome sponge to drink. I sank back in relief, and slept again.

I awoke to find the governor himself at my bedside, with a small regiment of slaves behind him.

'Good afternoon, my friend,' he greeted me. 'I trust you wake a little more refreshed?'

I moved my head and limbs exploratorily. I ached in every fibre, and my chest felt as if it had been carried in a brazier, but my body seemed to answer to my will, and although it was acutely painful, I could move.

'I think so, Excellence,' I said, struggling to sit up. It seemed improper to be lying down while the most powerful man in Britain was standing at my feet. My mouth felt like a furnace, and I was grateful for the beaker of water which, at the governor's signal, one of the house-slaves pressed into my hands. Something occurred to me. 'Good afternoon, you say,' I said when I had moistened my lips. 'It must have been midday when I went to bed. 'How long have I been asleep?'

Pertinax's stern face softened in a smile. 'Only a day or so.' He must have seen my look of consternation. 'We have been watching you. The *medicus* thought you should be left to sleep, but I asked him to fetch me as soon as you awoke. He said that you were stirring, so I came. He will look in again tomorrow, he assures me.' He looked at me anxiously. 'For now, if you are sufficiently recovered, I want to hear your version of what occurred. I have heard some of it from my bargeman, of course. That fellow should be whipped for letting you be harmed.'

I drained the rest of the beaker in a gulp. I found that I was hungry, which was an encouraging sign. My recollections of the day before were hazy and confused, but I managed to piece together an account of the significant events. 'And do not blame your boatman,' I added. 'I owe my life to him.'

Pertinax nodded thoughtfully. 'Those two ruffians he captured are both dead. One of them never recovered from his injury, and the other was cut down trying to escape. A pity. We shall get nothing from them now.'

The words reminded me so forcefully of my own

experience that for a moment I felt quite faint again. 'What about Glaucus, Excellence? He was the one who tortured me. Have you captured him?'

The governor shook his head. 'Unfortunately not. I sent troops to arrest him at the *factio* – Junio said he was connected with the team – but I think he found out somehow we were after him. I've left a guard on the building where they held you, but he has not been back. He seems to have disappeared from the city without trace and taken Fortunatus with him.'

Something half heard drifted back to me. I hoisted myself higher on my pillows and tried to look intelligent. 'I think you will find them at Camulodunum next week,' I said.

Pertinax looked doubtful. 'I thought that Fortunatus was injured – or pretending to be.'

'He will be racing,' I said, with sudden certainty. 'No doubt he will grow a beard and dye his hair and be registered at the course under some other name, or perhaps he will just make a last-minute recovery, but he will race, I'm sure. Just as I'm sure that Citus, the Reds' new wonder horse, will mysteriously go lame, unless a careful watch is kept on his stable.'

'Glaucus told you this?'

'Not in so many words, Excellence. He was talking to his guards and he thought I was unconscious, as I nearly was. But that is what will happen, I'd put money on it. As I'm sure that Glaucus and his team already have.' I handed my empty cup to Junio, who refilled it instantly. 'As for Fortunatus, I have not seen the man, but I am almost certain that he feigned that accident at Verulamium. And the team coach knew it, too. Someone paid them handsomely for that – Glaucus himself, no doubt.' My brain seemed to be functioning, if nothing else was. 'He does more than run the team's finances, Excellence: I think he runs a private gambling syndicate – and tries to improve his chances by ensuring the result.'

Pertinax looked grave. Both of these things were crimes, with serious penalties. 'You think the whole Blue *factio* are involved in this?'

'I doubt that very much. The fewer people involved, the greater the share of the profits and the less chance of someone betraying the rest to the authorities. But there is a lot of money in this, Excellence. Glaucus talked of making thousands from one race – and that was for each of them!'

'Could he be sure of that?'

'I think he could. All the money was on the Blues at Verulamium – so anyone who bet *against* them stood to win handsomely. At Camulodunum the opposite applies. The Reds are clearly favourites there, with Fortunatus hurt – and they have their wonderful new horse as well. Of course, Glaucus plans to tamper with the horse, just to make sure. Hardly anyone will be betting on the Blues at that meeting – their substitute driver is virtually unknown. So Glaucus will wager for the Blue team at the course and get attractive odds. Meantime, his illegal syndicate will privately take huge bets for the Reds. Both ways, they win.'

I turned myself tentatively on the bed, and tried to sit upright. My chest protested violently, but otherwise I seemed to be in working order. Pertinax watched me anxiously.

'Thousands upon thousands of *denarii* – certainly enough to kill men for. You think they murdered Monnius?' he said.

'Perhaps they did not kill him, Excellence; they were at Verulamium. But there is some connection, I am sure. Everyone jumped like guilty fleas as soon as I mentioned his name.'

'We shall find out,' Pertinax said grimly, 'when we get our hands on Glaucus. And we will. I'll send a messenger to every legion and garrison in the province. He won't get far. A racing fraud – the soldiers won't think much of that. They'll bring him in, if he is anywhere to be found. And when they do he'll wish he'd shown a little more respect for my warrant. As for Fortunatus, if you are right we can pick him up at the race.'

'If you time it carefully, Excellence, you could catch them in the act. Trying to get to Citus, for example. Otherwise all this might be difficult to prove. The attack on me is a different matter. I could testify to that – but there is no proof that anyone other than Glaucus was involved. And if we can't find him, I can't bring a charge. Now, if you will permit it, Excellence, I should like to try to stand on my feet again.' It would not have been polite to make the attempt without his agreement.

He gave it readily, but was gratifyingly anxious for my strength. I lowered an exploratory foot to the floor. The world had not come apart, I discovered, and I cautiously allowed my second foot to follow the first.

'Men who have been in slavery develop fortitude,' I said, as Junio knelt to fasten on my sandals.

Pertinax nodded. I reached out a hand to Junio and another slave also came forward to assist me. Leaning heavily on their shoulders, I forced myself upright. The room swam, but I steadied myself and I was standing, rocky but vertical.

Pertinax smiled grimly. 'You are a stubborn man, Libertus. In the circumstances, I have news for you. At first I thought you were not well enough to hear it. But since I find you determined to get up . . .'

I sat down again. 'More trouble, Excellence?'

He laughed softly. 'Some men might think so, though after what you have been through it seems trivial enough. Annia Augusta is here. She has been asking to see you – if "ask" is the appropriate word. I sent to tell her that you'd been badly hurt, but she only insisted all the more. She has a sovereign remedy for burns, she says, and now she has sent back to the house for that. She was not content to send a message to you, either – she insists on seeing you in person. She is outside now, in my reception room, no doubt terrorising the servants. I would have sent her away but she is a determined woman. She threatened to create a disturbance in the street and I believed her.'

I found myself frowning. What possible circumstance could drive Annia Augusta – a mother in mourning for her son – to abandon her home and come storming to the governor's palace in search of me? She was in danger of undoing all the purification rites for the funeral. What did she want to tell me which one of her household servants could not have come and told me just as well?

I asked, 'Has Caius Monnius been cremated yet?'

Pertinax looked surprised. 'I believe the funeral is scheduled for tonight. I suppose I shall be expected to attend, or at least to send a representative . . .' He stopped. 'I see! She has left the house, so the matter must be serious. Nevertheless, citizen, I can have her sent away. You have been injured.'

I shook my head. 'As you say, Mightiness, Annia Augusta is formidable, but after Glaucus . . .' I let the sentence hang unfinished in the air. 'Perhaps a little sustenance, and then I will see the lady – and her remedies.'

'My dear friend, of course. It shall be done at once. I have ordered something for you on the instructions of the *medicus*. It should be ready for you now.' Pertinax clapped his hands and a servant scampered off to the kitchens at once, to reappear a moment later with a tray. It was the sort of soft food I have seen served to invalids – eggs whisked and cooked with herbs, barley gruel, hot milk and honey.

The governor made his farewells – 'I am leaving some of my servants with you as well as your own slave. If there is anything you require, you have only to ask for it' – and I was left to enjoy my nursery meal in peace.

It did not take long. I was not as hungry as I thought I was, but I ate most of the egg and I was as ready as I'd ever be to face the formidable Annia.

Formidable she was. She swept into the room like a black barge under full sail, towing a laden maidservant in her wake. Annia was veiled and cloaked, but hardly had the courtesies been fulfilled when she bundled off her constricting outer garment and thrust it unceremoniously at the slave. Then she folded her arms grimly and stood looking down at me.

'Hmm,' she said (I was reminded of the chicken-buying cook again), 'you're looking very pale. They told me you were hurt.' She strode over to the bed where I was sitting. 'Get rid of some of these slaves and let's have a look at you. The governor has given his permission. All very well on a battlefield, these army *medici*, but when it comes to domestic injury you want a woman's touch.'

I thought, rather sourly, that deliberate torture hardly came into the category of 'domestic injury' and if the woman in question was Annia Augusta her touch was likely to be – at best – robust. But I had no chance to argue. Most of the waiting slaves had already disappeared, and her maidservant, having disencumbered herself of the cloak, was juggling a variety of bottles, phials and bowls out of the woven basket she was carrying.

'Take off that tunic and lie back,' Annia said, and I found myself obeying – to the evident amusement of Junio who was grinning widely as he assisted me. I was glad that, in putting me to bed, the *medicus* had left my underbritches on.

The grin faded, however, as Annia peeled back the bandages. The linen strips had stuck in parts and I heard her tut to herself impatiently, but there was nothing impatient about the way she soaked the cloth ('cooled boiled water, brought a flagon with me, much the best') and eased it gently away with surprisingly expert, reassuring hands. It was like being under the care of my grandmother again.

'Just as I thought,' she muttered. 'Those cuts are healing well. But the burns – no idea, some of these military men. Lavender and true aloe, that's what we want here. Bring me that purple salve, girl, and the drops in that tall phial on the end.'

She might be poisoning me, for all I knew, I thought: but there were too many witnesses for that. Besides, the salve that she applied was blissfully soothing, and by the time she had bound my wounds I was feeling more comfortable than I had done all day. Even then Annia Augusta was not satisfied.

'Sit up and drink this,' she said, pouring a thick vile-looking yellow liquid into the goblet I had used earlier.

It smelt almost as evil as it looked, and tasted even worse, but – as I realised afterwards – it was effective, too. At the time, however, my only sensation was of a revolting taste and a consistency almost impossible to swallow. Not until I had signalled furiously to Junio and gulped down another half-pitcher of water did I feel able to look up and meet Annia Augusta's eyes.

She was looking at me complacently, her ample hands clasped at her ample chest. 'Well?' she demanded. 'How are you feeling now?'

I muttered somewhat ungraciously that I was still alive. In fact, I realised with surprise, I was beginning to feel a little better.

She nodded. 'Very well, young man. You'll do for now – especially if I keep an eye on you. Get on your clothes and come with me. You can't walk anywhere, of course – I've got a litter waiting. We've got all sorts of problems at the house, and I think you should come and talk to Fulvia yourself.'

It was so unexpected that my mouth dropped open and for a moment I was speechless. Not merely that she had called me 'young man' (no one had done that for twenty years) but the calm assumption that I was now at her disposal, and could simply rise up from my bed of pain and accompany her as if nothing had happened.

Annia Augusta, though, seemed unaware of my amazement. She had turned away and was packing up her potion basket again: flapping away the efforts of the slave to help, as though she trusted the job to no one but herself. 'I sent a message to you the other day,' she was saying, 'but you didn't come, only that silly stuck-up palace-slave. I told him then – I thought you'd want to know. Filius heard it somewhere – you know what he is like about chariots. Fortunatus was supposed to be at some big race meeting somewhere the night of the murder, but he wasn't. He was here in Londinium all the time, claiming to be seriously injured, though Mars alone knows if it is as bad as he pretends. Of course, Fulvia heard of this and insisted on talking to the messenger, so the goddess knows what garbled version of the tale you heard.'

I managed to mutter that the story had reached me much as she had told it. If I had stayed in Londinium, I thought, this amazing woman would have brought me the information which I had travelled so far and worked so hard to find.

'Of course,' Annia went on, putting down the basket and holding out her arms to have her cloak put on, 'I don't believe a word of it myself. I know what Fortunatus was up to that night, if you don't. Only of course, Fulvia refuses to admit it. Goes on insisting that it was some stranger who broke in. And that's the problem, citizen. She claims that somebody is still trying to kill her.' She plonked herself down on the stool so that her servant could adjust the heavy veil over her face.

'Has there been another attempt to knife her?' I asked.

Annia snorted. 'Not that, citizen. But she has insisted for days that someone is trying to poison her – she even started to use that old slave of hers, Prisca or whatever her name is, as a poison-taster. Just the sort of thing that you might expect from Fulvia – my poor Monnius lying there dead, and she begins upsetting the house and making herself the centre of attention. Of course we are not eating prepared meals until the funeral feast, just dry bread and fruit, but she is still insisting on having hers brought specially, won't drink water from a jug and all that sort of nonsense. The priest had to have a word with her – you know how mourning rituals have to be observed, just so, in the right order, or the whole thing is invalid and you have to start again. Monnius had a perfect fear of bad omens at a funeral, and she seems determined to bring it about. Well, you can see for yourself.' She got to her feet. 'Put on a warm cloak, citizen. You'll find it cold outside after what you've been through, and you can hardly travel through the streets, like that, dressed as a palace-slave.'

While she was talking I had permitted Junio to ease me painfully back into my borrowed tunic. I could see what she meant, but I had no intention of going with Annia in any case. For one thing, I was still unsteady on my feet, and for another I was sure that Glaucus had known Monnius, and I didn't wish to encounter him again except in the safety of an imperial courtroom.

'Madam citizen,' I began, in my most formal apologetic manner, 'I am flattered by your confidence in my powers, but I fail to see what I can do to help. Fulvia is taking every precaution, and unless something further untoward occurs it seems my presence would only interrupt the rituals still further.'

Annia Augusta stared at me. She was veiled, so I could not see her face, but I could feel the contempt through several layers of net.

'Untoward?' she said. 'Of course it's untoward. That's what I have come here to tell you. I don't know how it can have happened – I was sure that the whole thing was nonsense – but it seems there might have been something in it, after all.

Prisca was found last evening outside the study, dead. She seems to have been poisoned tasting Fulvia's food. Now, are you coming, citizen, or not?'

Chapter Twenty-one

Our appearance at Monnius' house occasioned quite a stir.

The excitements of the funeral preparations – the comings and goings of priests, mourners, pipers, augurers and slaves – had drawn the usual little gaggle of onlookers and curious passers-by, who were being entertained when we arrived by an ancient itinerant viper-tamer. He had evidently seized the opportunity to set out his stall before a captive audience and was coaxing a less than impressive performance from a lethargic snake in a basket.

'Drugged,' Annia Augusta hissed at me, as she descended from her litter and prepared to follow her slave into the house.

The viper-tamer glared at her, but the crowd had lost interest in him anyway. I was lying on a carrying bed borrowed from the palace – my first attempts to climb into an ordinary litter having been conspicuously unsuccessful – and when that was borne along the street and up to Monnius' door, with Junio trotting obediently alongside, everyone on the pavement turned to stare. Not surprisingly perhaps, people being more accustomed on the whole to seeing bodies carried out of a house of death than into one, but it made me feel very conspicuous. Even the appearance of a pair of city councillors, in their chalk-whitened robes, come to pay their official respects to the corpse and carrying a model of a corn officer's *mobius* as a grave-offering, passed almost unnoticed in comparison.

My unusual litter caused almost as much consternation inside the house. As soon as we crossed the threshold, Lydia came hurrying out to meet us. She was wearing a different robe of faded black today, even more unattractive than the last, and was in her usual state of nervous indecision.

'Oh, dear madam,' she exclaimed, wringing her thin hands. 'I got your message from the palace, that the citizen was arriving on a bed. I have been in such a quandary wondering what to do. Where can we put him, do you think? I thought of the *triclinium* at first, but the servants are preparing for the funeral feast and the priest has already purified the room. It would all have to be censed and sprinkled again. Poor Monnius' body is in the atrium. Obviously the litter can't go here.' She shook her head. 'Should I find somewhere in the annexe, do you think?'

During all of this she addressed not a word or glance in my direction. I felt like a piece of awkward furniture, for which space has unfortunately to be found. It was as if the cloak and tunic had rendered me invisible, like a character in a fable. She would never have ignored me in this way if I had been wearing my toga. Even Junio caught my eye and grinned.

Annia Augusta could be placating when she chose. 'My dear Lydia, do not distress yourself so much. The *citizen*' – she stressed the word – 'is hurt but he is not incapable. Monnius' study seems the obvious place.'

'But is it big enough? It will not take the carrying bed. The Egyptian writing table is in there already, and a stool. And all those documents . . .'

I was struggling upright on my pillows to protest that although I could not comfortably walk, a stool would suit me splendidly, when Lydia began wailing again. 'We have had such problems since you left, with Fulvia. You cannot imagine, lady citizen! Crying and wailing and insisting –

insisting! – that the undertakers bathe and anoint her servant's body too. I tried to protest – it wasn't fitting, I told her – but she simply tossed her head, and said it was her house now, and her money, and she would do as she pleased. Of course, it isn't even true – the house was promised to my Filius. Everyone knows that Monnius changed his will. She'll enter a *querela* in the courts, and then . . .' She broke off, snivelling.

I motioned to my bearers to put me down. The carrying bed was in the way in the corridor, but I could hardly expect them to stand here, holding me all day; and this conversation was too interesting to miss. They put me down and Junio and one of the bearers helped me unsteadily to my feet, while Lydia pulled a linen handkerchief from her sleeve and sniffed into it.

'Oh, Lydia!' Annia Augusta was less patient now. 'Of course she won't contest the will. Fulvia is headstrong but she is not stupid. No one would benefit from a *querela* except the imperial treasury, she knows that as well as you do. Don't upset yourself. We'll see this citizen settled in the study – he'll need to speak to all the slaves this time – and then you can take some strengthening cordial and I will speak to Fulvia myself.'

I was mentally applauding this intelligent approach, but Lydia let out a doleful cry. 'But Annia Augusta, you don't understand. Fulvia has been impossible. She came out here, making such a scene, demanding honours for her stupid slave when the men were here to make Monnius' *imago*! She interrupted them while they were doing it.' She dabbed at her pink nose and watery eyes again.

Annia's lips pursed at this and I saw her ample bosom heave with indignation. I was not surprised. I had heard of funeral masks, though one rarely sees them in Britannia. It used to be the custom in Rome, however, that magistrates –

and only magistrates – were honoured with a wax mask at their death, moulded on their dead features and displayed thereafter in the family atrium as a perpetual tribute to their memory. Monnius, whether because of his position or of some earlier tenure as a magistrate, might have a claim to similar distinction and someone (I suspected Annia herself) had given orders that it should be done. In interrupting the creation of the mask, Fulvia had been guilty of dreadful disrespect.

But worse was yet to come. 'A dreadful omen! If only you'd been here, Annia Augusta. I hardly knew what to do. I had the priest of Jupiter called at once, to offer a propitiatory sheep. We had to abandon the lamentations and leave poor Monnius to the servants, while we attended the sacrifice and were sprinkled with the blood to cleanse ourselves. Even then all the purification rituals had to be done again. I even had to change my robes – my best black stola – and now I shall have to attend the funeral in this!'

Annia frowned. 'Just because she intervened? I hardly think . . .'

Lydia shook her head. 'She did more than that, most honoured madam. Thanks to her interruption, the mask was dropped. It had only just been finished, and it broke. Think of that!' She deployed the handkerchief again. 'Poor Filius – what an augury for him! Although he is too young to understand – poor boy, he was at first inclined to laugh. That was the shock, of course. But when we had to go and change our clothes, and sprinkle perfumed water on our heads and fast the whole remainder of the day, he saw how serious it was. We almost thought the funeral would have to be post-poned. And all this for a wretched slave, who could be washed for burial just as well by any servant in the house, and could have waited in the yard until after the ceremony was over – the slaves' guild won't come for the body till tomorrow night.'

She gave a helpless sob. 'Oh, Annia Augusta, if only you'd been here.'

'Well,' Annia Augusta said robustly, 'I'm here now, and it seems you handled matters very well. Now, attempt to control yourself a little – I will send a little cordial to restore you, presently. But we are being discourteous to this gentleman. I have brought him here to find the truth about this poisoning and if it is to be done before the funeral he will have to begin.'

Lydia gave a shuddering sigh. 'Ah yes, the poisoning. Another terrible omen, citizen. Do you not agree?'

'I do.' Especially for the old nurse, I thought wryly, but all I said was, 'We shall avenge her spirit by finding the culprit.'

At the mention of spirits Lydia rolled her sheeplike eyes, then fixed them lugubriously on me. 'You have your suspicions, citizen?'

I had no clues whatever, although I didn't want to admit that. I said, with an attempt at solemnity, 'I suspect everyone.'

Lydia turned to Annia Augusta and let out a doleful wail. 'He suspects everyone! Oh, madam citizen . . .'

'Do not be foolish, Lydia,' the older woman said sharply. 'The citizen does not mean you! Obviously not – you were performing the lament at the time, in full view of everyone.'

'But Filius . . .'

'I can assure the citizen that it wasn't Filius either – he was with me from the time Prisca herself brought the bread and water to us in the annexe until after her body was found.' She turned to me. 'I kept him deliberately under my eye – I did not want him wandering into the kitchens and being tempted to break the ritual fast.'

I nodded. In Annia's position I would have feared the same thing. 'The other servants will no doubt vouch for that?'

'Oh, Minerva . . .!' Lydia began, but Annia cut her off decisively.

213

'Oh, Lydia, for the love of Mars! Don't wail! Of course the citizen must confirm my story. And we cannot keep him waiting any more. Besides, we are blocking the passageway – those councillors will finish their lamentations any minute and they will be wanting to leave. I will accompany the citizen to the study and go and have a word with Fulvia.'

She suited the action to the word and began to lead the way. I waved aside the carrying bed and followed her on foot, assisted by Junio and one of the bearers who had brought me here. The other three removed the litter hastily, while Lydia trailed behind us, still protesting feebly.

Annia gave instructions as she walked. 'This citizen has been hurt – he needs a stool at least,' she motioned to a slave, 'and no doubt the kitchens can provide some dates and wine for him, even if we cannot partake of them. Or,' she turned her head to look at me questioningly over her shoulder, 'perhaps he would prefer a little cordial tonic too?'

I ceased my stumbling walk to murmur that I would be much obliged. I am, as Junio was well aware, no great enthusiast for sweet fat Roman dates and thin sour Roman wine, but the idea of rest and refreshment was becoming increasingly attractive.

'The distilled water of wild poppy flowers, I think,' the older woman said briskly. 'That is a strong remedy for frenzies and a wonderful restorative besides. I'm sure I have some in my bedchamber. I think I may even take a little myself.' She nodded to her handmaiden, who was attending her, and the girl set off to the annexe at a trot.

'But Annia Augusta, madam citizen.' Lydia's voice was again a wail. 'The augurer insists that we must fast. No meat or drink of any kind until after the funeral, and then the first thing we eat after the graveside rituals must be the flesh of the sheep that was sacrificed. Otherwise, who knows what trouble will befall this house.'

Annia was losing patience, I could see. 'To take a medicine is not to break a fast,' she snapped, ushering me at last into the study, where I sank down on a welcome stool. 'But you are right about one thing, Lydia. That story of the broken *imago*. Fulvia may be Monnius' official widow, but it was most improper of her to interrupt his funeral rites in that way. All that fuss, and for a slave-woman, too! She had no right to do it, and I shall tell her so.'

Lydia flapped her bony hands. 'Well, most honoured citizeness, you may try.' She had turned an unattractive shade of puce. 'We have all of us attempted to speak to her – Filius, myself, the priest of Jupiter, even the servants. But she insists that someone is trying to kill her. I have tried to reason with her, but the death of her nursemaid has only confirmed her opinion.' She shrugged her bony shoulders under the dark cloak. 'But you will see for yourself. She will spoil the whole funeral, if she continues. She has barricaded herself into her bedchamber and refuses to come out.'

Chapter Twenty-two

Annia Augusta was not impressed. 'Barricaded herself in?' she said. 'We shall see about that! She cannot keep it up; her attendance is required at the funeral. Meantime, I shall have the slaves sent here and the citizen can start on his enquiries. Ah, here is the girl with the cordial I sent for.' She motioned to the slave-girl to pour me a cup of the poppy-water cordial, which Junio brought to me.

I was cautious, after my experience with Annia's concoction earlier, but this one looked appetising enough, and I was woefully weak. Even that short walk had taxed my strength. When I took an exploratory sip I found it tasted wonderfully refreshing and I drank the rest gratefully. Annia sipped her own, but when Lydia was offered some she shook her head, and folded her arms like a rebellious child. For the second time, I saw a resemblance to Filius.

But there was little time to think of that. Annia was right. If I was to interview the servants and try to discover what had happened to the nurse, I would need to be quick about it. There was not much time before the funeral.

I had Junio round up the servants and bring them to me in batches, once Annia and Lydia had gone. There were a good many servants in a city household of this size, and they obviously could not all be spared at once, but their duties were limited, and I confined myself to questioning them according to their tasks: kitchen-slaves, handmaidens, page-boys, messengers, gatekeepers, and all the rest.

The borrowed tunic (and my consequent apparent lack of status) had almost prevented Lydia from uttering a word to me, but I hoped that now it would help to loosen tongues, and indeed there was no lack of willingness to talk. However, no one had anything significant to tell me. No one had seen anything suspicious, and all agreed with Annia Augusta's assertion that she and Filius had been in public view, and Lydia had been lamenting throughout.

One of the little pageboys gave the most helpful account. 'We were the ones who found the body, citizen. Poor old Prisca. She was just lying there, outside the master's chamber, her face all screwed up and blue and her eyes protruding, and foaming at the mouth like frogspawn. It gave me quite a shock, and Parvus here' – he indicated the fellow pageboy at his side – 'had never seen a poisoned body before. He had to be given water to revive him.'

I was not altogether surprised at his reaction. The last time I had seen Parvus he had been tasting Fulvia's drink himself.

But the other boy seemed oblivious. 'Of course, we should have expected something of the kind. Poor Lady Fulvia has been worried for her life ever since she was attacked – insisting on sending us out for bought bread from the market instead of eating anything from the kitchens. Even then, she refused to touch it unless Prisca tried it first. And it was the same with wine and water – hers had to be the second drink poured from any jug, with one of us pageboys standing by to make sure no one tried to poison the cup.'

'But someone did,' I said.

He shook his head, perplexed. 'I don't know how,' he said. 'We were right beside Lady Fulvia while she ate, in the *triclinium*. I brought the tray of food to her myself, and Prisca tasted everything before she ate it.'

'And there was no sign of a problem then?'

He shook his head. 'Everything seemed to be in order,

although now I come to think of it the lady Fulvia did say that the water tasted a little bitter, and refused to swallow any more of it. But we thought nothing of it at the time – she has been suspicious of everything for days, and Prisca seemed to be all right. Then our mistress decided to retire, and her nurse went off to prepare the bedchamber.' He shrugged expressively.

'And then?'

'That was the last we saw of her alive. She was gone so long that Lady Fulvia sent us after her – and there she was in the passageway, stretched out, obviously dead. Parvus here let out a screech, and then of course everyone in the household came running to have a look, except Lydia, who was doing her part in the lament. Even Filius and Annia Augusta came.'

'And the lady Fulvia?'

'She didn't come. She was too horrified to move, I think.'

'So you went back to tell her what you'd found?'

'We did. I had to break the news – Parvus was still babbling with shock. Poor lady, she was terribly upset. And, of course, more worried for herself than ever. She made us stand beside her bed all night, with lighted lamps. And she has not eaten since. In the morning even Annia Augusta agreed to send for you.'

I nodded, and was about to dismiss the boys when a sudden thought struck me. 'There was no one else in that part of the building at the time?'

The two pages looked at each other and then at me. This time it was Parvus who spoke. 'No one that we noticed, citizen. Of course the servants' stairs go up from there, and anyone could have slipped up there for a moment. Or gone out into the garden and the shrine – but certainly we did not see anyone.'

'And what happened to the body afterwards?'

'It was taken to the servants' hall to wait. Fulvia went in this morning to the undertakers and insisted on a proper cleansing. Lydia made quite an uproar about it, but the lady Fulvia got her way. She paid them handsomely to do it, I think – with oils and everything. Quite an honour for a poor old nursemaid, with not a *sestertius* in the world.'

There were a few more questions, but they could help no further, and this time I did let them go. For form's sake, I spoke to the undertaker's man who had prepared the body. He was a big, rough fellow, with hands like corn scoops and a wind-scarred face, but he confirmed the pages' story.

'First time I've ever been called on to do it for a slave-woman, and an old, ugly one at that. Waste of time of course – the household isn't paying for a funeral, and the slave guild simply picks the bodies up, throws them all together on one pyre, and sets fire to them. What's the point of elaborate preparations for a funeral like that, when there's no public exhibition of the body – not even any mourners to speak of?'

I thought for a moment that he was about to spit for emphasis, but he seemed to recollect himself.

'Going to put it out the back first, when they found it, out of the way. But the widow-lady, the pretty one, insisted that we took it upstairs. She'd got it into her head that it was her fault or something – and then this morning she came in, offering silver for us to prepare it for burial. Mad as a satyr, of course, but you don't argue with a bag of coins! So when the mask-makers were here I went upstairs and dealt with the thing – gave it a quick wash and oil, and got it tidied up a bit. Hadn't been dead long, either, when we took it up there – the body was still warm. You notice that sort of thing in this job.'

I remembered that I had failed to notice something similar myself.

220

He seemed to take the colour in my cheeks as a sign of personal enthusiasm, and he went on with professional relish. 'It's still up there, if you want to see it. Not that there's very much to see. There were no marks on the body, citizen, if that is what you are thinking. Some pink patches on the skin – I've seen them before with people who've been poisoned – but no bruises or any sign of force. Ate, or more likely drank, something that was poisoned, and a few minutes later she fell to the floor foaming.' He shook his head. 'A nasty way to die, citizen. But we did a nice job on her, if I do say so myself.'

He bent towards me confidentially. He smelled of death – herbs, oils and corruption. I almost found myself leaning backwards to avoid it. I put on my most official manner and briskly asked another question. 'And the body had not been tampered with overnight?'

He straightened up and shook his head. 'Just as we left it, citizen. Covered with a cloth and all that, and I'd stake ten *denarii* that no one had been anywhere near it. The servants were frightened out of their wits, as it was, with having a corpse up there – we put it in an alcove, but I noticed this morning there were prayer plaques nailed to the door, and herbs and salt on the floor as if someone had been doing a purification rite. And they all keep away from us undertaker-slaves as if we are plague-carriers.'

I nodded. I rather sympathised with their position.

'Believe me, citizen,' he went on heartily, 'they wouldn't tamper with that body willingly. There aren't even any of the right herbs up there to burn, and the corpse'll be beginning to stink by this time. Besides, what would be the point of touching her? The poor old soul had nothing to steal.' He flashed his remaining teeth in a crooked grin, as though we were comrades in complicity. 'You just say the word, citizen, and I'll take you up there and explain the whole process, step by step.'

I hastened to tell him that would not be necessary, and his face fell a little.

'All the same, citizen – anything you want to know about the business, you come to me. Now if you are sure . . .?'

I was sure, and at last Junio was able to hustle him out of the door, taking the odour of mortality with him. The pageboy, Parvus, hurried in.

'A messenger has come for you, citizen, from the governor himself. One of his own bodyguards, I think.' The boy's eyes were round as a discus. 'He says he has important news for you.'

'Show him in,' I said, and a moment later one of the giant Nubians was kneeling before me. He was making an obeisance, but at the sight of my palace tunic his black eyes twinkled in his dark face and the lips that murmured courteous greetings were visibly trying not to smile. The hand that pressed mine to his lips was so enormous that it could have crushed me like a walnut in a press, and his strength seemed twice as great in contrast to my current weakness. I felt foolish, and we were both aware of it.

I signalled to the man to rise – a mistake in itself since he now towered over my chair like a basilica. 'You have news?' I enquired, with such remnants of dignity as I could muster.

'His Excellence the Governor, Publius Helvius Pertinax, instructs me to inform you that two people whom you were seeking have been taken under arrest.' The Latin was perfect, cultured, and spoken with a clarity and accent which would have made many students of oratory seem only half civilised.

I gawped. Could that be Glaucus and his corrupt team manager Calyx, I wondered. 'Two people?'

The Nubian giant inclined his head in assent – to say that he nodded would be to understate the gravity of the gesture. 'One of them is unknown to me, although I understand it is

222

someone well known in the city. The other is one Lividius Fortunatus, a gifted pilot of the chariots. I have myself been known to venture a *denarius* or two on his abilities. You wish to speak to him, I believe? His Excellence, as supreme governor of the province under His Imperial Mightiness the Divine Emperor Commodus, enquires what you wish him to do with these two persons.'

'Do with them?' I said foolishly.

'Would you prefer him to imprison them – neither, I think, is a Roman citizen, so they could be interrogated by the state, if you wish – or would you rather he should send them here, so that you can question them yourself? Under guard, naturally.'

I found myself smiling childishly. I confess to a sudden and unworthy desire to see Glaucus – if this was indeed Glaucus – brought in under arrest and finding himself answering to me. An opportunity to speak to Fortunatus – and in Fulvia's company – would be interesting too. Perhaps even Filius would emerge from his annexe to see his hero and I would have the chance to learn something there. And – some inner demon asked me – what would Annia Augusta say if she saw the charioteer?

I smiled more broadly. 'My thanks and greetings to the governor. Have them brought here,' I said, and he bowed himself out, while I returned to my enquiries.

There was little left to do. I questioned the last remaining servants – a couple of garden-slaves who tended the plants, cleaned the pool and swept the paving stones. They had little to add. They had not been working in the peristyle, they told me, since their master's death, apart from cutting a few plants for the undertakers. Their services had been required elsewhere, strewing aromatics in the street outside, and fetching extra water for the kitchens. In any case it would have been difficult to see into the house – the shutters in their master's *cubiculum* had been kept closed since his death, and the ones in Fulvia's bedchamber had been shut and bolted by the pages.

I dismissed the gardeners, feeling very little wiser, and heaved a dispirited sigh.

'You are tiring yourself, master,' Junio said anxiously. 'Should I send for the litter for you, or a mattress so that you can stretch out on the floor?'

I shook my head. 'But since you mention the floor,' I said, 'there is something that I'd like you to investigate. You will do it more easily than I will, and I think that there is time before we are interrupted again. There, underneath the table – you see where the square in the design has a deep space around the border?'

Junio was on his knees in a flash. 'You think . . .?'

'It lifts,' I said. 'I know. I moved it once before – and I think that you will find underneath it the solution to Eppaticus' missing money.'

He flashed me a cheerful grin. 'We'll see.' He inserted his fingers in the crack as I had done, and once again the central section moved. 'It's too big and heavy,' he said. 'I can't grip it. I could get it up at one end, but I need something to prop it with.' He looked around as if for inspiration.

'That gong stick on the wall outside?' I said, suddenly remembering.

He nodded eagerly, and soon came back with it. It was a strange shape, almost triangular, but when Junio lifted one end of the floor panel, and inserted it, the gong stick acted as a perfect wedge. It was exactly the right weight and width to slide under the aperture – almost as if it had been designed for that very purpose. With one end now propped open it was easier to lift the other, and a moment later the cavity was revealed. It was cleverly made: lined with wood and a stone floor set into it, it would have been a dry and certain hiding

224

place for anything. And it was spacious too – just as I had remembered it.

Except that this time the cavity was empty. It was so surprising that I staggered from my gilded stool to look. There was no mistake. The coins had gone.

Chapter Twenty-three

'Empty, master?'

'There were coins in there, Junio,' I said, clinging to my dignity. 'I'm sure it was the money owed to Eppaticus. So what has happened to it now? It was there after the murder. If Fortunatus did come here and strangle Monnius, he certainly hasn't been back to take the money.'

Junio looked at me. 'Perhaps poor Prisca stumbled on the hiding place. Look at the way those men treated you. And Superbus, too. They wouldn't hesitate over an ageing nurse.'

I shook my head. 'This death was different. Poisoning has to be planned.'

'Then why Prisca?' Junio said.

I sighed. 'I wish I knew. Perhaps the poison was designed for Fulvia, as she claimed. In any case, we'd better put the lid back on the hiding place. I don't want the thief to realise that I know. That way I might startle a confession from the one who took it – if I ever discover who it was!'

The lifting section of mosaic went back more quickly than it had come out, but even so Junio had scarcely time to hang up the gong stick and take his station behind my stool again before Annia Augusta swept into the room, followed by her apologetic maid.

'Lydia is right,' she announced, without further ceremony. 'That wretched Fulvia, may Dis take her, has barricaded herself into her room. Literally barricaded herself. I've knocked and shouted, but she refuses to reply, and it seems she has even pushed something behind the door so that it cannot be opened from outside. That heavy storage chest of hers, I imagine.'

She looked like an avenging fury, with her folded arms and dark flowing robes. I said, diffidently, 'You tried the door from Monnius' chamber, too?'

She looked at me as though I were a toad, suddenly discovered in her bedchamber. 'I would have, though it seemed disrespectful to the dead. But she has blocked the door from the corridor into my son's room as well – put something heavy just where the panels would fold. And she will not even answer when I call. Great Minerva, citizen! They will be beginning the eulogies in an hour or so, and we cannot start the funeral without her. What are we to do?' She glared at me, as if I were personally responsible for this affront. 'And you? Have you made any progress here? Perhaps if we can discover who killed her maid, you will be able to persuade her to come out, like a civilised woman!'

I remembered the ladder leaning on the wall. Had Fulvia thrown caution to the winds and run away? Fortunatus had not been alone when he was arrested. I countered with a question of my own. 'Have you any idea, madam citizen, who might have killed the servant? Or wanted to kill Fulvia, perhaps?'

She drew herself upright. 'What are you suggesting, citizen? Are you accusing me?'

Of course, that was a possibility. Annia Augusta had made no secret of her animosity to Fulvia – but she must have known that the widow was employing a poison-taster. I tried a little hasty flattery. 'Not at all, madam citizen. I am simply interested in your perceptions.'

Annia Augusta was not placated. 'I wonder why? You've not been interested in what I thought till now. Besides, I have nothing to suggest. I cannot imagine who would be interested in a worthless slave, so presumably the poisoned draught was meant for Fulvia. Perhaps I should have paid more attention to her claims. I confess I did not believe there was any threat to her, despite her protestations. Even now, I do not understand it – unless that Fortunatus fellow has some other woman in the town, and she somehow managed to smuggle poison in.'

I thought of Pulchrissima. 'And how would such a person arrange that Fulvia would take it?' I said.

'Fulvia did insist on sending out for everything herself. It might have been contrived.' Annia lost patience suddenly. 'I don't know how. You are supposed to be solving this, not me. I am simply attempting to see that my son has a decent funeral, without its being interrupted any more than necessary. By his widow, among others. If he'd listened to his mother, and stuck to Lydia, none of this would ever have happened.' She broke off as Fulvia's pageboy, Parvus, came into the room. 'What has happened, boy? Has your mistress finally consented to come out?'

'There is a detachment of soldiers outside, mistress, asking to see the citizen. They say he is expecting them.' He looked at me. 'Should I let them in?'

Annia Augusta echoed in amazement. 'Soldiers? Here?'

Parvus nodded. 'They've got two prisoners under escort.'

'Prisoners!' Annia rounded on me, furious. 'You have allowed them to bring prisoners here? In the middle of our mourning, too. This is an indignity – an insult to the dead. Lydia is right, the auguries are frightful. And in front of all those spectators outside, as well. Jupiter alone knows what everyone will think – that these are mourners coming to the funeral, no doubt, and my son has only criminals to weep for him.'

I made a deprecating noise. 'On the contrary, madam citizen. They are more likely to suppose that Monnius' killer has been caught. You might think so yourself. One of the prisoners is your charioteer.'

Her indignation vanished like a sneak thief at a fair. 'So you have taken my opinion seriously at last? I see. In that case have them brought in here by all means. I will stay and listen, citizen. I shall be very interested to hear what Fortunatus has to say for himself.'

I nodded to the page, who hurried off, and Annia glared at me. 'I know you think I am an old fool of a woman, citizen, and you are still not convinced that Fortunatus was behind the murder of my son. But I am sure of it. If he did not do it himself, he contrived to have it done. And the poisoning of the old nurse too, perhaps, though I fail to see how that advantaged him. I would put nothing past him. I told you, I do not trust his face.'

That face, when it arrived a few moments later in the company of the rest of Fortunatus and two hefty guards, was rather as I'd imagined it: young, bronzed, and broodingly attractive, with that expression of petulant vanity that young men sometimes develop when they know that they are irresistible to women. I waited for the other prisoner to appear, wondering if it would be Fulvia after all, but there was no sign of anyone else, and I turned my attention to the charioteer again.

He was a handsome figure. His body was surprisingly slim, but the muscles on the chest and shoulders rippled under the blue tunic he wore, and the legs and arms were strong and taut as whipcord. His dark hair was short and curled, and he wore a cloak of fine cream-coloured wool, clasped at the shoulder by a heavy pin, with a gold medallion hanging round his neck. He looked exactly what he was: fit, wealthy, successful, self-confident and not a little put out to find himself a prisoner, with his hands bound in front of him and a dagger at his back.

He was glowering at Annia Augusta, and if a man ever looked capable of murder, I had to admit that it was the young charioteer at that moment. 'This is your doing, madam citizen!' he hissed.

'On the contrary,' I told him, from the comfort of my stool. 'You were brought here on my orders.'

He gazed at me, taking me in for the first time. In the borrowed palace tunic and with parts of my body bandaged as if in the last stages of some terrible disease, I suppose I hardly looked a figure of authority.

'You?' He could scarcely conceal his contempt.

'Allow me to introduce myself. Longinius Flavius Libertus, Roman citizen, at your service – or rather at the service of the governor. This is not my own tunic, as you might deduce – my toga required some attention after an unexpected meeting I had with a certain Glaucus, in a cellar. Your cellar, I believe. I think this Glaucus is a friend of yours?'

The face of the charioteer had turned first white, then red, and now was fast becoming the chalky colour of his cloak. He said nothing.

'His Excellence the Governor will be interested to hear your answers,' I said. 'No doubt he will be prepared to use persuasion, if necessary.'

Fortunatus glanced at Annia, who was smiling with grim satisfaction. 'Of course I know Glaucus,' he muttered reluctantly. 'He is provisions officer for the Blues. As to the cellar, I have no idea. The house is in the process of repair – they are putting in some drains. I have recently bought it but I do not live in it.'

'So I understand,' I said. 'You have been staying at an inn, I think? I am so glad to find you so fully recovered from that dreadful accident at Verulamium.'

He almost stepped backwards in dismay, but the dagger at his kidneys stopped him short. He shrugged helplessly.

231

'It must have been a tricky thing to stage,' I said conversationally. 'Very dangerous for you. I do hope Glaucus paid you well for it. Or did he just permit you to bet against yourself? I presume the syndicate had money on the Reds?'

Fortunatus could have raced for the Reds himself, without a uniform, at that moment. He muttered, 'I'm a team driver. I just do as I am told.'

'And what they told you,' I said, 'was to lose that race, and make yourself scarce for the rest of the programme in Verulamium, while they spread rumours about how badly you were hurt. Then, when it comes to Camulodunum, you will appear and win the race – with Glaucus having doped the rival horse, just to make certain of your victory.'

He stared sullenly at the floor. One of the soldiers cuffed him on the ear. 'Well? Answer the citizen. Or would you prefer us to take you to the prison and have their interrogator talk to you?'

Fortunatus looked at me sourly. 'There is no need to call the torturers,' he said. 'You seem to know all about it already. Though I don't know why you have arrested *me*. It was hardly my doing.'

The soldier cuffed him again, harder this time. 'Don't speak to the citizen like that.'

The charioteer's voice became a whine. 'But it is true. I drive to a contract – all right, I've bought my freedom now, but I'm still not much better than a slave. If Calyx and Glaucus command me to take a fall, I take it. What else can I do? I don't enjoy it; it makes me look a fool in front of all my fans.'

'But they persuaded you to do it all the same, because they paid you well?'

'Perhaps they do pay me well, but I don't earn as much as they do, by a long way.' He looked at the daggers pointing at his vitals, and seemed to come to a decision. 'Glaucus not only lays bets himself, he runs a betting booth as well. Illegal, but he has rich backers in the city. High stakes and high returns. The syndicate makes sure that the gamblers win sometimes, of course, but more frequently they lose. That is where the real money comes from. When I fell in Verulamium, for instance, they paid me a bonus equal to the prize, but they themselves made thousands of *denarii* – both on what they won, and what their clients lost. And I take all the risks. I am tired of it. That is why I bought myself a house – so I can pay off my contract as soon as possible, give up racing and retire.'

'With your lady-friend?' I asked.

Annia Augusta stiffened. 'Indeed! Your lady-friend. Now we are coming to the truth. That was your plan, was it?' He was pinioned by the soldiers, and she came close up beside him and poked him violently with her forefinger. 'A monster, that's what you are. Abusing Monnius' friendship in that way! You come here, eat his meat, drink his wine, and then seduce his wife. But not even that was good enough for you. You wanted more – a rich widow to help you buy your freedom and retire. I see it now!' She punctuated each word with a stab of her finger, and each time I saw Fortunatus flinch.

'I didn't mean . . .' he began helplessly

'Didn't mean?' she imitated mockingly. 'Hardly an accident, was it? You crept in here at night, when everyone supposed you were at Verulamium, stabbed my poor Monnius, and even pretended to attack Fulvia so no one would suspect her part in it. Well, this citizen and I were too sharp for you. Why did you kill the old nurse, though? She would have faced the beasts for Fulvia. I do not underst—' Her voice broke off.

I followed her gaze. The other prisoner had at last arrived. Not Fulvia. Not even Glaucus, or Calyx, as I'd half expected.

233

The newcomer – bound, bleeding, cursing, dragged between six soldiers and still struggling – was an unmistakable giant of a figure, with a shaved forehead and Celtic pigtail. Eppaticus!

He had not come without a struggle. Several of the soldiers, I noticed, were breathing heavily, and one had a reddening bruise over his left eye. The room was full of people now, but they got their captive in somehow and thrust him roughly to the floor.

'Not! Not!' he was still protesting volubly in his inimitable Latin. 'Nothings I have done deserving this. Only an honest trader – nothing tricks . . .' The tirade ceased as one of the soldiers placed a heavy foot on his neck.

'Apologies, citizen,' the senior soldier said. 'He took us by surprise. He was quiet enough when we arrested him, but as soon as we got outside this house and he saw where we were bringing him, he suddenly tried to make a break for it. It took all six of us to bring him down and get him under control.'

I made no answer. I was looking at Annia Augusta. The arrival had taken her by surprise. For one brief second she had caught her breath, pressed both hands against her face and widened her eyes with a kind of appalled horror. She regained her self-control at once, but I had registered that immediate response – like some kind of allegorical statue representing Guilt.

'You know this trader, lady citizen?' I enquired, rather pointlessly.

Before she could utter a word, Eppaticus lifted his head with an effort and began again. 'Nothings. I know nothings. Just is a business – come here for my money and now happening all this . . .'

The soldier moved to silence him again, but caught my eye and instead tugged at his bonds and allowed him to scramble to his feet.

234

'Eppaticus,' I said, when he had struggled upright. 'What was it that you sold to Monnius?'

The great Celt looked discomfited. He dropped his head and gazed at the floor but did not answer, even when the soldier kicked him savagely.

I repeated the question, in Celtic this time.

Then Eppaticus did raise his head and glanced at Annia. 'A private matter,' he replied unwillingly, in his quaint version of the same language. 'It was a business accommodation, that is all. I have done the same thing for Monnius before.'

'A business arrangement with those female slaves you had for sale?' I prompted. 'Setting up a *lupanarium*, perhaps?' Five thousand *denarii* would have been a high price to pay for a brothel and its inmates, but I was convinced that the arrangement was something that Eppaticus found embarrassing, and the setting up of a whorehouse was a possibility. A potentially lucrative business, but something which the Trinovantine might prefer not to discuss openly in front of his partner's mother. We Celts do not share the robust Roman acceptance of these things.

Eppaticus shook his head and mumbled. For a moment I thought he might be about to tell me.

But all this conversation in a language that he did not understand had angered Fortunatus. He had lost his earlier shame-faced air, and now began to berate me angrily.

'Enough of this nonsense! Why have I been brought here? Of what am I accused? Killing Monnius? That's a monstrous lie. If I am to be charged with deliberately falling at the races, very well – let me go before the council and stand trial. I have admitted it, and I will pay the fine – and take the flogging too, if that's the penalty. But to be brought here at swordpoint and accused of killing a citizen! There is some mistake. Someone will pay for thi—'

He broke off in surprise. Eppaticus had struggled free and

with a furious effort had broken from his guards. Before anyone could stop him, he had launched himself across the study at Fortunatus, raised his bound hands with a snarl and sent him reeling sideways against the wall.

'You fall deliberate? And all my money lose! And I here risk myself to come to this house two times, even when man is dead – only for find some way of pay my debts. I kill you, son of a pig!' He raised his hands again as if to bring them down on the charioteer's head with murderous intent.

It was doomed, of course. There were too many soldiers and he was hampered by his bonds. The nearest soldier solved the problem with professional skill. He raised the heavy baton that he held and hit the Celt neatly and hard behind the ear.

Eppaticus pitched forward with a soft moan and this time he did not get up again.

Chapter Twenty-four

There was a sudden hush. The little *librarium* was crammed with people, but all of them were suddenly silent after this casual display of force, and were watching me warily.

I looked at the gigantic figure on the floor, which (to my relief) was already beginning to stir slightly. Whatever else, the Celt was strong – the blow he had received would have half killed a lesser man. I made a decision

'Take him outside,' I said to the soldiers who had brought him in, 'and when he has come round a bit, I want you to escort him to that warehouse of his. Have a look around. I want to know what he sold Monnius. He seemed strangely reluctant to tell me. That is curious. Don't let him mislead you.'

'I know where the warehouse is, master,' Junio said unexpectedly. He was still standing behind my stool and I realised he had been waiting for some opportunity to make himself useful.

'Then you go with them, Junio,' I said. 'Take that wax tablet from the writing desk. I want a list of everything he stocks. In particular anything that might be worth several thousand sesterces. I remember you saying there was no sign of grain? Check that. It would have seemed the obvious commodity.'

Junio nodded importantly. I had taught him to read and write, and he was proud of his accomplishments. 'He has some slaves there – I will talk to them,' he said, picking up

237

the writing tablet and the stylus. 'He's keeping them chained up at one end of the warehouse. If he sold something significant, recently, they may be able to tell us what it was.'

I glanced at Fortunatus. He was sullen, but not subdued. 'Don't look at me. I don't know what he had. I tell you, the man was only at my house to sell me furniture and dishes – he had some Samian ware, he said, extremely cheap, and some inlaid cabinets from Egypt. He came to see me at the inn and we went to the house together to see if the larger chest would fit in my new *cubiculum*. He was recommended to me by Glaucus – I have never seen the man before. I do not understand what any of this is about.'

'The night that Monnius was murdered, a large amount of money disappeared,' I explained. I did not add that it had disappeared again. 'This man appeared next morning claiming that it had been owed to him.'

Annia Augusta fidgeted, and seemed to be making up her mind to speak. She was watching Eppaticus, who was beginning to open his eyes and shake his head dazedly. She cleared her throat. 'You need not concern yourself with that, citizen. There was a debt from Monnius to this man. But it is paid. The man has called here since and I have settled the matter myself. With money of my own.' She smiled, doubtfully. 'Not a wholly regular arrangement, I know, since it was civic money which Monnius owed, but I did not want questions raised about the will. There would have been claims against his private estate – how much he was personally responsible and every kind of fuss. You know how these things are.'

I did. Any debt unpaid at a person's death could be claimed for in the courts – always a long and expensive business, which can eat up much of the estate. If this was not simply a private debt, but one involving civic tax money, the courts would make a showpiece of it and spin the hearing out for weeks, employing their most eloquent orators. Any citizen could understand the impulse to settle such a matter, quickly and privately, before the whole inheritance found its way into the public purse.

I nodded. 'So you can tell me what Eppaticus did not? What did Monnius owe the money for?'

She gave a would-be helpless shrug – unconvincing as a goose pretending to be a sparrow. 'I did not ask him, citizen. I supposed it was something to do with corn – that was my son's customary business. I did not enquire further. It was enough to pay the debt and remove the problem.'

From many women, I might even have believed it – the avoidance of long, costly wrangles in the courts at any price. But Annia Augusta, I recalled, managed her own estates. I did not believe that she would part with five thousand *denarii* without requiring at least some evidence of the original bargain – and properly witnessed proofs of payment, too.

'Forgive me, madam citizen, but I know that a large sum was involved. You had that kind of money in your possession?'

Her eyes flickered – only for a moment, but I was sure they flickered – towards the lifting mosaic in the floor.

I was instantly alert. I was sure that the last time I was in this room Annia Augusta had not known the hiding place was there. Also, she did not bridle, as she normally would, at my impudent enquiry, but gave me that imitation shrug again. 'I do have money, citizen, from my estates. My steward has recently sold a large quantity of produce, on my instructions. It was most fortunate.'

Too fortunate, I thought. By now my suspicions were thoroughly aroused. It seemed much more likely that she had paid Eppaticus with money she had discovered in the hiding place. Perhaps I had even led her to it myself. But that did not explain why the money had disappeared from Monnius' desk and been hidden in the first place. And what about that missing document? Was this one of Eppaticus' less than legal deals?

I said, watching Annia closely, 'I would still like the warehouse searched.'

Annia was not good at hiding her emotions, as I had just seen, so I watched her closely this time for some slight start of guilt or gesture of unease. However, there was no change in her expression of Vestal innocence, and my hopes of finding anything at the warehouse dimmed. I looked at Eppaticus, who was conscious now and must have heard the whole exchange, but he seemed entirely occupied with collecting his wits and not at all concerned about the proposed search.

Whatever that transaction with Monnius had been, I thought, there was no evidence of it left. But I had committed myself. I nodded to the escort.

'As you command, citizen.' The senior soldier stirred Eppaticus with his boot. 'On your feet, you Trinovantine dog!' The Celt struggled unsteadily upright and spread his hands expressively at Annia.

'You see what happen, lady,' he muttered indistinctly. 'I told you this. No paper for the warehouse, make trouble for us all. Monnius every time, fix documents.' He stumbled forward as the soldiers tugged his chains, and forced him, still reeling, from the room. Junio raised his eyebrows at me, after this most interesting outburst, and followed them eagerly.

Annia Augusta did not wait for further questioning from me. 'Instead of wasting time on that rogue, citizen,' she demanded, 'why do you not send this lying charioteer to the torturers? My son's spirit will rest more easily if you expose the truth about how this man came skulking back from Verulamium and killed him while he slept.'

Fortunatus gave a bitter laugh. 'Madam citizen, I did not kill your son. The day I returned to Londinium I was with

Pulchrissima all night, as I've no doubt she will tell you, if you send for her.'

Annia Augusta snorted. 'Pulchrissima?' she said, in tones of disbelief. 'What kind of name is that? Some paid girl from an inn who would say or do anything for a *quadrans*? What court will pay the slightest heed to her? A prostitute has no rights under law. Do not believe him, citizen. Fulvia . . .'

Fortunatus turned to me. 'The lady Fulvia will not like to hear it, but it's true, citizen, as Jove lives and rules. I came back from Verulamium to the team headquarters, gave my orders to my slave, and then went straight to Puchrissima at the inn. I have not left her room until today – any of the girls who work there could tell you that. In fact, we made ourselves the subject of ribald gossip, because we scarcely even troubled to send out for food and wine. Ask anyone in the tavern. A memorable few days, citizen. I am sure Pulchrissima could give you a detailed account.'

The two soldiers were examining their feet by now, trying to suppress their grins, but Annia Augusta was not amused. 'You have the habits of a satyr, charioteer. Could you not confine your attentions to this Pulchrissima before, instead of dishonouring the wife of a respectable citizen?'

Fortunatus flushed slightly and answered with some spirit. 'I dishonoured nothing. The lady Fulvia was a most unhappy bride. If it had not been me she welcomed to her bed, it would have been someone else. It was scarcely serious – we were very discreet, and I have managed similar affairs before.' He shrugged his supple shoulders with a rueful smile. 'I hope I do not shock you, citizen. This is not unusual, in my profession. And not without its benefits. Fulvia Honoria is very beautiful. And enthusiastic too. Since Monnius is dead it hardly matters if I confess that now.'

I looked at the young man with contempt. He and his Pulchrissima were well matched, I thought, in more ways than one. 'You confessed it earlier, I think,' I said drily. 'To your team-mates in the barracks of the Blues. She could not get enough of you, you said. Yet when you came back to Londinium, you did not go to her.'

He had the grace to look discomfited. 'She was getting too demanding, citizen. Wanting every minute of my time – insisting that I call on her whenever I was free from racing or the team. Sending messages and presents, in broad daylight too. She was becoming careless.'

'Great Mars!' Annia Augusta cried. 'It *was* you who attacked her after all. You had had your fun with her, and when you tired of it you tried to kill her to get rid of her. You viper! Not even Fulvia deserved to be treated in that way.'

Fortunatus ignored her. He addressed himself to me. 'I tried to tell her, citizen, but she would not listen. It was impossible to go on as we were – her husband would become suspicious, I would be disgraced, she would be exiled if not worse – and Glaucus and Calyx would have punished me severely for breaking my contract for training with the team.'

'Besides, you were in danger of losing your golden fleece,' I said. 'Monnius already suspected, and had changed his will, leaving much less to Fulvia. Asked you to witness it, I think, to make quite sure you understood.'

Annia Augusta gasped. 'So when you came back from Verulamium you crept in here and tried to kill them both?'

'By all the immortals!' he exclaimed. 'I did nothing of the kind. I did not tell Fulvia I had come back. I went straight to the inn and found Pulchrissima. It was only the day after the next that Fulvia heard about my accident and tried to contact me – she sent a letter to Blue headquarters by one of the governor's own palace servants. My team-slave came scampering over to the inn to alert me.'

I nodded. My reasoning about Superbus was confirmed. Annia Augusta had summoned him to the house (as she'd told me) and while he was there Fulvia had given him a message for Fortunatus. That had no doubt pleased him, since he knew that I had gone away on a fool's errand to Verulamium. But I could imagine what alarm it had caused when he turned up at the *factio*, in palace uniform, after I'd been asking questions at the races, in Pertinax's name. Glaucus had already come hurrying back to alert the camp for spies. So the unfortunate slave was taken to the cellar to find out what he knew, and had fallen to his death. Poor Superbus. I could imagine how self-important he had felt, taking that message to the charioteer. I hoped it had afforded him a little pleasure, at least, before he died.

I turned back to Fortunatus. 'Fulvia didn't come to you today?'

He looked almost as startled as Annia Augusta did. She clasped her hands and cried, 'What do you mean?' and he said, 'Dear Mercury, I hope not. Did you think she might?'

'She's locked herself into her room,' I said. 'Or appears to have done. I wondered if in fact she'd run to you.'

He shook his head. 'Not that I know of, citizen. I was not expecting her. No, she can't have done. She'd have come to the house, and these soldiers would have found her there. She wouldn't go to the headquarters, she knew that was forbidden, and she doesn't know the inn exists. You're sure she isn't in her room?'

'On the contrary,' I said, getting to my feet urgently, 'I'm beginning to believe that's exactly where she is. And her serving-woman was poisoned yesterday.' One of the soldier escort stepped forward to assist me, but I brushed him aside. 'I'm starting to be alarmed about her. Her own door is blocked, and so is Monnius'.'

'You think she's drugged herself to sleep?' Annia said. 'She should be here by now – it is time for all of us to purify ourselves. The mourners will be congregating at the door.'

243

I looked at Fortunatus. 'The window to the garden? Is it possible?'

He nodded. 'There is a stone shrine built into the further wall. The niche has a projecting canopy – if you are very determined you can scale the wall and let yourself down by standing on the arch.'

'As you have often done,' I said, and it was not a question. 'Could Fulvia have got out the same way?'

He shook his head. 'You need a ladder to reach the roof of the niche from the inside. I do not believe that Fulvia could do it, citizen – it is an energetic climb, even if one is not wearing a stola! It makes demands on me, and I am a fit man.'

'Then she is still there,' I said.

He looked at me. 'You want me to scale the wall and get her out? She would listen to me, I think, if no one else.'

'Especially as she has no idea about Pulchrissima?'

He coloured. 'That may be so, citizen, but it is to our advantage now. If you will call your soldiers off . . .'

I nodded. 'Escort him to the wall.'

'The people in the street!' Annia Augusta cried.

'See that the crowd is moved round the corner,' I instructed. 'Then Fortunatus can climb up, and if necessary force the shutters for us. Unless you have sufficient strength to force the door? Annia Augusta couldn't do it.'

'I could try,' he said, and everyone fell back to let him pass. He went to Fulvia's door, with the confidence born of familiarity, and hammered on it.

'Fulvia! It's Fortunatus! I'm here. Let me in.' He rattled the panels of the door but there was no answer at all from within. He put his shoulder against one of the hinged folds and the door gave slightly, but he shook his head. 'There is something heavy just behind the door. Annia Augusta is right – it's impossible to move. I'd have to smash the wood.'

Annia frowned. 'That seems unnecessary.'

He shrugged. 'Then I'll try the window route. Wait here.'

He led the way, followed by both the soldiers, although they had sheathed their daggers by this time. We waited in the passageway for what seemed a long time – long enough, in any event, to remind me that I was still weak from my recent ordeal. I put my ear against the door, but there was nothing to be heard.

At last there came a heavy scraping from within, as if someone was dragging something across the floor. The door opened back, and there was the charioteer. He looked shaken and pale.

'You had better come in, citizen,' he said. 'She's dead. Someone has stabbed her through the heart.'

Chapter Twenty-five

The scene that met my eyes will haunt my dreams for ever. Fulvia's beautiful room, furnished with such restraint, looked like a butcher's shop. The floor was covered with the splintered fragments of the phials and vases from the shelves, their precious oils and unguents staining the tiles: a half-full goblet had been shattered into a thousand pieces by the bed, and splashes of blood bespattered everything.

Fulvia was stretched out on her pillows, the centre of a dreadful spreading stain. It had soaked the dark stuff of her mourning clothes, seeped across the blankets of the bed and was making an obscene stain on the white bandage round the outstretched arm. A pitcher of whatever she had been drinking still stood on the small chest beside the bed, but the hilt of a dagger protruded from her ribs, under the swell of her once lovely breast. Her neck, too, had been savagely slashed.

Annia Augusta had followed me into the room. She sat down heavily on the wooden chest, which stood now in the middle of the room, where the charioteer had dragged it away from the door. She looked old, suddenly, and defeated. 'This is my fault, citizen,' she said. 'I should have listened to my daughter-in-law. She said she was in danger, but I did not believe it – even after the death of the old nurse. I was so sure that Fortunatus . . .' She buried her head in her hands. 'Dear Jupiter, what an awful scene. And I did nothing to protect her. Perhaps I am the old fool that you take me for.'

Fortunatus spoke with difficulty. 'Do you think, citizen, she might have killed herself? Suppose she *had* heard about Pulchrissima, after all. She barricaded the doors herself, we know. Perhaps took one of her potions to give herself courage, and then rammed home the knife with all her force?' His voice shook and he kept his back turned to that awful figure on the bed.

Annia Augusta raised her head and spoke with something of her old spirit. 'You overestimate your charms, I think, charioteer. Fulvia was not the sort of woman who would die for love. She might kill herself, but only if it would avoid more dreadful pain, like being thrown to the beasts. And she would choose an easy way, poison perhaps, and put it in a sleeping potion first. Not this – it is a dreadful way to kill yourself. Supposing that the wound had not been fatal? That might mean hours of dreadful agony!'

I could not have put it more cogently myself. As a solver of mysteries, however, I felt I should add something to her words. 'Besides, look at her hands – they are spread out, not clasped against the knife.'

Fortunatus shifted uncomfortably. 'It was just an idea, citizen. So there was someone from outside after all. It was simply that I could not think who it might be. Who would want to murder Fulvia? I suppose it is possible. The killer could have escaped through the garden – the shutter in Monnius' room was slightly open.'

'Open?' I said sharply. It should have been closed, by custom, in a dead man's room.

'That was how I got in. I couldn't open this one, it was bolted from inside. And the doors to the corridor were barricaded too. You don't suppose . . .' he dropped his voice and looked around uneasily, 'that we have something supernatural here? That Monnius . . .?'

I looked around the blood-splattered room. Parvus, the

248

little page, had insinuated himself into the room and was sitting by the bedside, holding Fulvia's hand and weeping helplessly. 'I think this was a human being at work,' I said grimly. 'Supernatural retribution is generally more inventive. But you are right, chariot-driver. The question of the barricades is interesting. How were the doors wedged shut?'

'That wooden chest in this room,' he replied, 'and in the other someone has blocked the door with a statue. See for yourself.'

I walked to the interconnecting door. It was open, and with the shutters pulled back I could see the situation for myself. It was Priapus, of course, still on his marble plinth but now lying on his back beside the door. Bizarrely there appeared to be a silken cord tied around his most outstanding feature, and the wooden bowl – without its feathers now – was lying in the corner where the statue had once stood. The painted satyrs leered down from the walls.

It was indecent in a room of death. I went over and righted the statue. It was top-heavy and fairly difficult to move, especially in my weakened state, but I managed to do it and opened back the door of the bedchamber. As I did so, it was to find Lydia in the passageway outside, hurrying towards me with Filius at her skirts.

'Citizen!' she exclaimed as soon as I appeared. 'What is going on here? There are mourners congregating at the door already. I went out to speak to them, but the soldiers came and herded them away, and made them go off and wait further down the street. Oh, sweet Minerva!' She lifted her bony hands in a gesture of despair. 'Poor Monnius – and poor, poor Filius. What an appalling omen for his adulthood – this is his first public duty as the head of the household, and here we have funeral guests driven from the door, while arrested criminals are invited in.'

Fortunatus had followed me through into Monnius' room,

and the sound of voices had brought Annia Augusta and her maid into the passage too.

'What is this uproar, Lydia?' the older woman said.

Lydia gave a little sob, while her son stood mulish and stolid by her side. 'Madam, it is time to start the rituals, and neither you nor Fulvia could be found. But I see the door is open now. Has Fulvia consented to come out?'

I looked into that pinched and anguished face. 'There has been an accident,' I said inadequately. 'Fulvia is dead.'

The pale eyes opened wider and the corners of her lips drooped downwards in an expression of dismay that made her look rather like a fish. 'Dead? She can't be. I saw her just before she locked herself in there, and she was quite well then.'

Annia Augusta said quickly, 'Lydia, be careful what you say.'

But I had already seen the implication. 'Then you were the last person in the house to see her alive. When was that, lady, and what happened then?'

A faint flush coloured Lydia's thin cheeks. 'This morning. Fulvia was very upset after the death of her maid, and what happened with the mask. She said that she was going to her room until the funeral.' As she spoke she was pulling her fingers till they cracked. 'She sent one of her pages to ask me for some reviving cordial – I brought it to her myself, and tasted it for her – she would not have trusted it otherwise. She took it from me, then ordered me away, and I heard her barricade the door behind me.' She dabbed her face with her linen handkerchief. 'Oh, this is dreadful, dreadful. And what about my husband's funeral? There has been so much disrespect – his death is unavenged – we shall have his spirit walking the corridors. And if he is not decently laid to rest tonight . . . Oh, Annia Augusta, what are we to do?'

It was Filius who spoke. 'I don't know why we can't just go

ahead as planned. Fulvia could be quickly washed and salved
– the undertaker did that for the slave this morning, and it
did not take very long. They've got that old nurse's body up
there on a funeral litter of sorts: we could have Fulvia put on
that, and taken to the pyre with my father while we are about
it.' He looked at the shocked faces around him. 'Well – that
would have happened if she'd been murdered with him, or if
she had killed herself for grief. I suppose there's no chance
that's what happened, by the way? It would save us so much
trouble if it were – even the mourners would understand if
there was a short delay.'

'Filius!' Lydia's voice was a horrified whine. 'Do not speak
so!' She turned to Annia Augusta's maid. 'Go, quickly, bring
some water, salt and fire. And some refining herbs. The
undertakers will give them to you.' The girl scuttled off.
'Such dreadful disrespect. It must be purged. We need some
Vestal virgins here to chant! . . . Oh, great Minerva, pardon
Filius – I promise to perform a sacrifice . . .' She was burbling.

'Lydia!' Annia Augusta broke into her lament. 'Control
yourself. A pity you can't take some of your own restorative.
Or did you give it all to Fulvia?'

Lydia shook her head.

'When my slave-girl comes back, send her for some. And
as for the funeral, perhaps Filius is right – Fulvia has no
family left alive. It would fall to this household to organise a
wake and that would only lead to more expense. Who profits
by delay?'

Lydia let out a wordless wail, and buried her face in her
handkerchief.

'Annia Augusta is right,' I said, feeling that some leader-
ship was necessary. 'A little restorative would do you good.
You took Fulvia a great pitcherful; she did not use it all.
Fortunatus, fetch some for the lady. You will find a small cup
in the chest that Annia was sitting on.' The charioteer looked

doubtful, but I frowned at him in my best official manner and he went. 'In the meantime,' I added, 'let us repair back to the *librarium*. We are all distressed, and I am feeling in need of my stool again.'

The little procession followed me into the study. Fortunatus was not far behind us, bearing the half-full pitcher and the drinking cup. He poured a little of the liquid out and handed it to Lydia. She smiled at him wanly, raised it to her lips and would have drained it at a gulp if Annia Augusta had not intervened.

'Don't drink it, Lydia. Don't be such a fool!'

Lydia lowered the cup and looked at her in surprise.

'Fulvia is dead, for Mars' sake, Lydia!' Annia Augusta said. 'Who knows what is in that cordial! Do you wish to follow her to the grave?'

Lydia gaped. 'But I prepared the potion with my own hands,' she wailed. She turned to me. 'You think that Fulvia was poisoned, citizen?'

I thought of that blood-stained figure on the bed. 'I'm sure that she was not,' I said. 'Given a sleeping potion perhaps, to keep her quiet before she was attacked.'

Lydia sniffed at the liquid expertly. 'I'm sure there is no sleeping draught in this.' She took a tentative sip. 'No, I am certain of it. This is just the potion I prepared. But perhaps you are right, lady citizen – it is better not to drink.' She gave Annia Augusta a wan smile, and handed back the cup to Fortunatus. 'I am recovered now.' She turned to me. 'You say that Fulvia was murdered, citizen? Someone escaped through Monnius' window-space? But who could have done it? You think that Monnius' killer struck again?'

Like the hiding place in the study floor, the whole section of mosaic suddenly slipped neatly into place. 'Hardly that,' I said, slowly. 'Annia Augusta was right. I think that Fulvia murdered Monnius herself.'

If I had been an actor in a Roman tragedy, I could hardly have hoped for a greater response. Annia Augusta gasped, Lydia did her impression of a fish, and Fortunatus muttered, 'By all the gods!'

Filius screwed up his unattractive face and said thoughtfully, 'That would be parricide, wouldn't it? Murder of one of your immediate family? Does that mean that she will have no claim on any of the estate?'

'She will inherit nothing anyway,' I said, 'since she's already dead. Nor could you bring a case against her, as you cannot take her to court. But if you wish to raise a question before the magistrates, I am sure they could find some way of delaying the will and relieving you of your money, as your mother always feared.'

Filius retired in a sulk.

Annia Augusta said, 'I cannot believe it – I thought that it was proved that she and Fortunatus . . .'

'That was our mistake,' I said, 'yours as well as mine – supposing that Fortunatus was involved. In fact, I see now that was part of Fulvia's plan. She knew that you would suspect him at once. So she chose to kill her husband on a night when – as she thought – Fortunatus was safely in Verulamium, racing a chariot in front of hundreds of witnesses, and could not possibly have been here. What she did not know was that her lover was engaged in a gambling fraud, and was going to throw himself deliberately from his chariot to ensure that his team lost. He was in Londinium that night, not injured as he claimed, and that fact confused me in my enquiries.'

'But why did she do it?' Fortunatus asked.

'She wanted you,' I said, and saw him flush. 'You told me she was getting indiscreet – and Annia Augusta had made her opinions clear to Monnius. If he divorced her for adultery she would end up, at best, exiled to some barren island for the rest of her life. She would not even have her tiny dowry back. She would have nothing. She told me that her husband tolerated her unfaithfulness, but I don't believe that. And he knew about it, thanks to Annia.'

Annia gave an affronted sniff.

'He did change his will,' Fortunatus said. 'And asked me to witness it. That was to warn me off. I told her that, but she ignored me. She seemed to think she'd still get half of his estate. Of course, she might have been right. I couldn't prove that he had other witnesses – and as you know, to be completely secure in law, any will must be confirmed by seven citizens.'

'Even if he had changed his will, she still had much to gain,' I said. 'At least a country house and – she thought – a handsome husband too. Much to be preferred to a life of penury and exile.'

Lydia whimpered into her handkerchief. 'But what about the man who came in through the window and slashed her arm?'

'My dear Lydia,' Annia Augusta said severely, 'do try to concentrate. Of course there never was a man. Fulvia invented the whole story, and no doubt damaged her own arm to make it look convincing. I always thought there was something strange in that. Why should a man who strangled twice suddenly resort to using a knife, and run away just because a woman screamed? Naturally, I assumed that the intruder was Fortunatus, and she had let him in. But I can see she might have done it all herself – though I am surprised she had the courage to cut herself. When did you first suspect her, citizen?'

'From the very first. Monnius was murdered in his bed, while the servants who were on duty were all drugged. I thought at the time that Fulvia had best access to their wine – and she had that sleeping potion too. She was cunning there – she deliberately bought a draught that Lydia had made, in

254

case suspicion was ever aroused, and then made sure that everyone knew that the liquid in her phial had been exchanged for water. I began to think that my first suspicions were wrong.'

'Dear Minerva! My sleeping draught would not have drugged those slaves so deeply,' Lydia cried.

'Of course not,' I agreed. 'But that was not the potion that she used. We know that she had skills with herbs herself. What she put in the servants' wine was far, far stronger – the same potion that she doubtless used to make sure that everyone was sound asleep whenever Fortunatus came to visit her over the garden wall. Don't argue, Fortunatus – it is clear you knew the route.'

He coloured, mumbled something indistinct, and fell silent again.

'Of course,' Annia said, 'the slaves who were not on duty that night would not have drunk the potion – or very little of it – so they would waken when she screamed. Wicked, but clever. I always knew she was a schemer! But would Monnius listen to his mother? Doted on her completely, foolish man!'

I nodded. 'Up to the very end, I think. He was killed, after all, by someone who managed to put a necklace round his neck. He was a big man, and even in a drunken stupor he would never have succumbed to that without a struggle. But if his wife came in – whom, as you say, he worshipped – and put a playful hand under his neck . . .'

Lydia looked appalled. 'You mean she went in to his bed, uninvited?'

'He often summoned her to him. We have the old nurse's word for that. If he was as drunk as people say that night, I doubt he even stopped to question why she came. She put the necklace round his neck and pulled it tight. But she was not certain of killing him – he was not like the little slave-boy in the corridor. It seems he struggled. She had to kneel on him and hold the pillow over him to make sure that he was dead.

Again, that did not sound like our supposed intruder. Fulvia talked about a "big man", but any fit male – like Fortunatus here – could have throttled a drunken Monnius with own two hands. Certainly he would not need to finish off the victim by holding down the pillow until it split its seam. And why bother with the necklace? Why not use the knife?'

'Because it was my necklace,' Annia Augusta said. 'Just as the sleeping draught was Lydia's. Fulvia had one just like it of her own, but she could produce that with a flourish, and look innocent.'

'Exactly, madam citizen,' I said. 'That was the way throughout – everything would point to Fulvia, but then another explanation raised its head. A kind of double-bluff. Your Glaucus would approve of that, Fortunatus. Like the chariots of Calyx, you should not bet on what you think you see.'

'More clever than I took her for,' Fortunatus said, and there was admiration in his voice.

'Not as clever as all that,' I said. 'That necklace had been with the silversmith for mending. If anybody asked Annia about it, as I did, she would reply that it was not in the house. That would raise all kinds of suspicions, naturally. But that was Fulvia's mistake – the necklace was returned that evening at the feast, and only she and Monnius were there. No one else could even know it was back.'

'Someone could have found it, I suppose,' Fortunatus said. He seemed disposed to argue for his erstwhile lover suddenly. 'No doubt Monnius took it to his room. Just as they must have found the knife.'

'Do not be absurd, young man. You think they found the necklace first, and then went into the corridor and throttled the pageboy with it before returning to Monnius?' Annia Augusta's mind was sharp. I was beginning to have a certain respect for it.

Fortunatus shook his head. 'I suppose you're right.

And throttling the pageboy first suggested that the killer came from the corridor.' He frowned. 'But she *didn't* come from the corridor. How did she come to kill the pageboy first?'

I smiled. 'But she did come from the corridor. She had been here, in the *librarium*, hiding the money from the chest – another ploy to allay suspicion, suggesting that there had been a theft. It was her nurse, Prisca, who alerted me to that possibility – her mistress often paced the corridors, she said. Fulvia tried to shut her up at the time. I did not see the importance of her words. But I have thought about it since. And there was something else. There was something peculiar in the wine, Prisca said. She tried to warn the boy, but said he was asleep before his head had touched the floor. That suggests that she was *not* asleep. And when the servants rushed downstairs to help, there was Prisca, tending Fulvia. Clearly she didn't drink the stuff herself.'

'So you think that she was awake all the time? She witnessed what Fulvia was doing?'

'I believe so. Fulvia didn't realise that, of course – until the old nurse began to babble on to me. I think she often feigned sleep when Fulvia thought her drugged. Of course, Prisca would have faced the lions for Fulvia – she was finding excuses for her even then. Monnius was a monster, a brute – she was telling her mistress that she understood. But she was a danger all the same. She let slip to me that Fortunatus was Fulvia's lover – not intentionally, perhaps, but that was worse. She could not be relied on to be discreet. She sealed her own death warrant with that mistake.'

'Fulvia killed her too?' Lydia's question was a yelp. 'But she loved Prisca.'

'Fulvia loved no one but herself,' Annia Augusta snapped. 'I always said so, even to Monnius.'

'But see how she had the body anointed and prepared,' Lydia insisted.

'She was playing the part of the distraught mistress. Ruthless,' I put in. 'I knew she had a heartless streak – I once saw her force her page to taste a potion. Of course, she knew that it was only water – she put it there herself – but the poor little lad did not know that. Yet he drank it for her. She seems to have inspired that kind of loyalty. And by making Prisca taste her food thereafter, of course she made it easier to poison her – and claim Prisca's death as proof that she was in danger herself.'

'Poor Prisca,' Lydia lamented. 'All that poison-tasting too. I'll sacrifice a pigeon for her tomorrow.'

'And there's another thing. Why should a woman who has been attacked with a knife seek to defend herself by installing a poison-taster, rather than, say, a bodyguard? But Fulvia contrived to make it seem quite logical. Like that arm of hers – scratched just enough to make a lot of blood. We never saw the wound. And it was her left arm – most people raise their right hand to defend themselves. She was right-handed; I saw her tie her belt. I should have noticed at the time, but somehow she charmed me too.'

Annia's maidservant chose that moment to return with her handful of salt and her little bowl of coals. She stopped at the doorway, while the undertaker's assistant hovered behind her with a bowl of water and a bunch of herbs. Annia Augusta looked at me. I nodded.

'Go to the lady Fulvia's *cubiculum*,' she said. 'Purify the room and prepare her for burial at once – she will accompany her husband to the pyre.'

'But surely . . .' Lydia began, 'now we know . . .'

'My dear Lydia, what is to be gained? Monnius' murderer is dead. What could be more fitting than to burn her on his pyre? She was attacked when Monnius was killed, and since has died of her wounds. That is all that anyone need know – except the governor, of course. There will be no trial, there is nobody to charge. Let us resolve the matter, once and for all. You think that might be permitted, citizen?'

I nodded. 'It would put a stop to rumour and unrest. I think His Excellence would approve. Some things remain to be resolved, but this is the funeral of an official, so soldiers will accompany the cortège – I do not foresee any difficulty there. Let the slave-boy close his mistress's eyes and mourn her. There is no one else to do it. Unless . . .' I looked at Fortunatus.

He looked away, and shook his head. The maidservant bowed her way out of the study, followed by the undertaker's man. A moment later, from Fulvia's room, there was the scent of burning herbs and the pageboy's faltering voice began a heartfelt, sobbing lament.

'Now, if you will pardon me,' I said, 'I will return to the governor. He will be awaiting my report, and there are matters on which he may wish to act.' I looked from Annia Augusta to the floor, and saw her look of consternation. My surmises were correct, I thought. 'Send my slave after me when he arrives.'

'But,' Lydia protested, after a moment's pause, 'I don't understand. If there was no intruder at the feast, who was it who stabbed Fulvia again?'

'You have just answered that question for yourself,' I said. 'I suspected it before, and now I'm sure. Annia Augusta knows the answer too – that's why she's raised no question of her own. You did it, Lydia. How else would you have known that she'd been stabbed? We told you Fulvia was dead, but no one mentioned knives.'

She pitched forward in a graceless faint. Fortunatus caught her before she hit the floor.

Chapter Twenty-six

'Well, pavement-maker, welcome. Prepare him a place there, slave.' Helvius Pertinax, resplendent in a coloured dining robe, gestured graciously to a *triclinium* couch. He helped himself from a tray of pork and leeks, which a small servant-boy was offering to him, and gestured capaciously to me to do the same. 'A simple meal – I hope it meets your taste.'

I rose from my kneeling position and sank down on the proffered couch, glad of an opportunity to recline. I was exhausted, but damnably hungry, and Pertinax's 'simple meal' smelled like ambrosia to me. In my old toga, bathed and shaved, I felt like a human being once again.

A long time later, the governor turned to me. 'Glaucus has been captured, did you hear? Unfortunately, dead. The soldiers who arrested him had lost too much money on the chariots, I fear. They may have been a little over-exuberant.' He held out a goblet to his serving-boy, who filled it to the brim with watered wine. 'I hear you have done well today. And it was a domestic murder after all, not a political one. That news is doubly welcome.'

I had waited for this moment. Like any civilised Roman, Pertinax preferred philosophy to business as a topic of dinner conversation. Until the spiced fruits were cleared away, he had been discoursing learnedly on Homeric verse. Now, though, he had signalled he was ready. I outlined to him the events of the day.

He heard me out, gravely and courteously, nodding from

time to time. When I had finished he said, 'So Lydia betrayed herself, in the end.'

The servant filled my goblet in its turn. 'I had my suspicions before then, but that slip about the stabbing confirmed them. I was sure that it was someone in the villa. The statue had not been *pushed* behind Monnius' door, it had been propped up on the wooden bowl and *pulled* over by that cord. It was very top-heavy, so it was not hard to do, although it must have created quite a crash. She has described it to me since. She went into the passageway, shut the door as far she could, then pulled the cord behind her. She hoped it would come free as the statue fell, but it didn't, so she stuffed the end back through the crack, and latched the door. The statue prevented anyone from entering the room, which was what she intended. She hoped to rescue the cord again before it was discovered, but if not it was Fulvia's anyway, the girdle cord she always took off when she went to rest.'

Pertinax sipped his wine, and picked up a pickled nut. 'So it was someone in the villa. But why were you so sure that it was Lydia?'

'She went to Fulvia's room, she told us that, with the potion she had prepared. A sleeping draught, of course, although she denied it later. Probably in the goblet rather than the flask, since she was so ready to drink from that herself before Annia Augusta stopped her – but in any case it would have done her little harm.'

Pertinax nodded. 'She might even have smashed that drinking glass herself, to deflect suspicion. But it did not deflect you, my friend.'

I smiled under his praise, but honesty prompted me to add, 'But who else could it have been, Excellence? All the slaves adored Fulvia, as we know. Fortunatus was not in the house. Annia Augusta was here with me when her daughter-in-law was killed, and Filius was sulking in his room. There was no one else. Lydia, of course, believed the story of the intruder and did not see the risk.'

'So that is why she chose to use the knife? I wondered why she did not opt for poison. It seems an easier way, for a woman with her skills.'

'She thought that poison would be traced to her, and she might have been blamed for Prisca's death as well – although, as it turned out, she was wrong in that. If Fulvia had been poisoned like her maid, I might have believed she really had been at risk all along and that I was completely wrong in my suspicions. Then the truth might never have been discovered. But Lydia thought the story of the visitor was real.'

'So she tried to draw your attention to that window?'

'That was a mistake. Monnius' shutters *were* slightly open, but she could not have known that, unless she opened them herself. By custom they should have been closed – and yet she mentioned the window-space specifically. And another thing. I knew that whoever stabbed Fulvia must have been covered with her blood. That pointed to Lydia as well. It was that, and not the sacrifice she offered, which spattered her clothes and made her cleanse herself. Of course, the breaking of the *imago* gave her an excellent excuse.'

He nodded. 'There would have been a lot of blood.'

'There was.' Remembering that dreadful scene, I was glad of the glass of wine in my hand, although it is not my favourite drink. 'Will she be tried for murder, Excellence?'

He shook his head. 'Not unless one of the family brings a charge, and in any case Lydia could claim the law of *talio*, rightful retribution. Monnius was her protector and the father of her son. Fulvia murdered him, so she did have cause. It would be hard for any court to sentence her.'

'Except, of course, she did not know that at the time.'

He gave one of his rare smiles. 'So why did she do it? Jealousy?'

'She was afraid that Fulvia would bring a *querela* against the changing of the will. Lydia kept talking about the courts. It did not occur to me at first, but the law requires seven witnesses. We know that Fortunatus was one of them – but he is not a citizen. He bought his freedom, true, but he has no voting rights. There would be cause for question in the courts, and you know what that can do to an estate.'

'I see. Filius would inherit at least half, of course, since he is the eldest son, but if Fulvia got the town house, as she clearly thought she would, Lydia would find herself without a home. I don't imagine Fulvia would welcome her.'

'I think she did it for Filius, not herself. She claims it was for him, and I believe her. Half his inheritance was at stake – and his dignity. Fulvia took his rightful place in the procession, too. I think it was that, above all, which sealed her fate. I noticed that Lydia was holding herself oddly when she came out of Monnius' room. Obviously, she was hiding the dagger under her cloak then – it was in Monnius' room, but it was to be offered as part of the grave-goods so no one would have noticed it was missing. I suspected nothing at the time, and Lydia is so ungainly that her awkwardness was not remarkable.'

Pertinax popped another pickled nut into his mouth. 'So she will claim *talio*. She will be banished from the town, at worst. But the family would be chased out anyway. People do not take kindly to a *frumentarius* who cheated them – and Annia Augusta was implicated too, you say?'

'I'm sure of it, Excellence. I knew it as soon as I saw her with Eppaticus, though I was exceptionally slow in working it out. She was the one who started the alarm, you will remember, both for the money and the missing document. We know that Fulvia hid the money, and why, but that did not explain the document, nor why the money disappeared again.'

'Annia Augusta found it, I assume?'

'I led her to it, without meaning to. She found me on my knees, and when I had gone she discovered the hiding place herself. Then, when Eppaticus came back, she paid him what was owed. She admitted that. So why did she not simply tell me so? Why not restore the money to the estate? And why was there "no paper for the warehouse" as Eppaticus said? She must be hiding something – perhaps for Monnius, but he was dead. More likely for herself.'

Pertinax was watching me intently. 'Go on.'

'I began to see how pieces of the pattern linked together. Annia Augusta had a large estate, which she insisted on managing herself, through a steward, often against Monnius' advice. It was "towards the sea", you told me, which must mean to the east, because we drove to Londinium from the setting sun, and met no oceans on our way. But I learned from the warehouse I visited that there had been bad rainstorms in the east, and many harvests were ruined in their stacks.'

'Including hers?'

'That seems most probable. It was common knowledge in the household that Annia had scorned to use Monnius' drying floors. Your boatman had the answer, Excellence. He complained of sacks of grain half rotting when the baker got them home, and I know how it was done. The chief clerk at the warehouse wearied me with his account of corn, but I am grateful now. Damp rye or barley can be mixed with spelt, which must be roasted before it's threshed. The spelt is placed at each end of the sack and does not rot, although the poor grain in the middle sprouts and spoils. And the buyer cannot see it. Of course it is an easy matter, with the distribution chutes, to fill the sacks like that. And once the grain is sold, it is remarkably difficult to prove.'

Pertinax was frowning. 'And what has Eppaticus to do with this? It was Annia's corn.'

265

'He bought the crop from Annia, and sold it back to Monnius. That way, if there were complaints, it could not be traced back to the family. It was a huge risk for Eppaticus, of course – you know the law. The bargain had to be settled in cash, and once the money had changed hands the owner of the corn was legally responsible. No wonder he panicked when Monnius was murdered before he paid.'

'Yet he came back to the house a second time?'

'He was desperate for the money to pay his gambling debts. Men like Glaucus are not patient with those who owe them money – especially large sums of it. He must have been delighted when Annia found the money and agreed to pay him – he was already down by the whole price of the transaction, since he was obliged to pay her in cash in the first place, to make the contract legal. But he was worried at not having a receipt, and no warehouse records. Without the documents he had no proof of anything.'

'That was why Annia removed the documents? To see to it that he was still legally responsible?'

'I don't think so, Excellence. She was simply worried that any investigation into Monnius' death – and the stolen cash – might bring to light the business of the corn. When the money went missing, she hid the documents. I have no doubt they'll be found among her things. There was a lot of money at stake – it represented a whole season's earnings for the farm. Of course, there was a profit for the warehouse too.'

Pertinax looked grim. 'Buying half-rotten corn cheap, and selling it at the proper price – there was a little fortune to be made. The warehouse supervisor had to know, that's clear, and he doubtless got his share of the profit. I shall have him arrested instantly. Odd that I have never heard complaints.'

'There have been murmurs, Excellence. Of course, the army and the racing teams would always get the best, but the baker and his like can complain all they wish – nobody pays attention until there is a riot.'

'But there are laws. Interfering with the corn supply is a serious crime.'

I grinned. 'I know. The warehouse supervisor must have been terrified when we turned up and he had to show us round, though he avoided taking us to the particular grain loft in question. I did find damp rye and spelt grain mixed. I'm sure the system had been perfected many times. The only difference on this occasion was that the rotten corn was Annia's own. No doubt, like any owner of a farm, she was glad to get any price at all for her worthless crop. Monnius saw that she did not lose, even though she had ignored his advice.'

Pertinax sighed. 'Well, all those responsible will be charged at law. Eppaticus too. There will be heavy fines. Upsetting the supply of corn can destabilise the whole city.'

'Poor Eppaticus! I doubt he ever saw the grain, although he stood to make a very neat profit by buying and selling it without asking too many questions. I don't think he has even got anywhere to store it. That is what I sent Junio to confirm.' I frowned. 'What has happened to Junio, by the way? I saw him briefly when he first came back, but he went scuttling off again saying he had a mission to perform for you, and I haven't seen him since. I hope nothing has happened to *him*?'

Pertinax smiled in earnest then – a warm, pleased smile that transformed his face. 'He is a clever boy, that serving-lad of yours. When he checked the warehouse of Eppaticus he talked to the slaves and discovered something of great significance. He took it on himself to come and report his findings straight to me, and I have authorised him to go and act on my account.'

I found myself frowning. I would do much for Pertinax,

but if he took a fancy to purchase my slave I would find it very hard to forgive him. Yet this must be something of the kind – a slave is not often empowered to act for the governor.

Pertinax seemed to read my thoughts. 'Do not be alarmed, my friend. But it is clear that after your ordeal you are not well enough to accompany me to Eboracum, as I promised you, and with my new appointment overseas I cannot delay my visit there any longer. I am sorry to disappoint you. I wished to offer you some other reward, and Junio has made a good suggestion. There was something at Eppaticus' warehouse that he thought you would particularly like. I have instructed him to purchase it for me. I believe he is in the palace with it now – although there is no obligation on you to accept. Would you care to see?'

My mind was racing. Inlaid cabinets and Samian ware? Such things were beautiful, but had no place in my humble workshop home. Perhaps there had been tiles or marble in the warehouse which I could use for pavements – that would be a valuable gift. I could trust Junio. I said, 'I should be honoured, Excellence.'

He clapped his hands and sent a servant running. I took a sip of wine, and waited.

Not for long. Junio appeared at the door, his face a huge wide grin. And behind him . . . the glass slipped from my hand . . .

'Gwellia!'

Chapter Twenty-seven

She was exactly as I remembered seeing her that last cruel time, when each of us was tethered to a cart, and for a few heartbreaking seconds I met her eyes and knew she was alive. Not the dark, lively beauty I had married but she still wrung my heart, though she was subdued and lined, bowed by a dreadful weariness.

I looked at her and saw the matching tears that welled up in her eyes.

'Gwellia!' I said again, in a voice that scarcely obeyed my will.

She looked from me to the governor, and seemed to hesitate. Then in a dreadful gesture of submission Gwellia came and knelt before me, bowing her head to the floor beneath my feet in the eternal sign of servitude. I do not think that I have ever seen a sadder thing.

'Master?' she said, and I thought my heart would break.

I took her by the hand and raised her up, but she evaded my eyes. I saw the tears on her lids. 'You were one of the left-over slaves?' I said gently. 'One of the ones that Eppaticus had for sale?'

She nodded, and then said in that beloved voice, from which all laughter had fled, 'Few people want an older female slave – we are too frail to work, too old to breed.'

A glimpse of what those years of servitude had been for her almost broke my heart. How many children had she borne, I wondered. How many owners had pawed that lovely frame? 'Oh, Gwellia,' I sighed.

Pertinax looked at me anxiously. 'The gift displeases you?'

I shook my head, almost incapable of speech. 'These tears are pleasure, Mightiness,' I managed at last and saw him smile with satisfaction.

It was the same that night, in the *cubiculum*. I called her to me. She came and stood beside the bed, silent and shivering, to await my next command. For a moment I caught her eyes – and saw, or thought I saw, the ghost of the old fire that once had sparked between us. Then it was gone, and she was once again a picture of obedient resignation, tinged, I saw, with fear.

'It's all right, Gwellia,' I said softly. 'Lie down.'

She took up station at my feet, as Junio did.

'You are my wife,' I said. She shook her head.

'That was dissolved,' she murmured brokenly. 'I could not have borne the shame of my life else.'

She was right, of course. Once we were taken into slavery the marriage between us was not recognised in law.

'But I have found you now,' I urged.

The phantom of a smile touched her lips. 'I am happy just to be your slave,' she said. 'They told me I was purchased for Libertus, but I did not know the name. What should I call you?'

'Don't call me master,' I said. But she was right again. The old name she had called me in my youth belonged to other days, another life, when we were free and young and full of hope. ' "Libertus" if you must.'

'Then, sleep well, Libertus. Thank you for your care.'

'I have dreamt of you every night,' I said, my heart thumping.

'And I of you,' she said. She gestured to the bed. 'Libertus . . . if you wish . . .'

It was tempting, but I had read those eyes and I knew better now. 'Not like this,' I said. I kissed her on the head.

'When you are ready, Gwellia. Not before. And never as a slave. I'll take you to the courts, and set you free.'

She looked at me warily, those years of use and torment in her eyes. 'And until then?' she said.

I laughed. All desire left me and I felt only a great welling surge of protective love. 'Until then, I am an old man,' I said gruffly, 'and I have had a difficult few days. Go to the servants' room and get some rest. And send my slave – my other slave – to me. I want him to help me to undress.'

Her eyes lit up with a little of the old tenderness. 'You understand! I didn't think you would. You're still the same man that I always knew.'

She left me with a smile. Junio, proud to be still wanted at my side, was grinning like a fish when he came in, but he had the grace to look surprised.

'Master?'

'I have waited for my wife for twenty years,' I said. 'I can wait a little longer. She will come to me one day, in her own time. Willingly.'

And she did. It was worth the waiting for.